"It'll mean she will have destroyed my identity," whispered Julia aloud. "All day she's been building up in the minds of strangers the picture of a girl who isn't remotely like Julia Ross. I don't believe for one instant she wrote to Mrs Hurst. If you say 'Julia Ross' to her, she'll stare and pretend she's never heard the name.

"That's why she wanted someone who hadn't any friends, anyone to start inquiries if she disappeared. That's why we've come to this old place. Before I get a chance to see anyone she'll have told her story. It's tragic, but I have delusions. And whatever I say no one will believe me."

So that first night she began to traverse the path of understanding the appalling thing Mrs Ponsonby meant to do . . .

Anthony Gilbert (1899–1973)

Anthony Gilbert was the pen name of Lucy Beatrice Malleson. Born in London, she spent all her life there, and her affection for the city is clear from the strong sense of character and place in evidence in her work. She published 69 crime novels, 51 of which featured her best known character, Arthur Crook, a vulgar London lawyer totally (and deliberately) unlike the aristocratic detectives, such as Lord Peter Wimsey, who dominated the mystery field at the time. She also wrote more than 25 radio plays, which were broadcast in Great Britain and overseas. Her thriller *The Woman in Red* (1941) was broadcast in the United States by CBS and made into a film in 1945 under the title *My Name is Julia Ross*. She was an early member of the British Detection Club, which, along with Dorothy L. Sayers, she prevented from disintegrating during World War II. Malleson published her autobiography, *Three-a-Penny*, in 1940, and wrote numerous short stories, which were published in several anthologies and in such periodicals as *Ellery Queen's Mystery Magazine* and *The Saint*. The short story 'You Can't Hang Twice' received a Queens award in 1946. She never married, and evidence of her feminism is elegantly expressed in much of her work.

By Anthony Gilbert

Scott Egerton series

Tragedy at Freyne (1927)

The Murder of Mrs Davenport
(1928)

Death at Four Corners (1929)

The Mystery of the Open
Window (1929)

The Night of the Fog (1930)

The Body on the Beam (1932)

The Long Shadow (1932)

The Musical Comedy Crime
(1933)

An Old Lady Dies (1934)

The Man Who Was Too Clever
(1935)

Mr Crook Murder Mystery series

Murder by Experts (1936)

The Man Who Wasn't There
(1937)

Murder Has No Tongue (1937)

Treason in My Breast (1938)

The Bell of Death (1939)

Dear Dead Woman (1940)
aka Death Takes a Redhead

The Vanishing Corpse (1941)
aka She Vanished in the Dawn

The Woman in Red (1941)
aka The Mystery of the
Woman in Red

Death in the Blackout (1942)
aka The Case of the Tea-
Cosy's Aunt

Something Nasty in the
Woodshed (1942)
aka Mystery in the Woodshed

The Mouse Who Wouldn't Play
Ball (1943)
aka 30 Days to Live

He Came by Night (1944)
aka Death at the Door

The Scarlet Button (1944)
aka Murder Is Cheap

A Spy for Mr Crook (1944)

The Black Stage (1945)
aka Murder Cheats the Bride

Don't Open the Door (1945)
aka Death Lifts the Latch

Lift Up the Lid (1945)
aka The Innocent Bottle

The Spinster's Secret (1946)
aka By Hook or by Crook

Death in the Wrong Room (1947)

Die in the Dark (1947)
aka The Missing Widow

Death Knocks Three Times
(1949)

Murder Comes Home (1950)

A Nice Cup of Tea (1950)
aka The Wrong Body

Lady-Killer (1951)

Miss Pinnegar Disappears (1952)
   aka A Case for Mr Crook
Footsteps Behind Me (1953)
   aka Black Death
Snake in the Grass (1954)
   aka Death Won't Wait
Is She Dead Too? (1955)
   aka A Question of Murder
And Death Came Too (1956)
Riddle of a Lady (1956)
Give Death a Name (1957)
Death Against the Clock (1958)
Death Takes a Wife (1959)
   aka Death Casts a Long
   Shadow
Third Crime Lucky (1959)
   aka Prelude to Murder
Out for the Kill (1960)

She Shall Die (1961)
   aka After the Verdict
Uncertain Death (1961)
No Dust in the Attic (1962)
Ring for a Noose (1963)
The Fingerprint (1964)
Knock, Knock! Who's There?
   (1964)
   aka The Voice
Passenger to Nowhere (1965)
The Looking Glass Murder
   (1966)
The Visitor (1967)
Night Encounter (1968)
   aka Murder Anonymous
Missing from Her Home (1969)
Death Wears a Mask (1970)
   aka Mr Crook Lifts the Mask

The Woman in Red

Anthony Gilbert

An Orion paperback
First published in Great Britain in 1941
This paperback edition published in 2019
by Orion Fiction,
an imprint of The Orion Publishing Group Ltd
Carmelite House, 50 Victoria Embankment
London EC4Y 0DZ

An Hachette UK Company

10 9 8 7 6 5 4 3 2 1

A CIP catalogue record for this book is
available from the British Library.

ISBN 978 1 4719 2055 4

Printed and bound in Great Britain by Clays Ltd, Elcograf S.p.A.

www.orionbooks.co.uk

EVER SINCE DAWN it had been the most extraordinary day. By six in the morning the sky was covered by a yellowish light that crept across its pallor like a cloud of gas. There was no wind anywhere; no leaf stirred on the trees; dust lay undisturbed in the gutters; smoke rose upwards in a perfectly straight line. About midday thunder sounded like the rumble of guns, coming gradually nearer, passing over and breaking among the distant hills like a regular fusillade of shellfire. And now at six o'clock in the evening when by rights the air should be cooling it was hotter than ever. Being in London streets was like being enclosed in a brick oven; a copper-colored glow had appeared behind the clouds and there was an atmosphere of tension abroad. It was the sort of night when anything could happen.

Julia Ross, the twenty-three-year-old typist whose name was to be familiar in so many households during the next few weeks, had been going the rounds of the employment agencies since ten o'clock; she had travelled from Lancaster Gate to Bloomsbury, from Bloomsbury to Paternoster Row, from Paternoster Row to Belgravia, and now, when in thousands of homes people were turning on the six o'clock news and mixing drinks and setting out patiences, she found herself on the threshold of the Victoria Employment Bureau, wondering hopelessly if it was worth risking another five shillings for the registration fee. Nine hours of walking through the sun-baked streets, descending stairs, waiting for tubes, riding up on escalators, waiting in a line to be interviewed by prospective employers, had sapped her courage and resource. For nine weeks she had been out of work and her savings were practically exhausted. For the past month she had

1

been living on a regime that even the patriotic Food Controller would have considered inadequate; she had no relations and no friends who could guarantee her a week's board and lodging. Her best shoes were at the cobblers and would remain there until she could find four-and-sixpence to redeem them; almost everything of value was at the pawnbrokers. She had lunched lightly on a glass of milk and a penny chocolate biscuit; she would dine on a fried egg and chips. Tomorrow, unless she landed a job, she would probably have to cut out lunch altogether. All this explains why she paid her fatal visit to Mrs. Ponsonby.

Mrs. Hurst of the Victoria Employment Bureau knew nothing of Mrs. Ponsonby beyond the fact that she required a secretary-companion at short notice. Mrs. Hurst explained this with some care, to avoid possible future responsibility, but added that she lived in Henriques Square, which, she said, speaks for itself. She made it clear to Julia that if she did not at once seek an interview the Victoria Bureau would prove one more broken reed. She had, of course, accepted the registration fee before she so much as mentioned Mrs. Ponsonby's name. That was ordinary business, as she and Julia understood it. Your five shillings was a gamble; it might land you a fine job that lasted for years or it might be so much money thrown down a drain. So far most of Julia's five shillings had gone, if not down drains, into the comfortably-lined pockets of other Mrs. Hursts.

Jobs were at a premium in the late spring of 1940. A good many firms had closed down altogether, others had reduced their staffs. Every one agreed that the young women were all right; they could join the A.T.S. or the W.R.N.S. or get jobs at F.A.P.s. Any positions that were going were usually snapped up by the older women. Julia, having mutely parted with five shillings that she could ill afford, sat looking hopefully at Mrs. Hurst. Mrs. Hurst had immaculately-waved white hair and a dress from Hanover Place. Her hands were manicured and she flicked over the pages of her ledger with the most casual air in the world. Her manner suggested that she did this sort of thing for a hobby and it was ridiculous to expect her to take applicants seriously. Women in her position know at once whether a newcomer is a prospective employer or a mere job-seeker; they have

2

separate manners and ways of speech for these two classes. As soon
as Mrs. Hurst set eyes on Julia she selected her bland casual front and
said, before the girl had taken a chair, that times were very bad because of the war.

"I know," said Julia. "I had a job before the war."

"When did you leave it?"

"About two months ago."

"Did you give notice?"

"Mr. Kennedy said he was reorganizing the staff and he thought
it fairer to keep the older women who couldn't join the war services."

"You haven't thought of joining them yourself?"

"I couldn't pass the medical board. I had an operation for appendicitis last autumn that left complications."

"Have you thought of applying for a paid post with the A.R.P.?
I assume you've taken your certificates."

"I have, but I can't live on two pounds three and a penny a week."

Mrs. Hurst's brows lifted. A pert backchatting young woman, she
registered. She flicked over another page.

"Let me see—bookkeeping?"

"Simple."

"Then I'm afraid that's no good. Er—Spanish?"

"No."

"That's a pity. I had a very nice position. What salary were you
asking?"

"I got three pounds five with Mr. Kennedy."

"In that case it was a pity to leave. I have plenty of girls on my
books with better qualifications than yours ready to work for fifty
shillings."

Julia, well versed in the ways of women who run employment
bureaus, said nothing to that.

"I may be getting something else in tomorrow," suggested Mrs.
Hurst, gently.

"You've nothing at present—nothing at all?"

Mrs. Hurst frowned. She had taken an instant dislike to this trim
young woman with dark curls bunched on her neck and a clear direct
gaze. Girls who have been unemployed for two months and can
only give a vague reason for their dismissal—for reorganization is

3

taken at its face value at the bureaus—should be meek and eager. She said languidly, "I hardly think . . ." and then her expression changed. She looked contemplative and inquiring.

"I have one position," she admitted at last. "It only came in yesterday and I've sent two or three girls down, but I believe it's still vacant. Mind you, I know nothing about Mrs. Ponsonby. She's not a regular client, but she lives in Henriques Square, which speaks for itself. She wants a secretary-companion, someone young and without family ties."

"What does that mean?"

"I understand," said Mrs. Hurst coldly, "that her last secretary left her at very short notice to look after an invalid mother, and she naturally wishes to protect herself against a similar occurrence. You said you were free now and would take a residential position?"

"Yes," said Julia, unenthusiastically. "What salary is she offering?"

"That is to depend on qualifications. She is prepared to interview applicants until half-past six. If you go at once she would see you tonight." She was busily scribbling on a little pink card as she spoke. "Be sure to let me know first thing in the morning if you obtain the position. My commission is ten per cent on the first month's salary, calculated, naturally, on a board-wages basis."

Julia rose slowly to her feet; her eyes, as they met Mrs. Hurst's snapping black ones, looked bewildered, almost stupid. When she spoke there was a peculiar urgency in her voice.

"This is all you have," she said. "You're quite sure?"

"You can't get more than one position at a time," Mrs. Hurst reminded her, crisply. "Yes, that's all."

"I see."

"What's the matter?" demanded Mrs. Hurst with some exasperation. "Do you want a job or don't you?"

"I do—well, of course I do." She took the card and looked at it oddly. She was wondering why, when the name Ponsonby meant nothing to her whatsoever and when the address was, as Mrs. Hurst pointed out, so exceedingly respectable, she should be so convinced that nothing but harm, of actual danger even, could come of this venture. The door whispered itself shut behind her and she waited on the dusty pavement, jostled by passers-by, looking mutely into

4

the coppery heavens, her whole being shaken by a protest that was instinctive and illogical. In her brain a voice rang like a chiming bell. "Don't go," it pealed, "don't go, don't go, don't go."

Smothering an impulse to tear the card into four pieces and drop them in the gutter, she compelled her unwilling feet to turn into Victoria Station yard, where the big red buses waited. A No. 16 would take her within two minutes' walk of Henriques Square. One was just about to start. The conductor, seeing her approach, leaned down to help her on to the step. She hung back for an instant.

"Well, d'you want this bus or don't you?" demanded the conductor. "Make up your mind."

She drew a long breath; it was as though she said good-bye to hope. Then she climbed aboard and took a fare to Mount Street.

The houses in Henriques Square were tall, dark and dignified; many of them boasted tessellated steps; some of the basements were full of flowerpots and climbing plants; the curtains were heavy, expensive and discreet. The neighborhood had a queer old-world texture, as though it was full of ghosts—ghosts clattering by in carriages, being swung through the shadows in sedan chairs. Julia shivered, as though she had left the familiar world behind her in Mount Street. No. 30 stood back a few inches; it must, she thought, have been this that gave the house its odd effect, as though it were trying to huddle itself out of sight, drawing wings over itself to hide whatever was going on behind the glass and the brocaded tasselled curtains. It differed, too, from its neighbors in that its windows were a shade narrower, the porch a little darker, the basement more steep. Over the black front door a circular window stared out like a solitary eye.

"Go away," screamed the voice in her brain for the last time. Abruptly Julia silenced it; her worldly wealth consisted of two pounds in notes and eighteen shillings in silver and a set of old French paste that was often mistaken for emeralds. There was a family legend that whoever parted with that brought doom upon himself. Through all the difficulties of the past six years of wage earning, Julia had clung to her paste. Unless she got this job that would have to go to Kutnows, the Polish jeweller on Fourth Street, who already had the star-shaped gold locket set with seed pearls, the

5

gold and turquoise Maltese cross with earrings to match, the gold chain set with fire opals and the gold brooch with its design of double hearts in pearls, that were her sole treasures. Leaving sanity behind her, she mounted the tessellated steps and rang the bell. After that, it was too late. The wheel began to turn and she was caught up in the web of an intricate machinery that made small work of her and her efforts.

The door was opened so suddenly by a butler with a face like a white fox that it seemed he must have expected her. Yet when she offered the pink card he merely shook his head, saying, "We never buy at the door." But he made no attempt to move backwards.

"Never!" he repeated.

"I've nothing to sell," began Julia. And stopped. Because it wasn't true. She had come here to sell her abilities, her time, her person- ality—herself, in short. "I wish to see Mrs. Ponsonby," she con- cluded. "If you will take that card . . ."

The butler accepted it reluctantly from her outstretched hand. Reluctantly he moved back to allow her to enter.

The hall was long and narrow and unexpectedly dark. A vase of everlastings stood on a black oak chest against one wall; in the wan blue light that hung from a colored glass shade the outlines of oil paintings could be detected higher up. The hall narrowed beyond the stairs, becoming a mere passage, with a door at the end. The door, she supposed, led to the basement. The fox-faced butler had disappeared into a room on the left, muttering that he would ascer- tain if madam . . . the rest of the words were lost in a blurred shadow of a voice.

Julia looked quickly over her shoulder; some movement there must have been, something to attract her attention. But actually there was nothing there. She tried to fix her mind on the oil paint- ings, to discover their subject. Years ago a man had said to her, "If ever you're afraid, look hard at something close by, examine it, brood upon it. Then you can't brood on anything else." The first painting represented a man who looked down at her with a sideways leer; it was not a pleasant face; the forehead was low, the lips treacherous. Turning away hurriedly her attention was caught by the stairs. These were narrow like the rest of the house; they wound upwards into a darkness that was absolute. She found herself rigidly attentive, listening intently—for what? She didn't know, but the sound, whatever it was, came from the upper floors. In that darkness something moved, something invisible and hostile.

"It's the new one," mute voices were saying. And the presences withdrew.

A voice in her ear made her start so violently that her heart seemed to leap in her breast. The strange butler was at her elbow.

"Mrs. Ponsonby will see you now," he said.

The room into which she stepped from the dark hall was so bright, so commonplace, that it dazzled her. She hesitated, bewildered, on the threshold. Afterwards, she realized that her first sensation had been one of unreality. There was something removed from life about the furnishing, the garish curtains, the great blocks of furniture that massed the walls, the pictures, the fire that, even on so warm an evening, burned in the old-fashioned grate. Strangest of all was the woman sitting close by the fire, who swivelled round sharply as the girl came in.

Laura Ponsonby looked odd; she was a little plump body, something like a caricature of Queen Victoria, with the same dumpy body and sparkling eyes, the dominating nose, the imperious air. Yet the resemblance was far from complete. Queen Victoria would never have worn a bright red dress hung about with chains and amulets; her arms would not have been decorated with broad gold bracelets, each set with a huge colored stone. And certainly Her Majesty's hair would have been a decent grey instead of the curled red wig that tilted a little on Mrs. Ponsonby's forehead.

"I've made a fool of myself," thought Julia, and the relief that stabbed her was like a physical pang. "She's only mad, not bad, as somehow I've feared. No wonder the other girls Mrs. Hurst sent here didn't want the job. Most likely that butler is a kind of attendant; that's why he was so long explaining who I was. And perhaps that's why the house is so dark."

All maniacs, no matter how mild their condition, have some particular foible. Psychiatrists can give it a name. This extraordinary old woman probably cherished in her mind some secret, mean-

7

ingless to any one but herself; and the net result was the dark hall, the mysterious butler set against the vivid contrast of this room blazing with light and color. Mrs. Ponsonby had been engaged in a game of Miss Milligan when her visitor arrived. She used very large cards that entirely covered the surface of the old-fashioned sewing table that was drawn up by the hearth. The cards were so big that they seemed as much as her fat little hands could manage. But even here her love of color and display found expression. The box in which they were kept was of scarlet leather; the pattern on them was a brilliant flower design. When she leaned forward to move a card the firelight struck innumerable sparks from the jewels that she wore on her fingers. One great square emerald instantly held the girl's attention; it was so like the big paste ring in her top-drawer at the lodginghouse in Roland Street, the ring she would have to pawn if she did not get this position. The sense of unreality increased. It was like being in the pit of a dark theatre, watching a bizarre play unfold itself on the stage. And as that thought flashed through Julia's mind she began to wonder about Mrs. Ponsonby. Had she perhaps been an actress once and did she still retain her theatrical sense? In the girl's mind fear and excitement struggled together.

She came forward a step, her eyes passing rapidly from one object to the next; there were big brass vases full of flowers wherever the eye rested; but as she saw them more clearly she saw that they were all artificial. Huge red poppies nodded in one corner; red and pink roses were massed in another; delphiniums swayed in a white jar painted in vivid stencils; the old-fashioned easy chairs were almost hidden by the cushions piled upon them; and these cushions were striped and embroidered and fringed with red and green and blue. The general effect was hypnotizing. Julia felt as though she had left her everyday self in the hall, and someone she hardly knew came forward another step, forward to the little engrossed figure bent above its cards.

Laura Ponsonby's eye seemed to take in everything about her visitor at a single glance; it swept over the neat, tired figure, in its dark frock and small hat drawn well over the forehead; saw the dust on the well-mended shoes, registered the fact that the girl's gloves were made of dark-blue string. Only when her gaze lighted on Julia's handbag of scarlet leather did she begin to smile.

"Poor thing!" thought Julia, compassionately. "She's like a child or one of those birds that can't resist anything that glitters." And her voice was gentle as she said, "Mrs. Ponsonby? Mrs. Hurst of the Victoria Bureau told me to call. She said you were looking for a secretary."

Mrs. Ponsonby's attention seemed to wander; her little bright black eyes came back to the cards on the table in front of her.

"It's coming out," she announced, pouncing on a King of Hearts. "There's a space . . ."

She manipulated the cards so swiftly that it was impossible to follow her movements. In about a minute all eight piles were stacked up in orderly fashion. The little plump figure leaned back.

"So you've come about the situation," she said. "Come and sit here and tell me all about yourself."

Her voice was lively and warm; her beringed hand patted a long box ottoman, covered in cheerful sugar-stick silk. Julia sat down.

"I'm twenty-three and I'm looking for a job," she said. "Mrs. Hurst thought I might suit you. She didn't tell me very much or whether you wanted special qualifications, but I've had six years' experience and I could show you good references . . ." She had a dazed feeling; this was no way to open an interview. But then Mrs. Ponsonby didn't conform to type either. She should be asking specific questions, explaining what she required. Mrs. Ponsonby nodded.

"I don't mind about those. I'm accustomed to drawing my own conclusions. How soon could you come?"

"At once."

Mrs. Ponsonby softly clapped her hands; they were so plump it was like two little fat cushions being patted against each other.

"That's the sort of answer I like. Where are you living?"

"At Spencer House."

"What's that?"

"It's just a—a lodginghouse of sorts."

"A hostel for working girls?"

"Not that exactly. Mrs. Mackie just lets out rooms and you can have food if you want it."

"As I expect you do."

"Well, no, actually I don't. I get my meals out. It's—more of a change."

"Very wise of you." Mrs. Ponsonby nodded vigorously; one of the tight red curls unrolled a little and stood up like a question mark. "I suppose you have friends . . ."

"Not at Spencer House. It's a very keep-yourself-to-yourself kind of place. The regular lodgers who have meals with Mrs. Mackie know one another of course, but if you're out a lot, and don't eat with them, you really don't see any one to speak to at all."

"Have you been there long?"

"About four months."

"And what did you do before that? Live with your people?"

"Oh, no, I haven't any people. My parents were drowned when I was four years old. I was brought up by an aunt, but she died about six years ago, and I've been living on my own ever since. Actually, I haven't been in London long. My aunt lived in Edinburgh and I worked up there until last Christmas."

"And then you thought you'd like to come to town and see a little more life?"

"Yes," agreed Julia. She had never spoken to any one of the real reason for leaving Edinburgh. An unfortunate love affair, in which she had been serious and the man had not, had made her eager to leave the city and its memories and hopes. In London, where she knew no one, she could, she thought, begin a new life. Besides, in Edinburgh she might meet Hugh at any moment; her humiliation and suffering had been very great, and she had the sense to know that nothing could work so complete or rapid a cure as an entire change of scene.

"And you like London?" Laura Ponsonby was watching her with interest. Julia had the uncomfortable feeling that the little black eyes saw a good deal more than they were intended to. Again the thought of hypnotism came into her mind.

"She'll have me telling her the whole story in a minute," she whispered to herself, appalled. "And yet, I'm certain she's not sympathetic. It's just that she's got so much vitality she draws things out of you."

In reply to the last question she answered a little nervously, "It's still rather a strange city to me. It's fascinating, of course. I've spent most of my spare time exploring. And, of course, I had a job . . ."

"What made you leave that?"

"It was only temporary. I wasn't wanted for more than two months." That was a better reply than she had made to Mrs. Hurst.

"And what have you been doing just lately?"

All the employers asked that question sooner or later; it was the kingpin of the situation. When they heard that she had been unemployed for nearly nine weeks they lost interest. A girl with good qualifications, their manner implied, could always find a job. Either they set her down as inefficient or else they thought she had someone behind her, as one of the women at the agencies had phrased it. Julia drew a deep breath and began to speak very quickly.

"I've been looking for work. But it's not so easy as it sounds. The war has disintegrated a lot of businesses, and then employers for the most part seem to prefer London girls. Several of the agencies warned me of that. But if I could get started I know I should give satisfaction. I have a four year reference from my last position in Edinburgh."

"Why did you leave?"

"I—wanted to come to London."

Mrs. Ponsonby nodded. The long jade rings in her ears swung violently in opposite directions. "I understand. I don't want to probe into your personal affairs. You've a right to your own life. I can see, of course, that you're not being quite frank with me, but you have your reasons, and I can probably guess what they are. But tell me one more thing—are you engaged to be married?"

"Oh, no," cried Julia in a low voice. "Oh, no."

Mrs. Ponsonby's little fat hand stole out and rested on the girl's knee.

"So that's it? I wondered. But, if you'll take advice from a woman old enough to be your mother, try and believe that it isn't the past that matters but the future. No girl's life was ever ruined by a love affair unless she allowed it to be. Disappointments happen to every

11

one, but they pass. I know. Life hasn't always been easy for me. Now—do you think you would like to be my secretary? It's a very quiet life. I don't entertain much, and of course the war has hit me like every one else. What I want is companionship as much as anything else. Of course there would be my correspondence; I belong to various charitable committees and there are letters in connection with them; and there would be the household accounts, all that kind of thing. But nothing you couldn't manage perfectly easily. I'm offering a hundred a year and your keep, but I want to be certain of getting settled with the right girl. I had one who left me at practically no notice because of some domestic complication. That's very upsetting for me and for the servants. Peters—you saw him when you came in—has been with me for thirty years, and so has Sparkes, my maid. Thirty years is a long time. You become a creature of habit. I don't like chopping and changing, any more than I like modern furniture and modern clothes. If you'd told me you were thinking of getting married I wouldn't have offered you the post, because in a few months you'd be wanting to go off and leave me in the lurch. You must promise to stay a year, anyhow. I don't like these constant upsets."

It was all perfectly reasonable; Mr. Horncastle in Edinburgh had said the same. "If we give you a start here I don't want you leaving within six months because some other firm will pay you another half-crown a week. Actually, we're paying you while you get your experience, and we expect you to take that into consideration when you're worth more money." Mr. Horncastle had treated her well, and she had been happy there. Only, to be honest, she must admit that a good deal of her happiness had its source in Hugh. That must be the case, because when Hugh went out of her life she couldn't bear the office any longer.

Common sense told her to jump at the opportunity now being offered her. After all, there hadn't been so many people eager to employ her services that she had any justification for hesitating. And yet—and yet—— Her restless fingers pleated the fringe that embellished the ottoman. Someone had held a cigarette carelessly close to the covering and had burnt a little hole in it; unconsciously she explored the edges of the silk, feeling the soft stuffing, thinking desperately, "Why don't I say yes? Why don't I? Why don't I?"

She looked up from these doubts to see Mrs. Ponsonby watching her slyly. In the fireplace a coal fell and a flame shot up, throwing a ruddy glow on the little intent face and outstretched hand. It was absurd, thought Julia impatiently, to feel a sudden shock of terror at so normal a happening. Just because the flame and the shadow were red and the dress and wig were red, why should she suddenly think of blood that was red, too? To punish herself for her undisciplined mind she came to an abrupt decision.

"I'd like to come, Mrs. Ponsonby, if you'll have me. I hope I'll be able to please you. When would you want me to start?"

Mrs. Ponsonby twisted the little watch on her bosom. It hung from a red enamel bow. "It's just after half-past six. You could be here before nine, couldn't you?"

Julia stared. "You mean—tonight?"

"Yes. What would be so difficult? Have you an engagement for the evening?"

"It isn't that. No, actually I haven't. But it's rather short notice. I should have to give up my room . . ."

"How do you rent that?"

"By the week. As a matter of fact, I give a week's notice informally each Monday, in case something—like this—should turn up . . ."

"So you're due to leave on Monday in any case. And this is Friday. You don't stand to lose much."

"No, that's true. I thought perhaps tomorrow morning . . ."

Mrs. Ponsonby shook her head and again the earrings swung in opposite directions. "No. I have a lot of work to get through tomorrow, and I want to start early. It means wasting a whole morning. Can't you pack your belongings and be here by nine? Have you so much luggage?"

"I've only one suitcase," Julia confessed. "Yes, of course, I could come in tonight."

"Then that's settled." Mrs. Ponsonby leaned back and pushed an electric bell with one stubby little finger. "I'm glad to be fixed up. All this change is very disturbing."

13

The door opened and the manservant came in. "Peters, tell Sparkes I want her. This is Miss Ross. She'll be coming in tonight."

Peters turned and looked at Julia consideringly. Then with a murmured, "Yes, madam. I'll tell her," he went away.

"Tomorrow," said Mrs. Ponsonby, "you shall ring up this Mrs. Hurst and tell her I'm settled. I don't want a lot more girls coming round."

"She asked me to let her know . . ." murmured Julia, feeling that some response was expected of her.

"It's too late to write tonight. The last post goes out at seven-thirty. Besides, the morning will be time enough."

The door opened again and Sparkes came in. She was a thin dry woman of fifty, very upright, moving with the same curious silent step as the butler.

"Sparkes, this is Miss Ross. She will be taking Miss Hope's place. See that a room is put ready for her. She moves in tonight."

Sparkes in her turn surveyed the girl; then with a smile that had been kept on ice since the declaration of war, she said gently, "That'll be very satisfactory, madam. What time will Miss Ross be arriving?"

"Before nine." Mrs. Ponsonby turned to Julia. "I forgot to tell you—I keep very early hours. Peters has orders to lock up at black-out time, and I don't have the door unfastened again until the morning. In these days I don't consider it safe. One hears so many stories. So you'll be sure not to be late, won't you?"

She put out her hand and Julia took it unenthusiastically. The next instant she was stifling a cry. The little boneless hand seemed possessed of superhuman strength; the rings sank into the girl's flesh. Another flash of firelight passed over the woman's face, distorting it, so that its smile that had been one of pure friendliness a moment earlier now looked malicious and triumphant. Then the flame died down as swiftly as it had arisen and Julia saw that Mrs. Ponsonby's expression had not really changed. She looked pleased and tranquil; a rather tiresome domestic matter had been settled and now she could dismiss it from her mind. It meant no more to her than that.

Julia came back into the hall, with the long-coveted job in her pocket. For the next year, provided she satisfied her new employer, she was sure of a roof over her head and three full meals a day. In addition she would receive a generous salary. At the year's end she could leave, if she liked, with her savings, which should be at least half her salary. By that time, too, she would surely have recovered from her infatuation and its humiliating sequel. It was better than she had dared to dream. It was odd, she thought, that she shouldn't feel happier about it. She wished she were less lonely, could have had breathing space to discuss the proposition with someone else. Only there was no one—except Colin.

With a sudden lifting of the heart she decided to tell Colin about it.

2

TO THOSE WHO BELIEVE that there is a pattern behind this bewildering universe, it must sometimes be disconcerting to realize on what trifles the most momentous decisions may hang. Had Julia so much as breathed a word about Colin to Mrs. Ponsonby, she would not have been offered the position of companion-secretary, and the whole course of her life would have been different. She had not thought of mentioning him because, strictly speaking, Colin played no part in her plans. When she said that she had neither relatives nor friends she believed she was speaking the truth. A man whom one has casually picked up at a Lyons teashop and who is, on his own admission, engaged to a girl in Ireland, can hardly be called a friend. Yet he was the only person in whom Julia could confide.

She hurried through the dark hall and out of the door that the butler was holding open. In the street she was surprised to see how light it still was; the sullen glow had faded and the clear insubstantial light of evening filled the town. Glancing at her watch she saw that it was a quarter to seven. Seven o'clock was her usual dining hour. If she were much later she might miss Colin altogether. She decided, therefore, to go straight to Lyons and have a meal before returning to Spencer House.

Lyons at that hour was fairly full, but Colin had kept her a place at his table. They had fallen into the habit of eating together for some weeks now.

"Hallo!" he said as she pulled out a chair. "Wondered if you were giving me the bird."

"Had to see about a job," replied Julia laconically, wondering whether to choose fried egg and chips or baked beans on toast and treacle pudding and deciding in favor of beans. She gave the order to the waitress.

"Any luck?" asked Colin. He was a tall lanky young man with a thin face and a roving eye and a lock of fair hair falling into it.

"I start tonight."

Colin whistled. "You're a swift worker."

"Should you say two months finding a job was quick work?"

"I mean, when you do get on the track you don't lose any time. What's it like?"

"Secretary to a lunatic," said Julia more cheerfully. "What are you having?"

"Bacon and eggs. Shall you continue to dine here?"

Julia drew a long breath. "I shall dine—I hope—on roast chicken with bread sauce and French pancake and cream—with Mrs. Ponsonby."

"Is she the lunatic?"

"She is."

"Excuse my asking but have you a bias in favor of the unbalanced?"

"It doesn't sound so good put that way. Actually, she's the only person I've so far interviewed who is prepared to employ me."

"You're right," agreed Colin gravely. "It doesn't sound so good. I take it, you're living in."

"Right in. No latchkeys and the front door locked at nine."

"She's a lunatic all right. What does she expect you to do? Get out through the kitchen window?"

"I'm sure that'll be bolted too."

"Then perhaps there's a sympathetic parlor-maid."

"All I've seen are a butler looking like a fox in winter and a woman most inappropriately called Sparkes."

"Where is this desirable residence?"

"Henriques Square."

Colin nodded thoughtfully. "You're on the up-and-up all right. The very heart of Mayfair."

"If you said the Never-Never Land it would sound just as likely."

"Meaning?"

The baked beans arrived and Julia inspected them. "When I'm a rich woman, Colin, I'll never even expect my tweeny to eat these. Oh, just that it's queer. I mean, Mrs. P. sits in a room like the burning fiery furnace, but there's hardly a glimmer of light in the rest of the place."

"Patriotic," suggested Colin.

"It could be," agreed Julia. "I do hope she keeps a generous table."

Colin laughed; then sobered abruptly. "I'm going to miss you, Julia," he said. "There'll be no one to talk to at dinner any more."

"The world's full of girls," Julia rallied him.

"Will you get out ever in the evening?"

"Until nine o'clock."

He frowned. "Were you serious when you said she was mad?"

An odd smile curved Julia's lips; it gave a look of experience to her childish face. "She's rich, Colin. The rich can afford to be mad."

Colin said a sudden thing. "Chuck it, Julia. I don't believe your heart's in it."

"And who'll pay my rent? Don't be ridiculous, Colin." Her voice roughened. "I've got my living to get."

"But must it be with her? I believe you're going against your will."

"Well, it's not exactly an exciting household; a crazy old woman playing patience and two servants who've been there for thirty years and look as if they'd only stepped out of the tomb to say 'good-evening' to you. But it's a job, and they don't fall like plums from trees these days."

"I suppose not." He shook his head as though he were shaking off a sense of responsibility. "Do you remember the first night we spoke? You were so resentful I nearly took up my coat and went away. You said, 'Have you realized there are plenty of empty chairs in this res-

17

taurant, and if you like, I can occupy one of those?' You were very
distrustful, weren't you?"

Julia bent over her roll and sliced it in half. How could she say,
I was mistrustful of all men, after Hugh. Or, since Hugh fooled me
I didn't want to speak to another man. Lifting her head again, she
laughed.

"And all you wanted to do was to talk about Paddy. When are
you going to marry her?"

"As soon as I can. You'd like Paddy, Julia; she's what I've always
wanted in a girl. She's proud and she's brave and she's very good fun
and she'll be a fine wife . . ." He stopped, coloring a little. "You
think I'm mad, don't you?"

"I think Paddy's lucky," replied Julia in steady tones. For an instant she hated the girl she had never seen. Why did it have to be
her luck to get a man like Colin, who wasn't only faithful but had
that indefinable quality known as charm, while she, Julia, fell for a
man who only wanted a bit of fun and wouldn't have dreamed of
marrying a girl without a penny to her name? Her heart ached, and
suddenly she was glad she was going to Mrs. Ponsonby, to work and
forget, to sever herself completely from the life she knew, to be part
of a strange household; Colin was her last link with the past. After
tonight a new phase of experience would open. She said, "I haven't
long. I have to be in by nine and I haven't packed yet, or broken it
to Mrs. Mackie that I'm leaving. I only came to tell you, in case
you thought I was ill or something."

"Can't I come and carry your suitcase for you and give the old
lady the once-over? Then, if I don't think it's safe . . ."

"Colin, that's sheer melodrama. Of course it's safe. Safe and dull.
Besides, she doesn't approve of followers."

"Did she say so?"

"She doesn't want a lot of chopping and changing."

"You haven't tied yourself down, Julia?"

"I've said I'll probably stay a year. Well, I shall have to work somewhere and it's good pay as pay goes these days."

"I shall take you out on your day off," said Colin. "I feel responsible for you."

"That's ridiculous. Your responsibility is towards Paddy."

"She wouldn't mind," said Colin, quietly.

"I wonder if I'll ever meet her."

"I hope so. Give me your address so that I know where to find you. I don't like the way you're cutting yourself off."

She repeated the number of the house and watched him put it down in a little notebook. "Telephone?"

"I suppose so. She must be in the book."

"I suppose she must." He laughed again. "I was thinking of your face that first evening. You were wondering why I wasn't in uniform. You were afraid I was a C.O."

"You still haven't told me what you really do."

"A pen-pusher for H.M. Government. Not romantic, is it?"

"Someone has to," said Julia, briefly, taking a shilling out of her purse. "Good-bye, Colin. If ever I get the chance I'll look in here about seven o'clock and see if you're still alone."

"I'll have called to take you out before then. Au revoir, Julia. Be good to yourself."

But after she had gone he sat for some time, smoking cigarettes in sharp angry gasps, wondering about Mrs. Ponsonby.

It was nearly eight o'clock when Julia arrived at Spencer House where every one who was in dined at seven. In the hall she met Bertha, the new maid, a white-faced, secretive-looking girl who clearly disliked her job.

"Bertha, is Mrs. Mackie in?" she asked.

Bertha tossed her head. "Gone to the pictures with that Miss Waterer."

Miss Waterer occupied the first floor and was a favorite because she invited Mrs. Mackie up to her room for sherry and biscuits and discussions about life. Miss Waterer liked it to be known that she hadn't always lived on a small income in an obscure lodginghouse; she talked of 'me horses' and 'me father's yacht,' assuming an Irish brogue that sounded like the brogues you hear on the stage. Phoney, thought Julia. But she still had enough money to go out most evenings; and when no one better offered she would treat Mrs. Mackie. It was an investment of a kind. Miss Waterer's room had the least scrubby towels, the only scented cake of soap; Miss Waterer's plate held the choicest cuts from the joint, the largest baked potato, the most generous helping of coffee cream when the tinned peaches went the rounds. Her choice of a companion this evening, however, made Julia's position a little difficult. She had intended to explain matters to Mrs. Mackie in person, but it was now obvious that she must leave a note with Bertha. She went up to her room, aware that she had not much time. Fortunately her possessions did not take long to pack. The last of her treasures, the set of emerald paste, she put carefully at the bottom of her case, together with her identity card and one of her two remaining pound notes; the rest of her things were swiftly folded and put in, the lid fastened, and her coat and hat taken from the bed. She looked round the room she was leaving; it was small and uncomfortable, yet it had represented a kind of security. She thought of the dark house to which she was going and shivered. Seated at the little rickety table she scribbled a few lines to Mrs. Mackie. There were one or two minor accounts to be met—three shillings for laundry, two shillings Mrs. Mackie had paid the cleaners on her behalf, four breakfasts at ninepence each— gas-rings in the rooms were forbidden by the thrifty directors of Spencer House. Lodgers invariably took breakfast; girls with livings to get couldn't face the prospect of stealing out on black winter mornings into teashops where floors were still being washed in order to save coppers. Julia wrote her note hurriedly and put some silver into the envelope. She gave her address at Henriques Square in case any other accounts should be outstanding. Then she picked up the suitcase and came down to the hall.

A small lamp burned bluely in its shaded glass bowl; on every floor doors were closed; behind one or two she heard a wireless playing softly or voices murmuring; Bertha had presumably returned to the basement. Mrs. Mackie did a good deal of the cooking herself, with Bertha and a daily woman to look after the house that was not, of course, particularly well looked-after. The woman would have gone home by now; Mrs. Mackie was out; no one but Bertha remained. Julia pressed the bell and after a pause Bertha stuck her head round the top of the basement stairs.

"Bertha, I have to go now."

"What? For good?"

"Yes. I'm starting a new job tonight."

The rest of Bertha lounged insolently into view. New job nothing, said her attitude. We know that kind of job all right. Her eyes rested on Julia's suitcase.

Julia saw that look and interpreted it, but she choked down the rising tide of anger with the reflection that Bertha simply wasn't worth it. She was nothing but a slut who would probably only stay long enough to get herself into trouble with one of the tradesmen and then would be pushed out by a furious Mrs. Mackie to look after herself as best she could.

"Will you give Mrs. Mackie this letter?" Julia continued holding out the envelope. A moment later she experienced a pang of misgiving when she saw the sudden glint in Bertha's eye. It was obvious that there was money with the letter; Julia would have recalled the gesture had there been time, but it was impossible.

"I'll give it her," said Bertha, slowly. "What's the matter? Have you got to thinking I'm not honest?"

"Of course not," said Julia in hurried tones. "You must explain I had to go without warning—I didn't know she'd be out."

"And she didn't know you'd be going." Bertha slipped the envelope into the pocket of her apron.

"You won't forget," urged Julia.

"P'raps you'd like to call a policeman and tell him you think I'm a thief. Let me tell you, Miss Ross, my mother brought us up honest and decent . . ."

Julia went over to the door. "That'll do, Bertha. I never suggested you wouldn't give the letter to Mrs. Mackie. Ask her to send me the receipt to the address inside, will you?"

"Do I call you a taxi?" Bertha inquired, not moving from her stance in the back hall.

"Oh, no. It's not far."

Bertha nodded languidly. "O.K. And the case isn't heavy, I suppose."

Julia felt herself flushing at the implication. "By the way," said Bertha, "I meant to tell you—I found this outside your room this morning. You must of dropped it." Still without moving, she offered Julia a scrap of cardboard. Julia recognized it at once; there's some-

21

thing about a pawn ticket that screams its identity to the world at large. Julia snatched it out of the lazy unwashed hand.

"Oh—thank you—Bertha." She felt for her purse and took out a shilling. The girl had only been there a week and even a shilling was more than Julia could afford. Bertha took the money without comment and dropped it into her apron pocket. The battered grandfather clock struck three times. Eight forty-five! It was going to be a rush to get to Henriques Square. Perhaps she'd better take a taxi, after all.

It's on trifles that tremendous issues hang. If Julia had risked a florin and taken a taxi the driver might have been traced later on when people started making inquiries; but thrift was so firmly ingrained in her by this time that she decided to risk it. A No. 88 bus was passing and stopped a few yards from the door. At Marble Arch she changed to a No. 73; as she waited on the step of No. 30 Henriques Square she heard a clock somewhere begin to strike nine.

After the front door of Spencer House had clanged quietly behind Julia, the slovenly maidservant came into the hall and, standing under the shaded light, tore open the envelope addressed to Mrs. Mackie. She glanced cursorily at the letter, then greedily counted the silver. Eight shillings. She smiled and dropped the coins into her pocket to join the single shilling Julia had handed her. The letter she tore up and later burned in the kitchen grate. Mrs. Mackie and Miss Waterer returned at a quarter to eleven. Bertha by this time had gone to bed. Mrs. Mackie went into the room she called her office and set down her accounts, checking up the result with the money in her purse. She looked for any letters that might have come, but now that there was no evening post there was nothing. There was nothing on the hall table, either, where lodgers sometimes left notes for her. At eleven o'clock she bolted the front door and put on the chain. It was a rule of the house that the door was bolted at eleven, unless one of the tenants had given notice that she would be late (Spencer House only catered to women). No one had given notice or left a message, so Mrs. Mackie assumed that every one was in. She knew nothing of Julia's departure until nine o'clock the next morning by which time Julia was no longer in London.

22

3

PETERS WAS WAITING by the front door as Julia came panting up the steps; at the sound of her bell he let her in reluctantly, his manner saying more clearly than any word that she had run it exceedingly fine. After he had admitted her, he stooped to draw the lower bolt, stretched for the upper one, slipped on the chain and fastened the patent lock. There was nothing they had forgotten, Julia reflected, and suddenly she was thinking, wasn't it rather odd that in the heart of London, with policemen everywhere, a woman should take such elaborate precautions?

"And do they never have guests to dinner?" she asked herself. But that question she supposed she would be able to answer for herself in due course.

Peters, having completed his preparations for the night, took no further notice of the newcomer. Moving like a cat he went past her and into the basement regions; he must have told Sparkes that Julia had arrived, for a moment later the woman came gliding through the dim hall and paused at the girl's side, saying, "If you will come with me I'll show you your room." Julia hesitated a moment, glancing at the suitcase that she had set on a chair, but the woman paid no attention. So, picking it up, Julia prepared to trudge up to the attics. To her surprise Sparkes halted on the second floor.

"Madam's put you here," she said. "It's the room Miss Hope had."

If this room was typical of the treatment Mrs. Ponsonby meted out to her employees, Julia might have congratulated herself. It was clearly one of the two best bedrooms in the house, very finely furnished with a modern bed and a fine handsome carpet and fittings. There were no modern conveniences such as hot and cold water, but a painted glass basin and jug stood on a polished table and heavy fleecy towels were draped over a rail.

"It's a very nice room," Julia said, inadequately.

The maid did not reply. Instead she crossed to the windows and

23

began to close the shutters. These four windows filled almost the whole of one wall.

Julia moved quickly. "Oh, please, is that necessary? I like all the air I can get."

Sparkes paid no attention; she continued to unfold and bolt the shutters, fastening them with a broad metal bar fitting into a slot.

"Madam is very particular about light," she explained coldly, stepping backwards. "She doesn't like any window lights, either."

This was proved by the fact that the electric light socket above the dressing table was empty; the only other light stood by the bed and was a dull blue.

"Surely it wouldn't be seen from here," ejaculated the girl. "Not with all those shutters closed."

"Those are madam's orders," responded Sparkes, briefly. She moved towards the door, leaving Julia standing irresolutely by the foot of the bed.

"Shan't I—won't Mrs. Ponsonby want to see me again tonight?" she ventured.

"I'll let you know if she does."

This was very odd, reflected Julia, but then the whole household was odd. She exclaimed impulsively, "I hope—Mrs. Ponsonby isn't ill or anything?"

"Ill?" Sparkes stared. "Why should you think that?"

"Oh, I don't know. I thought perhaps if she didn't want to see me this evening she might not be well . . ." her voice trailed away into a lame silence. "Well, then, I'll get on with my unpacking until she's ready for me."

"Madam said there would be no need to unpack."

Julia jerked round. "No need? What does that mean?"

"Only just for the night. You'll be going away in the morning."

"Oh, no," said Julia, softly. "Mrs. Ponsonby didn't say anything about that to me. Or has something happened to make her change her plans?"

"I couldn't say," replied the woman in the same lifeless voice. "Those are madam's orders."

Like a parrot, thought Julia, only she's a lot more than a machine really. She knows what's going on, though she won't tell me. Why

24

didn't Mrs. Ponsonby explain about going away? She took a quick step forward.

"I'd like to see Mrs. Ponsonby at once. There's been some misunderstanding . . ."

Sparkes stepped on to the landing. "I'll come for you when madam's ready," she said, and closed the door.

Left to herself Julia stood panic-stricken for an instant. Not for one moment did she believe that anything had happened to change Mrs. Ponsonby's plans during the past two hours. No, she had intended all along to make this mysterious journey in the morning, that explained some of the strange questions she had asked.

"She didn't even mention where we were going. She wanted to be sure I had no ties. She was afraid of someone interfering, but why should she be, if it's all above-board? But, of course, it isn't. There's something odd here. Why am I given the best bedroom in the house? Answer: Because there are shutters and it's essential for her purpose that there should be. Also, this looks over the back. Even if I unfastened the shutters there would be no one in sight. I know these houses. Little patches of garden and the backs of the houses opposite. On the front there are policemen and taxicabs and people walking up and down.

"She's got me here like something in a trap, and she doesn't mean to let me go. But why? What possible use can I be to her?"

Whatever the reason, she was resolved not to spend the night under this roof. By this time she could read a sinister implication in the simplest development. When Sparkes returned at a quarter to ten with the news that Mrs. Ponsonby was now ready for her, she found that Julia had not so much as removed her hat. As the woman entered, Julia stooped for the unopened suitcase.

"You won't be wanting that," Sparkes suggested.

"There's been some mistake. I shan't be spending the night here. I—don't wish to leave London."

"That's no way to talk, miss," said Sparkes, coldly. "Mrs. Ponsonby offered you a position and you accepted it. You can't let her down now, not till she's got someone else."

"She didn't expect to get a secretary this evening. In the morning Mrs. Hurst will send her someone else."

"And madam doesn't like being kept waiting," Sparkes continued meaningly. Coming forward, she took the suitcase from the girl's hand. "If you do agree to leave, Peters will bring this down for you. But I should think twice. It might look a bit funny your going back to wherever you were living, saying you'd changed your mind. I don't think madam would like it, either."

Her mind a jumble of apprehensions and suspicions, the girl followed her guide down a flight of tall narrow steps into the huge double drawing room. Here Mrs. Ponsonby's love of light was emphasized by the two lamps with high-powered bulbs that were placed on each side of the chair in which she lay. These lamps were carefully shaded to prevent their rays being seen from outside with the result that they left a large part of the room in shadow. Standing for an instant in that shadow, Julia's conviction of unreality redoubled. The drawing room, in contradistinction to the emphatic Victorianism of the parlor, was Empire in period. Chairs, writing desk, draperies, had all been chosen to create an unforgettable picture. And here, as before, it was the personality of Mrs. Ponsonby that counted. Put her in a room of steel furniture, put her in a wigwam, and it wouldn't make any difference. It was the woman herself who was notable. Indeed, Julia had the hazy feeling that these surroundings only existed because Mrs. Ponsonby willed that they should; that if she rose and went away the room would dissolve into thin air. She even wondered whether she herself could continue to exist if the dumpy little woman in the red silk dress—for she wore red at night as well as by day—chose to forget her.

"She's dangerous," registered Julia's brain. "Thank Heaven I told Colin I was here." It occurred to her that until Mrs. Mackie returned from the pictures and opened her letter no one but Colin had any idea where she was.

Mrs. Ponsonby looked up. "So you're here. I began to think you were going to fail me. It was nine o'clock when you arrived."

"I had several things to do," protested the girl.

"Such as?"

"I had to pack and get some dinner and settle some small bills . . ."

"And ring up some friends, perhaps?"

"No, there wasn't time for that."

She was convinced it was not imagination that Mrs. Ponsonby's smile sweetened. *She doesn't want any one to know I'm here*, said a small merciless voice in Julia's brain. *That's why we're going away tomorrow.*

"Your maid told me not to unpack," she said clearly.

Mrs. Ponsonby seemed undisturbed. "It seems such a waste of time when we're going away in the morning."

"You didn't tell me that."

"You weren't in my service until nine o'clock tonight. Naturally I shouldn't discuss my plans with a stranger."

"I don't want to leave London. I shouldn't have accepted the position if I'd known."

"You told me you had no ties. Was that untrue?"

"No. I haven't. But . . ."

"Then why should you object to going to the country for a short time? As a matter of fact, my doctor has ordered me to take a rest. I've not been well. That's another reason why I want a secretary—to take the little anxieties off my shoulders. What's your real objection?"

She fixed Julia with a piercing eye. Julia felt helpless. She could find nothing to say. Mrs. Ponsonby went on, "I have had trouble enough as it is. Miss Hope left me with hardly a word of warning, and now, when I think I'm fixed up, you want to upset all my plans. If you hadn't told me you could come in tonight I shouldn't have arranged to leave in the morning. I hope you're not going to prove one of these temperamental young women. I thought you looked so sane. That's one reason why I offered you the position."

Julia looked at her dumbly; the situation seemed closed. Besides, her last words suggested that Mrs. Ponsonby was one of those unbalanced women who are accustomed to having their smallest wish granted, and are genuinely incapable of seeing any one else's point of view. Quite at random she had decided she was tired of London and wanted a rest in the country; obviously, therefore, her entire circle must be prepared to transfer themselves.

"And then, of course, she holds the purse strings, and that would count for a great deal with her," Julia reminded herself.

"It will be a nice holiday for you, too," the older woman continued. "I dare say we shan't be away long, but all the noise and bustle of the city exhausts me. I'm not so young as I was. I want some quiet." Her voice became more dreamy. "We'll find a little place in the country, away from the traffic and the bells and the telephones— and people everywhere, people prying and whispering and wanting to know things. It'll be nice to be in the country, away from it all."

Definitely she was a mental case, decided Julia, and for some reason her spirits began to rise. Sparkes must know the truth; probably she also was some sort of attendant. Julia felt sympathetic for the abused Miss Hope who had departed without notice. She wondered how long she had stood the strain. She didn't blame her, but her own fears sank. A doctor whom she had met in Edinburgh had once told her that she had the makings of an excellent mental nurse. "You're well-balanced yourself," he had said, "and that's of the utmost importance in controlling others; and I think you are naturally kind. That creates confidence." Julia remembered his words now. Mrs. Ponsonby, who had been watching her face, suddenly put out a hand and laid it on Julia's arm.

"You didn't really mean it," she suggested. "You don't mind coming to the country. It's only for a short visit. The doctor thinks I've been doing too much—all these war charities and the general strain. And I like the look of you. I hate having nothing but old people about me."

Julia's resistance softened. "Of course I like the country," she said. "Where do you think of going?"

"A very nice place," replied Mrs. Ponsonby vaguely, "very nice indeed. Nice and quiet. I don't like noise, you know. It upsets me."

As she spoke the telephone suddenly began to ring. Julia looked round quickly but could not detect the instrument. At the sound a change overspread Mrs. Ponsonby's little eager face. She put out the hand that hadn't been holding on to Julia and plucked an elaborate French doll from an adjacent table, revealing an old-fashioned black instrument. Whoever was at the other end of the line was not far off; the voice came through like the whisper of a ghost.

"Yes," said Mrs. Ponsonby, "this is Mayfair 00991. Who? No, I think it's the wrong number. No, we don't know that name at all. I'm sorry."

She replaced the receiver and fumbled for the French doll. When she turned back to Julia she saw that a change had taken place. The girl was white as paper, her eyes burned.

"Why did you say that?" she demanded. "That call was for me. I heard my own name."

"You were deceived," said Mrs. Ponsonby instantly. "The call was for a Miss Cross. There's never been any one here of that name."

"It was Ross," Julia insisted.

"That's impossible. Why, you told me yourself that no one knew you were here. Who could telephone you?"

Julia realized that she was caught in her own trap. The instinct she had been denying since six o'clock that evening clamored in her ears. Don't tell her about Colin, it said. With difficulty she managed a smile.

"You're right, of course," she acknowledged, "and I beg your pardon. It couldn't have been for me."

Besides, it was possible she was genuinely mistaken. Why should Colin ring her up within an hour of her arrival? Nevertheless, all her previous fears rushed back upon her. The ensuing silence was broken by the chiming of a French clock set under a glass cover on the white-painted mantelpiece. As the tenth stroke died away the door opened and Peters came in with two glasses of milk on a tray.

"Your milk, madam," he said.

"Is it ten o'clock already? Ah, you've brought a glass for Miss Ross. That was very thoughtful. It'll make you sleep," she added to Julia. "I wouldn't miss my glass of milk for anything."

Julia, who disliked hot milk, hesitated, but under the eyes of the two watchers her resistance weakened again. It wouldn't do to arouse suspicions in their minds. Already she was laying plans. It was too late tonight to do anything but appear to acquiesce in Mrs. Ponsonby's schemes; but she told herself that she had no intention of going with this strange woman and her sinister maid to "a quiet little place in the country where there will be no traffic, no people, no noise." Both women drank their milk standing, while Peters waited rigidly with the tray outstretched for the empty glasses. As soon as it was finished Mrs. Ponsonby said briskly, "That's all for tonight. We keep early hours here. I hope you'll sleep well and to-morrow we have a busy day."

Her words were a dismissal and as such Julia accepted them. She said good night and made her way up to her room. But she did not at once go to bed. First of all she opened the shutters and looked out. As she had expected, she saw nothing but the blind windows of the house opposite, and a little black garden in which cats rolled and loved noisily under the invisible laurels. The shrill scream of their amours broke up all the silence of the night. Drawing the curtains closely Julia switched on the bedside lamp; its blue gleam shone eerily in the big room leaving great patches of shadow in the corners. It occurred to her that she had forgotten to ask Sparkes the location of the bathroom, and she came out on to the landing to make the necessary inquiry. To her surprise the entire house was already plunged in darkness; yet she had heard no feet ascending the stairs, no doors close. The sense of being isolated in a strange place thickened; she tilted back her head as though she would pierce the darkness above her. She realized slowly that there were two floors at least up there. Who lived in those rooms? Or were they all empty? If the servants slept there, how was it that she had heard no one ascending? And why should everything be pitch dark?

"I can't stay alone on this landing," she muttered half aloud. "I must go down to where they all are. I believe she's evil, and I know Peters is, but all the same this loneliness is unendurable."

She had crept noiselessly down a few stairs when she became aware of a light moving slowly towards her. It was small and green and rose a few inches above the floor. Her blood turned to ice; she stood rooted to the dark stair. Then something touched her, some-thing soft and persuasive; a laugh choked in her throat.

"I'm going out of my mind," she warned herself. "Terrified of a cat, a walleyed black cat."

She stooped to lift the creature, thinking that any contact would be reassuring, but as her fingers touched the soft fur the animal glided away from her touch. She looked to see which way he had gone, but the green light had vanished as though someone had blown it out. Stealthily Julia descended a few more steps. Again she was arrested by a light, but this time of a different nature. A

30

wavering flame burned through the darkness, flinging the shadow of a huge menacing head on the wall; that misshapen head nodded at her as though it recognized her presence on the stairs; then slowly it moved on. After a moment it vanished downwards; Julia leaned over the staircase watching it go into the parlor.

"That was a candle," she thought, "but why, when the electric current is available?"

She was still pondering this peculiarity when a voice spoke in her ear.

"Did you lose your way?" it said.

Julia uttered a short cry. "I—I came to see if I could find someone. I don't know where the bathroom is," she stammered in desperation.

"If you'd rung I could have told you." Sparkes's voice was flat and inflexible. "Anyway, it wouldn't be on this floor."

"I suppose not," agreed Julia, her teeth chattering. "And then I nearly fell over a cat and that made me feel rather a fool." She was talking at random, her whole being chilled and horrified by the events of the last few moments. Yet when she was back in her room, she had to admit that her fears were absurd. She pictured herself telling the story to Colin, could see his astonished face.

"What on earth made you get in such a stew?" he'd ask. "It's normal to put out lights in the evening, and black cats are lucky. As for the candle, I suppose the old boy had forgotten something, and knowing that Mrs. P. was a terror for lights, he didn't dare switch them on."

Looked at like that, everything seemed perfectly normal. Yet she knew now that her first instinct had been correct. By coming to see Mrs. Ponsonby she had started the wheel spinning; it was impossible to guess what the pattern would be, only she was involved in it, whether it was for life or death.

"Certainly I'm going out of my mind," she told herself scornfully as she undressed, feeling suddenly extraordinarily tired. She was drifting into sleep when, with startling clarity, the thought came to her: That's what they mean me to do. Somehow I'm caught up in some hideous plot and they don't mean me to let me get away and tell the truth—to any one.

Exhausted though she was, Julia forced herself to get out of bed

31

and fix a chair under the handle of her door. She had already ascertained that there was no key for her protection, but no matter how deeply she slept she must be aroused by someone trying to force a way in. And it was a well-known gambit to steal into a room in the dark and contrive to terrify the occupant almost out of her wits. Thinking this, Julia put out her hand, half expecting another hand to reach out of the darkness and take it. When nothing of the kind happened her tortured mind suggested that the agony was being deliberately prolonged; while she lingered on the stairs someone had stolen in and concealed himself behind the curtains. The impression was so strong that she pushed the switch of the bedside lamp. Nothing happened; even the wan blue beam by which she had undressed failed to materialize. Then she understood the meaning of the candle. The electric current had been cut off.

When Sparkes had seen Julia safely back to her room she came downstairs to the parlor where Peters waited for her by candlelight.

"What did she want?" he demanded abruptly, as the woman came in.

"She was looking for the bathroom."

"I don't like it," said the man.

"I don't like it either," agreed Sparkes. "I never meant to get mixed up in—murder."

"Who's talking about murder?" Peters's voice rapped out the words.

"What else would you call it?"

"I wouldn't call it anything and nor will you if you've got any sense. Just you remember you know nothing—and that there's nothing for you to know."

Sparkes said fearfully, "A young girl—that makes it seem worse."

Peters's face darkened with rage. "You keep your mouth shut," he warned the woman. "Just remember you're in this with the rest of us. It's too late to start getting squeamish now. All you have to do is take orders. Leave the organization to us, see?"

Sparkes nodded slowly. "You needn't be afraid. It's not me that'll upset the apple-cart. All the same, I don't like it. And we're not out of the woods yet. This girl looks like trouble."

"We've had trouble before," said the man. "You'd better get back and make sure she's really asleep. We don't want any funny business here. When we're down there it'll be different. We can handle that all right."

Sparkes turned towards the door. "Did you know someone rang her up tonight?"

"Whoever it was won't have a chance to do that again, you take my word."

Sparkes left him standing in that crowded room, packed with the memories and lives of an earlier generation, the candle throwing monstrous shadows on the wall. Creeping up the stairs she hesitated at Julia's door and softly turned the knob. The door resisted and after a moment she stole away again. Another door opened and a faint pencil of light from a torch shone down the passage.

"Sparkes!" creaked Mrs. Ponsonby's voice.

"Sparkes, come in. We've got a lot to do before morning. We've got to make an early start."

4

FIGHTING AN OVERWHELMING DROWSINESS, Julia struggled with her plans for the morrow. Tonight Mrs. Ponsonby had won the first round, but tomorrow it would be Julia's turn.

"Get up very early." The words filtered through Julia's drugged mind. "Nothing to pack but a spongebag and hairbrush—get out before the old woman's down."

In daylight, surely, it would be less easy to hold a girl who desperately intended to get away. She had only to scream, to break a window—anything, she thought, no matter how undignified, so long as she escaped from this appalling house. She set her pocket alarm clock for six-thirty. By seven she would have left the premises. She could see no farther than that. The great thing was to get away.

Even if she had wanted to make more detailed plans it would have been impossible. The fumes of sleep came over her like waves of enemy bombers; no sooner did she drive off one attack than a second materialized. At last, exhausted by the experiences and alarms of the day, she let her head sink into her pillow and was swamped by sleep.

The black grandfather clock in the hall, with a foolish design of moons on its painted face, chimed the quarter. Someone gently tried the handle of Julia's door. Whatever obstruction had been placed against it the previous night had not been removed.

"What's wrong?" Like a shadow, Peters had materialized at the woman's side.

"Nothing. She's put the chest of drawers or something against the door. Doesn't trust us, I suppose."

"You'd better get her going. You know what it is. Someone doesn't like being kept waiting. Besides, the sooner this house is empty the better."

Sparkes shivered a little in the cheerful sunlight; her face looked like parchment, deeply inscribed with symbols. The hand she lifted to knock on the door shook a little.

Julia, waked out of a deep sleep, took an instant to realize her surroundings. Then, as her eyes took in the outlines of the furniture, the pattern of the carpet, the color of the quilt, her mind sharpened. Quickly she looked at the little clock on the bedside table. Eight-fifteen! She couldn't believe it. She even took up the clock and shook it despairingly. The alarm had not betrayed her, she noticed, so obviously she had slept through its chime, a thing that had never happened to her before. The person outside was knocking more loudly. A thin voice called, "Miss Ross! Miss Ross!"

Julia pushed back the clothes and swung herself out of bed.

"I'm coming." She dislodged the chair and opened the door. Sparkes was outside; of Peters there was no sign.

"I'm sorry to rouse you, miss," said the woman, civilly. "But Mrs. Ponsonby is planning an early start, as we've a long journey ahead. She's having breakfast already."

"I overslept," said Julia. "I can't think how it happened because I never do. Will you tell Mrs. Ponsonby I'll be down in ten minutes?"

After the woman had gone, the girl who was their victim crossed to the hanging mirror and stood staring at herself for a moment.

She saw a slender figure in green silk pajamas, her dark hair tumbled from the night, her cheeks paler than usual, shadows under her eyes.

"You're looking a regular hag," she told herself gloomily. "I dare say it isn't all Mrs. Ponsonby's fault. You haven't been having enough to eat for weeks. All the same, you can't be surprised if you are turned down for jobs, looking that way."

Stripping off her pajamas she began hurriedly to wash in cold water. As she dressed she was formulating phrases with which to assure Mrs. Ponsonby that she wasn't going to leave London.

"She can't force me," she urged, as she brushed out her hair and curled up the ends over a pintail comb. "She can't gag me and hurl me into the car. Of course, she can ring up Mrs. Hurst and make it pretty difficult for me to get another job, because half these agencies work in with one another, but that's her limit. And whatever happens, I'm not going out of London."

With this resolution firmly in her mind she came downstairs, her suitcase in her hand. Sparkes was in the hall.

"Madam's breakfasting in here," she said, taking Julia into yet another sitting room in this amazing house. "The car's due at nine o'clock."

Julia, wearing her hat and coat and carrying her gloves, came quickly in.

"I'm afraid I overslept," she apologized, not offering to take a seat. "I never do. It's very odd."

Mrs. Ponsonby didn't appear to think it odd at all. "Perhaps it was the hot milk," she said, smoothly. "If you're not used to milk at night it often has that effect."

Her eyes today were bland and as hard as agates. Julia felt a wave of real fear sweep over her.

"Of course," she thought, "the milk was drugged. She knew I might try and make a getaway and whatever happened she didn't mean me to go. Why does she want me so particularly? Because she does. That's obvious. She's going to stop at nothing to prevent my getting away. But I've got to outwit her somehow."

"Sit down and eat some breakfast. You've run it very fine," Mrs. Ponsonby was admonishing her.

Slowly Julia sat down. "It was rather strange about that milk," she suggested. "Don't you think so?"

"Not at all," was Mrs. Ponsonby's crisp reply. "A soothing drink and the knowledge that you had a safe position at last—it's quite understandable. But a little inconvenient because it's made us rather late."

Safe, thought Julia, in a daze, taking a piece of toast and a cup of coffee without realizing what she did. She said safe. Now's the time to tell her I can't come. As she opened her mouth to speak Mrs. Ponsonby said, "Here are the tickets. Take care of them."

Instinctively Julia took them. They were first-class tickets for Bournemouth, which wasn't at that stage a prohibited area. Mrs. Ponsonby handed her something else—a luggage label bearing the address of a Bournemouth hotel.

"You only had one case I think you said? Then, as soon as you've finished breakfast, tie it on and Peters can load it on to the car."

Julia found her voice. "Mrs. Ponsonby, I'm sorry, but what I told you last night holds good. I don't want to leave town."

"How long did you say you'd been earning a living?" asked her employer dryly.

"I—six years."

"I wonder any one kept you six months if you were as changeable as that. As for not wanting to go to Bournemouth, that's absurd. It's a delightful place, with pleasant walks and excellent air. You're looking peaked and no wonder. A holiday will do you good. Now finish your toast and don't talk any more nonsense."

Julia began to speak, hesitated and stopped. It was ridiculous, of course. This was London, where girls aren't kidnapped or compelled to go away against their will. And she, Julia, was young and strong and accustomed to looking after herself. Yet she felt like someone trying to scale a perpendicular cliff. Every time she tried to make a little headway, she found herself hurled back by Mrs. Ponsonby's impenetrability. There wasn't any conceivable reason for refusing to go to Bournemouth beyond the irrational one that she didn't want to. The door opened and Peters came in.

"Ferrers is ready, madam, when it suits you," he said.

Mrs. Ponsonby stood up, brushing the crumbs away from her knees.

"Ready? If you're hungry, bring a bit of toast with you into the car. What about that label?"

"I have labelled the young lady's case," said Peters. "It's in the car."

Mrs. Ponsonby bustled into the hall. Julia came with her, cursing her folly in leaving her case unprotected. Now, if she made a scene, it meant unpacking all the luggage of which a good deal was packed into the long black and silver Daimler drawn up before the door. The chauffeur, Ferrers, had come to meet them. He was a blond pleasant-looking person, unhampered by brains.

"Good morning, madam. It's a nice day for the drive."

The morning sunlight fell round them in a flood of gold. It struck radiance from the polished windows of the car and her immaculate paint work. It was an adequate background for Julia in her blue suit with its long white collar, white gloves, blue shoes faced with white. She looked, though she didn't know it, like someone from the cover of Vogue—until you saw her eyes, that were disquieting.

"Come along," said Mrs. Ponsonby, "we don't want to miss that train." Ferrers had gone down to the gate and was holding open the door of the car. Mrs. Ponsonby trundled after him. She had abandoned all her gay colors today and wore a black coat that accentuated her dumpiness and plainness. Julia felt like someone who has taken a drug. Just as that can soften muscles until they are no longer capable of resistance, so she now felt helpless, swept along on a tide that took no notice of her feeble struggles.

"It'll be better to wait till we get to the station," she told herself weakly. "Then, while they're fussing over the luggage, I can grab my case and somehow slip away."

But she felt less certain than she'd have liked. Suppose Mrs. Ponsonby engaged a porter—or even two porters—to collect the trunks and hat-boxes—and what a quantity she was taking for a short visit—would it be possible to detach one small slightly shabby suitcase from the ruck and take it in one's own charge? Suppose Mrs. Ponsonby said it was her case and started a scene? There was no limit to what she would do to attain her objective, Julia felt.

The car rolled on. Neither woman spoke. Mrs. Ponsonby was huddled in her corner, a big black bag on her knee; she grasped it firmly and appeared unaware of Julia's existence. Julia was making plans and discarding them. Whatever happened, she wouldn't leave town. She felt, superstitiously, that if she did, she was lost. Presently she began to wonder about Mrs. Ponsonby, the possible reasons behind her extraordinary behavior. The woman herself told you nothing, a little hunched black bird in the corner of the magnificent car. Yet even now strength came from her, a silent ruthlessness that would understand no appeal.

"What happened to Mr. Ponsonby?" Julia wondered. "Did he die of the strain or did he . . . ?" She stopped her thought abruptly. Even in your mind you didn't use words like murder. Yet she could see Mrs. Ponsonby looking with that same stony gaze at a man who had been a nuisance and had now been put out of the way.

Anxious to clear her mind of these reflections, Julia turned towards the window and looked out. To her amazement she saw that already they had left London behind. She jerked back to her employer.

"But—this is the Great West Road," she expostulated.

"Oh, yes." Mrs. Ponsonby didn't sound interested, yet Julia, shooting her a sharp apprehensive glance, saw that the lids were not fully lowered over the sharp black eyes, that the hands apparently so innocently clutching the shabby handbag were ready to pounce, that the whole body was taut with a suppressed excitement.

"And probably Ferrers is in the plot," thought Julia, panic-stricken as the realization of the simplicity with which she had been duped rushed upon her. "Now I'll never get away."

Desperately she struggled to keep her head. "You said we were going to Bournemouth—you gave me the tickets."

"Well?"

"But you go to Bournemouth from Waterloo."

"If you're going by train."

"Then—we're not?"

"I should have thought that was obvious."

"But—the tickets?"

"You'd better return those to me. I can get them refunded. Peters will see to it."

Julia hesitated. Once she yielded up the tickets she said good-bye to the last atom of proof of the story she might be going to tell—yes, if you get the chance, jeered her mind.

"I don't believe you ever meant to go to Bournemouth," she said.

"That's no way to speak. As a matter of fact, on a day like this, when I've got the petrol, it would be a crime to go by train."

"Then—we are going to Bournemouth?"

"Haven't you seen the luggage, all labelled?" She kicked a small case derisively with her shoe. Julia leaned back, a trifle reassured. Perhaps, after all, as she had told herself last night, Mrs. Ponsonby was only eccentric, a rich woman accustomed to her own way and inclined to be tyrannical if she didn't get it. Perhaps they really were going to the Albion Hotel, Bournemouth, and three months hence she would be laughing with Colin over these fears. But at that reflection she stiffened again. If all was well, why had Mrs. Ponsonby denied her presence in the house last night? And how about telephoning Mrs. Hurst to say that the post was filled? It wouldn't have been possible before they left, for these bureaus did not open until ten o'clock. And there had been no letters lying on the hall table, and Ferrers hadn't been given one to post. Be as optimistic as you pleased, everything pointed to one solution—that Mrs. Ponsonby wanted to spirit her away without any one realizing where she had gone. But why she should want to do such a thing opened the door to a far larger and more terrifying mystery. Whatever their destination, it was to be some quiet place, where no feet sounded and no traffic rolled, where there wouldn't be a telephone and there'd be no neighbors. In such a recess she might never be found—or found too late. Desperately she struggled against the rising wave of hysteria that threatened to engulf her. There could be no sense at all in the suggestion that Mrs. Ponsonby was carrying off a strange girl, of whose existence she hadn't heard twenty-four hours earlier, in order to do away with her. And yet—and yet—if everything was above-board and no danger threatened, why this secrecy, this deception?

"I'm a pawn in a game I don't understand," Julia told herself.

39

"My only hope is to get away somehow before we reach our destination. Even if I have to leave the suitcase it can't be helped. The main thing is to get away."

For some time she hoped the chauffeur might stop to fill up with petrol, but apparently he had been told the length of the journey and had made his preparations, for the car spinned past pump after pump. It was a perfect spring morning. The hawthorn and fruit trees were snow against the sky, a light wind blew, ruffling the leaves till the undersides showed silver; in the fields the lambs were sturdy and combative now; through little villages they slid, whose houses opened on to cobbled paths, and whose windows displayed the inevitable fern in a colored pot. Men lounged outside public houses, women carried big bags of vegetables and groceries in and out of the shops; two young men lounged on a bridge; a dog leaped frantically for sticks by the edge of a river; a flock of white ducks floated on a pond that reflected the blueness of the sky. The world was so normal that her own position seemed to Julia incredible. But she reminded herself that though they moved through this normality they were not of it; nor did they pause to share it. They left it behind and sped on—and on.

5

JULIA BEGAN TO PIN her waning faith on the lunch interval. They must stop somewhere for lunch, since a careful survey of the baggage revealed nothing in the nature of a hamper. And then, though it meant creating a scene and even attracting the attention of the police, she must break away before the gates of a strange house closed upon her, shutting her completely from the friendly and familiar world. She had a little silver in her bag and with this she could charter a taxi, demand to be driven to the nearest station where the pound note she carried for emergencies would, surely, purchase a ticket back to London. Once there she would find Colin—thought stopped at that juncture. It did not occur to her that in an adverse world Colin also might disappear.

Shortly after one o'clock the car glided into a prosperous market town and the chauffeur paused to ask his direction.

"We're going to have lunch here," said Mrs. Ponsonby, pleasantly. "You'll be glad of an opportunity to stretch your limbs." She looked with disapproval at the long slim legs in burnt-almond silk stockings.

"Yes, indeed," said Julia, telling herself not to look as though she were in a hurry, but to behave quite normally. "I'm hungry, too."

The car came to a standstill and Ferrers got down. Clearly he had his orders for he didn't open the door but instead went into the superior pastrycooks that advertised, "Luncheons. Teas. Ices." Julia watched him expectantly and put out her hand. Mysteriously, the car door was jammed. She twisted it more vigorously.

"Don't trouble," said Mrs. Ponsonby, dryly. "It's locked."

"Locked?"

"Yes. I was once in a car when a door opened by mistake and a woman was killed. Since then I've taken every precaution."

"But we're not travelling now. It would be quite safe to unlock it," Julia protested.

"Ferrers will unlock it when he returns. He's seeing about our lunch."

"Are we having something special then?"

"I'm having it brought out to the car. I don't like restaurants, big crowded places, people staring. I like privacy." She nodded at the girl, one conspirator confiding in another.

Julia's fears mounted; they were like a great fiery wheel turning in her brain.

"But—I shall want to wash my hands before lunch."

"Of course. But we must wait till Ferrers comes back. We can't leave the car unattended."

"I could go first," said Julia, trying to prevent her teeth from chattering.

"We must wait till Ferrers comes back because of unlocking the door," said Mrs. Ponsonby smoothly. "Ah, here he is."

Ferrers came out of the shop and came round to his employer's side of the car.

41

"Lunch will be ready in five minutes, madam. And the proprietress will let you use the private staircase."

Julia's brows drew together. "I thought we were lunching here," she began when Mrs. Ponsonby gave her a little push and Ferrers got back into his own seat and leaned across to unlock the door. Julia got out quickly, but Mrs. Ponsonby was quicker still, and was waiting on the pavement when the girl alighted. She slipped her hand under Julia's arm and led her, not through the door of the shop, but into a private entrance where a pleasant-looking elderly woman with white hair greeted them.

"Through this door," she said kindly, looking at Julia with undisguised interest.

"You go first," Julia offered. "I'll wait." But Mrs. Ponsonby's grip on her arm tightened.

"It's all right, dear," she said, and now there was a note in her voice the girl had never heard before. "You're quite safe with me. Nobody's going to stare at you or hurt you," and she smiled at the white-haired woman, who smiled back. Julia stood stock still; she believed that last night she had plumbed the abyss of fear, but now she knew she had only hesitated on the edge, peering uncertainly into the depths. What lay ahead was worse than anything she had conceived. She realized far more clearly than before the type of woman against whom she was pitting her strength. Mrs. Ponsonby left nothing to chance; she planned everything. The drugged milk, the suitcase removed before its owner could protest, the arrangements regarding lunch, proved that. Once again she had got in first. Nothing Julia said, no explanation, no matter how plausible, would now have any value at all. Let her try to explain that she was being kept against her will, and the two women would exchange another glance of complete understanding. Poor thing, that glance would say. So that's how it takes her. And if she persisted in her story, still no one would believe her. Mania. So sad. Quite young and not bad looking. What a responsibility for—what? Her guardian—aunt—mother?

"Come this way, dear." Mrs. Ponsonby was speaking again. Julia flung an anguished glance at the other woman, but on that bland, nicely-powdered face was only a reassuring smile.

42

"You'll be all right," she said. "There's no one there."

Julia made a last frantic bid for freedom. "I must go back to the car," she exclaimed. "I've left something . . ." Again the two women smiled. "Can't you see what she is?" Julia's heart was screaming. "That she's false? Evil? Dangerous?" But, no. Mrs. Rutland saw nothing but the sad spectacle of a young woman suffering from delusions, who must be coaxed and soothed into a semblance of normality. Her aunt's wonderful with her, Mrs. Rutland thought. So patient. Lucky they've got money. It does grease the wheels. And she thought it would be quite justifiable if she added a shilling for service.

"No one's going to hurt you," Mrs. Ponsonby repeated in a kind artificial voice. "I'm with you, dear. You're quite safe."

Inside Julia some change took place on the instant. It was as if a blast withered a flower, a healthy body suddenly rotted under the eyes from some nameless disease. Her courage simply rotted away and she accepted the inevitable. The hours of strain following weeks of disappointment and anxiety now took their toll. She accepted the fact that she was trapped, that she couldn't escape, that some frightful doom lay ahead that was inevitable. The change manifested itself in her face. All the life died out of it. She knew the despair of the prisoner the first time he understands that he can batter against his iron door till his hands are bloody, but there's no escape. In such a spiritless mood she followed Mrs. Ponsonby up the stairs.

Lunch was ready for them when they returned. Julia, her appetite destroyed, nevertheless tackled the wing of a chicken. At the back of her mind, so faint that she scarcely recognized it, the ghost of courage lingered. She was defeated today, but there would be tomorrow. She refused Mrs. Ponsonby's offer of anything to drink for a long time. "No," she said, "no coffee, thank you," but when the waitress returned with the bill she said suddenly, "I believe I am thirsty after all. I'd like a small bottle of ginger ale. Would you bring me the bottle so I can make sure it's the kind I like?" As she spoke she opened her purse to make it clear that she was paying for this herself. As Mrs. Ponsonby had smiled at Mrs. Rutland so now she smiled at the waitress. The waitress didn't look the least surprised;

she said soothingly, "Of course, miss," and brought a bottle, glass and opener to the car.

"You silly girl," said Mrs. Ponsonby indulgently. "D'you think someone's trying to poison you?" Again she sent a sympathetic glance to the waitress.

"There was that milk last night," said Julia in shaky tones.

Mrs. Ponsonby nodded and the waitress took Julia's sixpence and went inside. "Ever so sad," she told Rose, her special friend among the waitresses. "Such a pretty girl and quite dotty. Thinks every one is trying to kill her."

"You never can tell," said Rose darkly. Rose went to too many pictures and was always discovering sinister motives for the most innocent acts. And even that trivial conversation was to play its part in the astounding plot in which Julia was already enmeshed.

After lunch Ferrers drove more quickly. Julia tried to memorize the route he took, but he flashed by signposts before she could read them, and Mrs. Ponsonby insisted on drawing the side-blinds because of the glare of the sun, so Julia soon lost all sense of direction, which, of course, was what Mrs. Ponsonby intended. Her manner towards the girl was definitely changing. She no longer spoke like an autocratic employer, but rather like a nurse to a patient. Julia recognized the manner; she had seen it used towards young children and very old people who are too senile for sense. By this time she knew she was outwitted. She could shout her story from the village green, but no one would believe her. "This isn't Chicago," they'd say, "and anyway, where's the motive? A girl without a penny, without friends, without influence, a complete nonentity." Yet in her troubled mind she clung to that one fact—that it was because she was so utterly unknown, because no inquiries would be made for her if she disappeared, that she had been selected by Mrs. Ponsonby for whatever dreadful part she was destined to play.

"I'm not hysterical," she told herself desperately, "but if she wasn't trying to blot me out, why should she go to all this trouble? I haven't an idea what's behind all this, but I do know I'm in some appalling danger and at present I can't see any way out."

She must have dozed for a time, for when she woke it was evening and the shadows were closing over the countryside. She was startled to find Mrs. Ponsonby's arm round her waist.

"You've had a nice sleep, dear," said Mrs. Ponsonby. "I'm so glad. We shan't be very long now."

"What about tea?" murmured Julia, still not quite awake.

"They filled our thermos at that nice shop where we had lunch. We can't afford to stop again. It's getting dark very quickly as it is."

So that was that. Even Mrs. Ponsonby wasn't going to risk a second shop, a second attempt at confidences. This time Julia was forewarned and might get in first. So they would have their tea in the car. Julia played her last card.

"I'm awfully sorry but I feel a bit sick. I never am very good at long car drives. I wonder—if we pass a house soon—perhaps they'd let me sit down for a few minutes."

"I don't think there are any houses near here. This is a very lonely part of the country. Anyway, it might be rather difficult explaining, don't you think? But I'll tell Ferrers to stop and we can open a door and you can walk up and down a little bit if you think that would help."

Julia looked at the world beyond the glass. They were in one of those long English lanes with a hedge on one side and fields, now growing dim in the dusk, on the other. Work was over for the day. There was no one to shout to, even if shouting to a yokel would really do any good. Of course, there was a chance that a car might come sweeping round the bend and she might be able to flag it. She said, "Thank you. If you don't mind," and Mrs. Ponsonby took up the speaking-tube.

"Turn up the next corner," she said. "And stop for a few minutes."

Ferrers drove on for a couple of minutes, then swerved to avoid a grey car rounding the bend. When Julia saw it she cried out instinctively, but the driver of the grey car thought he was being abused for bad driving and accelerated. He didn't even see the passengers in the Daimler. Julia turned her head and saw him streaking through the half-light till the corner hid him from view. There was no other traffic on the road. Ferrers drove some way up the lane and then dismounted and unlocked the door. Slowly Julia alighted, assessing her chances of escape if she should make a bolt for it. A couple of hundred yards ahead of the car was a stile leading into a field that sloped down to the distant sky. The surface was rough with stones; a girl wouldn't make much of a pace over that, while a man like Ferrers, who had the obtuse muscularity of a bull, could overtake her almost at once. If she squeezed behind the car and ran towards the road, even then Ferrers would overtake her before she reached her objective. On the left was a hedge, very thorny and impenetrable. On the right a stone wall enclosed an orchard. There was no dwelling except a dilapidated shepherd's hut in sight. The forlornness of the empty landscape increased her sense of helplessness. For a minute she stood with her back to the hedge, her ears astrain for the sound of wheels. She took a few steps backwards. Mustn't hurry, she thought, just go to and fro like the Contented Bear. That may allay their suspicions. Then, if I hear wheels, I can dash, and they may be off their guard. She turned and came back to the car; when she would have turned back towards the road she saw that Ferrers had moved unobtrusively in that direction. The darkness was falling with disconcerting swiftness. Where a few minutes ago the shadows had been blue now they were smoky with night; a faint ground mist stirred at her feet. Mrs. Ponsonby put her head out of the car window.

"Do you feel better now?" she inquired. "If so, I don't think we should wait any longer. There's a sort of fog coming on and we don't want to spend the night on the road."

Julia climbed back into the car and resumed her corner. She felt tears welling into her eyes and hurriedly she blinked them away. The landscape grew hazy with mist and the shades of night; now and again the roof of a cottage appeared with startling suddenness, but it had disappeared again before she could so much as verify its existence. The world seemed full of vapor and the darkness and the queer sounds that belong only to the night. Almost, she thought, she could hear the slow invisible dropping of the dew. She looked across to where Mrs. Ponsonby lay, a bunchy little figure, in her corner. Owing to wartime regulations the light in the car was no more than a flicker; it was difficult to persuade oneself that what lay there so quietly wasn't just a bundle of clothes instead of an intensely clever and ruthless woman who had never taken her eyes off her passenger since the beginning of the journey.

By the time they reached their destination it was so dark that Ferrers had to shine his torch on the step of the car. By that evasive gleam Julia made out a dark wooden gate set flush in a brick wall. Mrs. Ponsonby, straddling out of the car, dipped into her big bag and produced a key that she handed to the chauffeur. With a little difficulty the man fitted this into the lock and swung open a pair of gates made of solid wood, so that, shut, nothing could be guessed of what they concealed. Leaving the car in the roadway Ferrers guided the two women up a stony path and through a kind of arbor leading to a front garden. Everything was going as if by machinery; one development led smoothly to another. It was like being part of a puzzle. You couldn't step out of your place or object to your position. Nowhere else would you fit with the completed picture. When Ferrers left them at the front door, having pulled an old-fashioned bell, he disappeared through the arbor. He was going to put the car away. Julia looked round her; she could see faintly against the dark sky a fringe of leaves from the climbing roses on the arbor and that was all. Beyond those pricking edges there was nothing but the great immensity of sky. It was too dark to make out much of their surroundings, but so far as she could gather there was not another building in sight. A hand on her arm made her turn sharply. The door had been opened and there, like a crêpe-clad needle, was Sparkes, standing aside and waiting for them to come in.

"Did you have any trouble getting a conveyance from the station, Sparkes?" Mrs. Ponsonby wanted to know as she walked into the lonely building.

"No, madam. There was a man there—five miles isn't much in this part of the country." Then she peered over Mrs. Ponsonby's head at Julia. "The young lady's tired," she suggested.

"She had a nice sleep on the way down," replied Mrs. Ponsonby with the bright, false smile to which Julia was becoming accustomed. "But perhaps," she added, turning to the girl, "you would like dinner in bed?"

Instinctively Julia negatived the suggestion. What lay ahead of her she could not guess, but she had no desire to find herself a prisoner in a strange room in a dark house.

"Very well then. We'll just wash and have something to eat at once. The journey took rather longer than I expected. Sparkes will unpack for you while we're eating," added Mrs. Ponsonby to the bewildered girl at her side.

"I can unpack," replied Julia, quickly. "It won't take me five minutes. I prefer to do my own unpacking." The thought slid through her mind that her identity card and spare pound were in that case, and she trusted the maid no more than she liked the mistress. Fortunately she had thought to lock her case, and it did not at that moment occur to her that an expert like Sparkes would make small account of a cheap lock.

"You can't unpack until Ferrers has brought in the luggage," Mrs. Ponsonby said good-temperedly. "It'll take him a little time to do that. Meanwhile, it's getting on towards eight, and we're both tired." She took off her black coat, twitched the dumpy black turban off her amazing red hair, and went into a room on the right that Sparkes indicated. Julia, not discarding any of her outdoor clothes, followed her. The thought had passed into her mind that perhaps they were not going to stay here long either. Perhaps, if her case did not appear, Mrs. Ponsonby would explain that it didn't seem worth while unloading all the luggage. There was a mirror at the end of the long room they had entered and Julia went instinctively towards it. Mrs. Ponsonby, she noted, looked as neat, unimpressive and unruffled as when she had set out that morning. Yet, in spite of her nondescript appearance, the girl had the same sense of a tremendous force that had assailed her the previous night. Apparently Mrs. Ponsonby could produce that effect without making any effort; she didn't rely on clothes or manner as do most women; her personality was so packed with energy and explosive force that the stranger felt as though he had been hit over the head and stunned when he came face to face with her.

Julia, putting this uncomfortable thought out of her mind, pulled a comb from her bag and tried to tidy herself. She thought she had changed in some odd way since morning, but that, of course, might be due to the oddness of the room's lighting. It seemed clear that they were far from civilization for there was no electricity, only lamps; the glass showed a greenish face staring back at her, a face somehow unfamiliar. The dark hair was disordered; what it wanted was not a comb but a vigorous brushing. Julia did her best, but the curls had become disarranged during her uncomfortable sleep and her hair stood out round her head in a sort of halo. A word raced into her mind. Fey. That was how she looked, someone not quite normal, not quite controlled. Any one meeting her for the first time would suspect something odd. And as she realized that she staggered backwards with shock. If it were true—and it was—it meant that Mrs. Ponsonby had won the second round, also. *Because that was how Julia was meant to look.* That was why she couldn't have access to her luggage; she wasn't to be given a chance to restore her appearance. Turning quickly, she found Mrs. Ponsonby watching her.

"You'll feel better tomorrow," said Mrs. Ponsonby. "Now come and sit down and we'll both turn in early."

Julia slowly crossed the big shadowy room. "You haven't said anything more about my duties," she remarked nervously.

"Your duty today was to accompany me here," Mrs. Ponsonby told her calmly. "Tomorrow there'll be letters and so forth. But neither of us is fit for anything but sleep tonight."

As though the notion had only just occurred to her, Julia exclaimed, "We never rang up Mrs. Hurst. We ought to let her know."

"I've attended to that," returned Mrs. Ponsonby in the same tone. "You've nothing to worry over this evening."

The simple meal was quickly disposed of and Julia received permission to go up to her room.

"Second on the right at the top of the stairs," Mrs. Ponsonby instructed her. "I've told Sparkes to leave a lamp there so you can't go wrong."

As before, she had been allotted a handsome room, well-furnished, but her heart sank when she saw that here also she was at the back of the house and that the windows were tightly shuttered.

"I'll wait till everything's quiet and then I'll open those," she decided, looking round for her case. But this had not yet arrived. Impatiently she walked up and down the room. She had no idea where they were; they had passed no vehicle on the last five miles

49

of their journey and when she stood still to listen it was like waiting for a world to be born. No movement, no sound, no struggle—a kind of deathly peace. Tiptoeing across the room she opened her door. Now faint noises reached her. Mrs. Ponsonby and Sparkes were conferring together. Julia tried to hear what they said, but the door was closed and only a faint buzz reached her ears. She came back into the room. The bed looked inviting and she saw the curve of a slack hot-water bottle under the sheets. If only she could have her case, could pull off her clothes and slip into her pajamas, she might sleep. And sleep she must. If she had to wait much longer her mind would become so active that sleep would be impossible. She was like someone sub-consciously warding off an attack of anticipated pain. Each moment sleep receded further from her. She opened the door again with a violent movement and found herself face to face with Mrs. Ponsonby. The woman had the gift for putting other people in the wrong, she reflected, as she stepped back with a muttered apology.

"I was only coming to see about my case," she explained. "I'm so tired, I . . ."

Mrs. Ponsonby nodded sympathetically. "It was about your case that I came to see you."

A fresh misgiving shot through the girl. "It's all right, isn't it?"

"Of course it's all right. You silly girl."

Julia breathed again. "Perhaps I am being silly, but for one moment I thought you were going to tell me that it had got lost in transit. I don't think I could have borne that."

Mrs. Ponsonby's thick black eyebrows, that were like woolly bear caterpillars under a tangle of scarlet undergrowth, lifted in surprise.

"My dear, don't be ridiculous," she said. "As a matter of fact, that's precisely what I've come to tell you. Oh, of course, it's only an accident. You'll get it in a day or two, but somehow or other Peters has bungled things and your case must have got left behind in Henriques Square. It's nothing to be upset about. I can lend you night clothes and I've even a spare toothbrush, and tomorrow we'll write for the case. It should be down the next morning."

50

"Tomorrow's Sunday," said Julia. "I don't suppose the local post office is open. Oh, but of course you can telephone."

A film of ice seemed to form over Mrs. Ponsonby's stubborn little features as she said, "I'm afraid we have no telephone here. But a letter will reach Peters on Monday and a packed suitcase cannot be easily overlooked."

"Which makes it all the more peculiar that it was overlooked in the first place. I heard your butler say he'd put it in the car . . ."

"Presumably there was a little readjustment and he took it off and somehow it got forgotten. However, there's no need for you to distress yourself. Your suitcase can be of no possible interest to any one but yourself. It's tiresome, but after all we're here for some time and it's not as though we shall be having visitors. You can manage in what you're wearing for the next day or two."

Julia said slowly, "I looked round before we left and my case wasn't anywhere. I'm sure of that."

Mrs. Ponsonby caught her arm in a firm grip. "Now, my dear, you're being babyish. You must pull yourself together. Of course it was somewhere, and I shall send Peters a telegram on Monday morning—that's better than a letter—and he'll send the case straight down. In fact, I shouldn't be surprised if he's sent it on already. He'll have found it when he was clearing up and he'll realize it was left behind by mistake. Now, I'm going to find you a nightdress— I'm afraid I can't oblige you with pajamas, I've never worn such things in my life. And if you take my advice you'll go quietly to bed, and when you wake in the morning you'll wonder what on earth all the fuss was about."

"I've wondered a lot," said Julia.

Mrs. Ponsonby smiled, but behind the smile was a warning. Take care, that smile said, if you probe too far you may find more than you've bargained for. Remember, ignorance is often bliss. Julia shrank back.

"Where are we?" she asked, catching her breath.

"The house is called Beverley."

"What's the name of the place?"

"King's Marlow. It's so small it's not on any of the maps." So small, thought Julia, you'd never think of looking for any one there.

51

After Mrs. Ponsonby had left her she began slowly to undress. She was convinced that there had been no accident behind the disappearance of her case. Probably long before this Peters had examined it—for what? The question brought her up abruptly. What value could it have for any one besides herself? A few clothes, a pound note, an identity card . . . Shock made her knees weak. She put out a faltering hand as she collapsed on the side of the bed. Suppose she was right in her conjecture, that the case had been deliberately lost? Suppose it never turned up? That would mean . . .

"It'll mean she will have destroyed my identity," whispered Julia aloud. "All day she's been building up in the minds of strangers the picture of a girl who isn't remotely like Julia Ross. I don't believe for one instant she wrote to Mrs. Hurst. If you say 'Julia Ross' to her, she'll stare and pretend she's never heard the name. That's why she wanted someone who hadn't any friends, any one to start inquiries if she disappeared. That's why we've come to this odd place. Before I get a chance to see any one she'll have told her story. I'm queer—it's tragic, but I have delusions. And whatever I say no one will believe me. It's one thing to say these things can't happen. I've often said it myself. But I've been wrong. They can. And now they're happening to me."

So that first night she began to traverse the path of understanding the appalling thing Mrs. Ponsonby meant to do.

6

ONE OF THE FIRST EFFECTS OF SHOCK is a dumb acceptance of situations hitherto considered unthinkable. For some minutes after Mrs. Ponsonby had left her, Julia sat on the edge of her bed, letting this new dreadful truth sink into her mind. As the clock moved from one figure to the next she saw clearly how well the woman had prepared the ground. In this remote village, who was likely to give a strange girl a fair hearing? Sparkes, of course, had been coached in her part. Before Julia had any freedom at all—supposing that the smallest measure of freedom was to be allowed her—the story would have gone round that she wasn't a person to be trusted. A whisper here, a hint there, and Mrs. Ponsonby's work would be done. She would be, not Julia but a person, someone to be watched curiously, not one of the normal army of mankind but marked, as Cain was branded on his forehead. Julia saw it all. After some time the first numbness wore off to be succeeded by a sense of amazement that such a thing could happen. Like thousands of other unhappy mortals caught in a relentless net, she was staggered by her own helplessness. There must be something she could do, some way out she hadn't so far discovered.

The door opened and Mrs. Ponsonby returned with a nightdress and a few toilet articles. Julia pulled herself together and began to speak in what she hoped was a normal voice.

"What a large house this is!" she murmured. "I hope I shall be able to find my way down in the morning."

"If you can't, I'll send Alice to guide you."

"Alice?" That was a new name.

"She's the girl who works here. Well, poor Sparkes could hardly do everything herself."

"Of course not."

"Though we shall be living very quietly indeed. That's what my doctor ordered. It'll be good for you, too. You're very highly-strung, aren't you?"

Again the flick of the whip! With an effort Julia kept her voice calm.

"I suppose we shall have neighbors."

"We'll be neighbors to one another," smiled Mrs. Ponsonby.

"But there must be someone else living here. This can't be a village of the dead." She shivered a little as she uttered the words. They sounded ominous and she wished she hadn't spoken them.

Mrs. Ponsonby put out her pudgy little hands and caught both of Julia's in them.

"You don't want to see a lot of people, dear. This craving for excitement is quite unnatural. Now, if you just rest and make up your mind to take things easily, you'll soon be better. Above all, don't worry. Worry's fatal."

Julia's heart jumped sickeningly. "Better? But I . . ."

53

"Just let yourself go," advised Mrs. Ponsonby. "You're all taut. You must relax, otherwise you may be really ill. Now this is the very place you want. Of course, it's not all in order yet, but we shan't mind that for a day or two, shall we?" She smiled again. She could say so much without uttering a word. "It's a good thing neither of us believes in ghosts," she whispered. "If we did, I'd say this was the very house for them."

Julia remembered sundry white-draped pieces of furniture on the stairs and in one of the big bare rooms downstairs. She resolved to be on her guard. Trying to frighten her out of her wits wouldn't be beyond Mrs. Ponsonby and she knew it. A wind had risen during the evening and it moaned fearfully at the windows. The shutters, that fitted less well than the shutters in the London house, creaked and whined, as though some living thing in the night outside sobbed for shelter. She glanced up apprehensively. Mrs. Ponsonby laughed, a cheerful full-throated laugh that seemed indecent in that solitary house.

"Mustn't be getting the jitters," she said, the slang word sounding incongruous from so Victorian a figure. "You'll soon get accustomed to night noises. If you hear anything, just tell yourself that this is an old house. Old houses have histories. They've seen so much. It would be absurd not to expect them to remember some of it, and now and again they may recall it. That explains the footsteps people hear in quiet houses like these, hands tapping on walls, or shadows moving for no reason that we can understand. Are you interested in old houses, by the way? They've always been a hobby of mine."

There it was, nothing you could really take hold of or quote as a threat to security, just a middle-aged woman warning a young one not to be nervous if she heard odd movements in the night. And if the young one didn't heed her advice, lost her head, or screamed, well, it wouldn't be hard to find an explanation. A nervous breakdown, perhaps. Young people were so reckless, burning the candle at both ends. Julia understood it all perfectly, as perfectly as she understood that any sounds that might be heard after dark wouldn't be due to ghosts, old timbers or the shutting of a window on badly-fitting casements. Mrs. Ponsonby was an artiste at her job, you had to admit that. She was overlooking nothing.

After Mrs. Ponsonby had disappeared Julia poured out some cold water and bathed her hands and face; when she dried her hands she found that they were shaking, and was glad there was no one to see her. Crossing to the dressing table she saw that she had been provided with a set of petit-point brushes and she picked them up with a sense of surprise. Somehow she hadn't anticipated these. Plain silver or perhaps ivory, slightly yellowed with age, would have been more in the picture.

"But no," she told herself an instant later. "If she'd produced those it would have been proof positive that she never meant to bring my case down here. These must be her own brushes. She'd never bring down a second set."

Faintly curious, she examined them. There was a monogram worked into the gilded decoration of the handle. Julia bent over it. The letters could be clearly distinguished, S.C. That was another strange thing. Mrs. Ponsonby's initials were L.P. Even if these brushes dated from a pre-marriage era the first initial would be L She thought of other explanations. Perhaps these had belonged to a younger sister whose Christian name had begun with S. The C. might stand for Mrs. Ponsonby's maiden name. She turned the hair-brush over. The bristles were new and unyellowed by time. Julia laid it down again and moved to the bed. An apple-green silk night-dress lay on the thick corded quilt. She shook it out. It looked a frivolous article for such a woman. Besides, she'd never get her plump proportions into that slender garment. Fat women can never wear clothes cut on the cross, she remembered. Then her heart jolted again. On the little pocket on the right-hand side of the nightgown was a monogram, S.C. Julia abandoned the idea of the cherished little dead sister. This was new, hardly worn, cut to a modern design. Hurriedly she examined the dressing gown hanging on the back of the door. This time she experienced no surprise when she found the monogram embroidered on this also, in the manner of a decoration. The immediate effect of these discoveries was to induce a desperate nausea. Hurriedly she crawled into the bathroom, that fortunately was adjoining, where she was horribly, frighteningly ill. Feeling as weak as a cat she crept back to her room. Mrs. Ponsonby's intentions were becoming increasingly plain.

Julia Ross had disappeared. In her place was a girl of weak mentality whose initials were S.C.

When she had given the household time to settle down for the night she went cautiously to the windows and unfastened the shutters. It was difficult to make out the nature of the countryside, for there was neither moon nor stars; but presently, as her eyes became accustomed to the blackness, she realized that the house was built on the side of a hill, and that below her window the ground dropped away almost as sheer as a cliff. After a time she could even discern the rough shadowy outlines of bushes and trees. Certainly there was no hope of escape from the house that way. Nevertheless, she remained at the window for some time. The cool night air subdued the fever in her blood, urged caution and tact. Precisely what ordeal lay ahead of her it was impossible to surmise, but she would need all her wit and coolness to meet it.

As she lingered there her eye was caught by a sudden light. For a moment she drew back. This, she thought, was history repeating itself. In the house at Henriques Square she had been startled by the green eye of a cat; this eye was green, too, but it couldn't be a cat. It moved first in one direction and then in another. Besides, it had too high a range. Suddenly it switched abruptly in her direction, and she realized that it was a torch. Someone was making a difficult way home. On sudden impulse she leaned out of the window and began to whistle—not too loud in case Mrs. Ponsonby heard it, yet loud enough for it to carry to the passer-by. Whatever was going to happen it might be a good thing for a stranger to be able to bear witness that someone had been in that room on the night of the 27th April. The torch however had turned away again and was slowly going out of sight; worse still, it was going out of earshot. In a burst of panic Julia whistled louder. But if she had shouted it wouldn't have made any difference to the passer-by, for he was as deaf as a beetle and had been for ten years past.

So engrossed had Julia been in her efforts to attract the stranger's attention that she failed to hear the door of her room open or the subdued rush of little fat feet across the floor. The first she knew of the invasion was when she felt small boneless hands grip her shoulders and heard the hiss of an infuriated voice in her ears. Instinctively she struggled, leaning farther out in an attempt to free herself. A voice called "Sparkes," and, as though she had been an actress awaiting her cue in the wings, the stringy handmaid came in and caught Julia round the waist. The affair resolved itself in an undignified scramble and a chorus of recriminatory voices talking incoherently. Then Julia felt the grip relax, the window was slammed down and she was face to face with a transformed Mrs. Ponsonby. The fat little personage was panting and scarlet; when she tried to speak at first she couldn't get her breath, but she nodded to Sparkes who caught Julia's arm and dragged her nearer the bed. Julia, angry in her turn, flashed into unwise speech.

"How dare you?" she cried. "Just because I wanted some air——"

"Air!" Mrs. Ponsonby had recovered her voice. "Don't lie to me. You saw for yourself, Sparkes. This can't go on. It's the second time."

Julia was silent in surprise. It was a minute before she found her voice.

"The second time? I don't know what you're talking about."

"It's too great a responsibility," Mrs. Ponsonby swept on. "You'll have to have someone to sleep with you. I hoped it was just a temporary brainstorm, but the risk's too great. Sparkes!"

"Yes, madam. I'll just put up the camp bed." In her night attire she was an extraordinary, a sinister figure. Over a calico nightgown she wore a black wool dressing gown and black felt slippers.

"No," said Julia furiously. "I won't have any one in here."

"It's for your own good, you foolish girl." Mrs. Ponsonby's voice was calm again.

"Do you think I don't realize what you're trying to do? But you'll not succeed. I leave this house tomorrow. I'd leave it tonight if I could."

Mrs. Ponsonby's face looked curiously flat in the light of the candle she had brought in with her and set down on the table.

"Who's to stop me?" Julia continued.

"The doctor, if necessary."

"Doctor?" It was like a dash of cold water. Julia's rage died and sheer terror took its place.

"Yes. If you have any more of these ungovernable fits I shall have

57

to call him in. We've done our best, brought you to this quiet place to give you every chance. It's not particularly convenient for me, but get this into your mind. If this doesn't prove a satisfactory solution, there'll be no alternative but the one I don't like to consider. I've every hope that the quiet and the solitude here will work miracles. But if you're going to be violent, then you leave me no choice. Only you've got to co-operate. Now do you understand?"

Before Julia could reply there came a gasp and a shudder from the doorway and the eyes of all three women turned in that direction. A sixteen-year-old girl with a face like a ferret was standing on the threshold, a skirt huddled over her nightdress.

"What are you doing out of your bed, Alice?" asked Mrs. Ponsonby, sternly.

"Heerd a scream," said Alice in sullen tones. "What you doing to her?"

"They're trying to drive me mad," said Julia, quickly.

"Come, come." Once again Mrs. Ponsonby caught her hands. "You don't know what you're saying. Sparkes, you'd better see if Ferrers has gone to bed. If not, tell him to come up here and screw down the windows. It's the only thing to be done."

The girl, Alice, spoke again. There was a soft gleefulness in her voice.

"You said she was ill. You never told me she was daft. My auntie (she pronounced it ante) was the same. They had to put furniture in front of the windows, but one day she got through a skylight on to the roof and threw herself right down. Ever so many people saw her. Made ever such a smack, she did. Mum had her picture in the papers afterwards."

"That'll do, Alice," said Mrs. Ponsonby. "There was no need for you to get out of bed, but since you're here you may as well stay just while Sparkes fetches Ferrers, in case I need you."

"I'll stay," said Alice, happily. She came farther into the room and seated herself, unbidden, on the bed. "I'm awful strong," she volunteered.

"I'm glad to hear that," observed Mrs. Ponsonby. "I'll remind you of it in the morning. There'll be plenty of work here."

The girl drooped a little. "It's my legs that get so tired."

58

"You can come and close the window," Mrs. Ponsonby told her. "No, not the shutters. Didn't you hear me tell Sparkes they were going to be screwed down?"

It seemed to the half-demented Julia a long time before Sparkes returned with Ferrers, looking unfamiliar now that he wasn't wearing his chauffeur's livery. His big blond face showed no surprise when he received his orders. Quite expressionlessly he set about his job, nailing down one window after the other till all four were hermetically sealed.

"I suppose," whispered Julia, "you realize I can take you to court for this?"

But Mrs. Ponsonby only said, "Quiet, my dear, quiet. You must keep calm."

"There was someone flashing his torch at the window," Julia persisted, but no one paid any attention. She saw that none of them believed her. Mrs. Ponsonby had won the third round. Both the chauffeur and the hired girl were genuinely convinced that she was out of her mind. Alice, dismissed, went reluctantly to bed. Sparkes stood by the door, like some hideous avenging angel, her black gown held tightly round her scrawny shape. At last Ferrers had finished and went away, apparently as incurious as ever. Mrs. Ponsonby said, "Get into bed—quickly—and Sparkes will bring you a glass of hot milk."

In Julia's brain a wheel clicked. Hot milk! She shook her head. "I won't drink it."

Mrs. Ponsonby remained imperturbable. "Oh, I think so."

"You can't force me," stammered the girl.

Mrs. Ponsonby was smiling again. "You think not?"

In Julia's brain the wheel began to turn faster, so fast that it was generating heat. She put up her hands to cover her face, but someone caught them. She found herself staring into Mrs. Ponsonby's small cruel face. The nightmare in which she was engulfed stretched and stretched. Desperately she fought to wake up. But it was quite useless. Dreadful stories read in the yellow press and never more than half believed came rushing back to her memory, stories of friendless women trapped by unscrupulous bullies and burnt, starved, beaten into submission. There had been Harriet Staunton who had died in appalling circumstances, while none of the neighbors knew of her existence. And there were girls caught by the white slave traffic and never traced. She remembered a paper-covered book her aunt had given her when she was sixteen that had kept her awake for nights. And now the thing you couldn't quite accept had happened to her, just as at this moment it might be happening to a hundred other people, equally defenseless.

A voice that she didn't recognize said, "All right, I'll take it."

Instantly the grip on her arm relaxed. "That's a sensible girl," said a relieved voice. "Now just get into that nightdress and pop under the clothes and Sparkes will be up in a minute. And if you promise not to give any more trouble you shall sleep alone. That proves I want to trust you, doesn't it?"

The sadism behind the last words was the most horrifying feature of the evening. Julia made no reply. Only, as her fingers slipped and fumbled with buttons and suspenders she knew that she was already lost. Presently she would begin to wonder if there really had been a Julia Ross, a Colin, a Mrs. Mackie, if it wasn't all the ravings of an unhinged brain. When that day came they could all lay down their cards, for Mrs. Ponsonby would have won outright.

Sparkes came back with the milk and Julia drank it docilely. When she had drained the glass Mrs. Ponsonby took it from her and went towards the door.

"Good-night—Sheila."

In spite of her exhaustion the girl started.

"Sheila?"

"Yes. Now come, you can't have forgotten your own name."

"I'm Julia Ross."

Mrs. Ponsonby shook her head. "I wonder where you heard that. No, no, you're Sheila Campbell. Why, you've got your initials on all your clothes . . ."

"My registration card . . ." began Julia.

"Oh, yes. I'd forgotten. You must have dropped it somewhere. I was going to give it back to you."

From the pocket of her wadded dressing gown she drew out the familiar buff card.

"Look!" she invited, advancing it to the girl so that she could see the name written inside it. "Sheila Campbell. Perhaps I'd better keep it in case you do anything—violent."

The instant after she had closed the door, Julia heard the key turned in the lock.

7

ON TUESDAY, April the thirtieth, Colin's uncle, Sir Wallace Roper, died at six a.m., after a protracted illness. On Wednesday, May the first, Colin examined the obituary notices in *The Times* for information regarding the funeral. For some reason the widow had not inserted the notice—not in that day's issue at least—but another caught Colin full in the wind and left him gasping.

Ross. On the 27th April, very suddenly, in London, JULIA, aged 23. No letters, no flowers.

Common sense told him, after he had recovered a little from the shock, that Julia Ross was by no means an uncommon name; probably, if he examined the telephone book, he would 'find a dozen. Nevertheless, the combination of details was disquieting. In London. Aged 23. Died very suddenly on the twenty-seventh of April, the day after he had last seen her. There was also the unexplained mystery of his telephone call. The way in which the woman, who was most likely Mrs. Ponsonby, had cut him off had roused his suspicions. Instructions from Headquarters had reached him early the next morning necessitating a journey north, whence he had returned on the night of the thirtieth, to find a message from his aunt, asking him to come round the next day.

"There's something fishy here or I'm a Dutchman," reflected Colin. "Why should she die suddenly? She wasn't any one's enemy, not even her own. She wasn't remotely important to any one at large; it can't be a case of someone being put out of the way because they know too much . . ." At this juncture it occurred to him that it might be a street accident.

He considered that for a time. "There's a flaw somewhere," he muttered. "I feel it, without knowing what it is." Presently he identified that, also. "If it was an accident, who put the notice in the paper?"

He remembered Julia telling him that she didn't even know the name of her next-of-kin. Perhaps this Mrs. Ponsonby, for clearly she had entered the woman's service, had got in touch with Spencer House. It seemed to Colin a reasonable step to do likewise. Recklessly hailing a taxi he drove first of all to Henriques Square. On the way he thought, "She must know about this. Julia was moving in that night. There's no reason why she should want to conceal facts. It's not her fault if the girl falls under a bus." He recalled Julia's description of her. "Quite mad," she'd said, and a new and horrible thought occurred to him. Had something appalling happened under that roof, something Mrs. Ponsonby's keepers would naturally try to keep dark? He fretted each time the taxi was held up by lights; but at last they turned into the square.

The taxi driver slowed down and pushed open the little window separating him from his fare.

"You said 30, sir?"

"Yes. Why, isn't there a No. 30?"

"There's a house all right, sir, but there don't seem to be any one at 'ome." He drew his cab to a halt, and Colin saw that the shutters of the ground and first floors were drawn and above that the windows were blank and curtainless.

"There must be a caretaker," he said. "Wait here and I'll ring."

Not even a ghost shuffled through the dust in the hall in response to his bell. Aware that he must cut a peculiar figure he stooped and peered through the slit of the letter box. What he saw startled him. The place was denuded of furniture, the doors swinging wide. Apprehension bit deep into his heart. Now he was convinced there was some sinister explanation behind the notice in The Times. A woman doesn't engage a secretary on Friday to work in London if she is proposing to clear out her house within the week. Slowly, he came down the steps and peered into the area. Although by now he knew it was a waste of time he rang the backdoor bell, too. He could hear the slow drip-drip of water somewhere, but that was all. The bell itself didn't ring.

"Electric current cut off," registered Colin's orderly mind. "Now did something frightful and unexpected happen on Saturday that sent the old lady packing in terror, or was all this planned?"

When he remembered his own telephone call on Friday night, he was convinced it had been planned.

Jumping back into his cab he had himself driven to Spencer House, where the door was opened in a leisurely fashion by the sluttish Bertha.

"Mrs. Mackie?" he said, crisply.

Bertha continued to stare at him. "I'll see," she offered. "But she don't take gentlemen."

"Kindly tell her I am here and I should be glad to have a minute with her."

"O.K. What name?"

"Mr. Bruce."

He was left waiting on the doorstep for some moments. Then Mrs. Mackie appeared. Nine-thirty in the morning was clearly not her best time; her hair was still confined in a silk net; her dress was a flowered overall with a dirndl waist that had been too stiffly starched and stood out like a miniature crinoline over spreading hips. When she saw Colin she said, before he could speak, "I'm sorry, but we don't take gentlemen. This is a ladies' club."

"I believe that, until last Friday night, Miss Julia Ross was one of your tenants."

The woman's eyes widened. "Are you the police?"

"The police!" Bewilderment in his voice gave place to alarm. "Why should you think that?"

"I don't know, I'm sure, but when people vanish the way she did you may be certain there's queer goings-on."

Colin said earnestly, "Look here, will you let me come in for a minute? It's just because there is something odd going on and I want to get to the bottom of it, that I've come. I'm a friend of Miss Ross and I'm anxious about her."

"I shouldn't worry," said Mrs. Mackie unpleasantly. "She can look after herself."

"Can she?" Colin's voice was as sharp as a chisel. "Have you seen *The Times* this morning?"

"I've no time for papers first thing. I have to get my reading done when my work's over."

"Then take a look at this." Colin lugged the paper out of his pocket and offered it to her. There was a short pause while Mrs. Mackie ferreted about for her spectacles.

When she had read the insertion she said flatly, "It can't be the same one."

"Why do you say that?"

"Why, she was here as well as anything on the Friday."

"That's why I say there's something odd."

This time Mrs. Mackie fell back and admitted him into her office.

"Of course, it may have been an accident."

"When she went on Friday night did she tell you where she was going?"

"She didn't so much as tell me she was going. First thing I knew was when Bertha took up her breakfast Saturday morning and told me the room was empty. She'd taken all her luggage, so her going wasn't an accident."

"Of course it wasn't an accident. She unexpectedly got a job and had to move in at once. Perhaps you weren't in on Friday evening?"

"Well, and suppose I wasn't? She could leave me a note, I suppose."

"And she didn't?"

"There wasn't a sign of one. Bertha says she never saw her go on the Friday. Well, she'd be down in the basement, and she wouldn't move if she did hear the door shut. My girls have perfect liberty to come and go as they please, within hours, of course."

"There was nothing in her room—in the way of a letter, I mean?"

"Neither letter nor money."

"She owed you something? Well, doesn't that prove there's dirty work somewhere? She's not the kind of girl to go away owing money. Probably she intended to come round on the Saturday and—something happened."

"Well, she might," agreed Mrs. Mackie, grudgingly. "All the same, she should have left a note to say she was going."

"Am I the only person who's made any inquiries so far?" Colin wanted to know.

Instantly Mrs. Mackie was suspicious again. "Who else should?"

"I was thinking about the notice—who would have put it in? Where are her belongings? Who arranged about the funeral?"

"Well, I suppose she had relations."

"None that she knew. She told me that herself."

"She was a sly one, all the same. Why, I didn't even know there was you."

Colin produced a card. "This is where you can find me," he said. "If anybody else comes inquiring, would you let me know?"

"I don't know who you are," demurred Mrs. Mackie.

"I'm going to marry her," said Colin briefly. "At least, I was."

"She never told me," gasped Mrs. Mackie.

"How could she?" asked Colin, simply. "Why, she didn't know herself."

Mrs. Mackie seemed only too ready to follow this red herring, but her visitor brought her sternly back to the important aspect of the affair.

"If any one should ring up or call or make any sort of inquiries, be sure and let me know," he said. And he went out. Mrs. Mackie thought more of Julia than she had done before. A man like that, a real gentleman, and the girl hadn't said a word. Then she told herself, "Going to marry her, was he? And she didn't know? Wonder if she's made herself cheap? Wouldn't be surprised. Never taking meals in, never talking to any one . . ." She abandoned the housework on which she had been engaged when Colin's bell disturbed her and hurried up to the first floor. She and Miss Waterer had a delightful morning's speculation. They were both astounded when they heard the clock strike twelve.

Colin found his taxicab waiting patiently by the curb. "Hallo," he said, "I'd forgotten you. Take me to 205 Bloomsbury Court."

The driver nodded complacently and drove off. He was reflecting that his wife had told him that morning they were going to have another baby, and he'd said, "That's a bit of bad luck," and now he was wondering if he'd been wrong. Perhaps the tide was going to

65

turn. A few more fares like this, clocking up threepences, and he'd do fine.

205 Bloomsbury Court was the address of Mr. Arthur Crook. It was ten o'clock when they arrived and the driver was disappointed to be paid off.

"Sure you won't want me again?" he suggested, but Colin shook his head. He wasn't really aware of the driver as a person at all.

Crook was seated at his desk, his plump form tightly buttoned into a brown suit of loud design, a brown bowler tipped so far over his eyes that it looked as though it balanced on the spines of his thick red brows. When Colin came striding in the lawyer pushed his hat back, nodded and said, "Well, well, well. So you've come to it. I always said you would. What is it? Murder, forgery, or sellin' Home Office Secrets?"

Colin said, going rather white, "It might be murder."

He was gratified to see Crook's expression change. "Might, eh? Your murder?"

"Not yet," said Colin, "but it might be."

Crook tipped his hat yet further back; he had a very broad skull with a good deal at the back of his head. It was this that kept the hat in place.

"Don't do it," he urged. "It's not safe. I don't mean I wouldn't do my best for you—I would, of course—but the police are getting stricter and stricter. Besides, you're only an amateur and you're so highly educated you'd be sure to bungle it."

Colin's attention was deflected for an instant. "You think an uneducated person has more chance of killing a beggar and getting away with it?"

"Well, of course, he has." Crook sounded surprised that the question should ever have been raised. "It's imagination that does your high-class criminals in. You see too far and too much. You're always preparing for something that's goin' to happen in the middle of the next week. And so, you see, it does happen. Ever read any crime reports? Unsolved crimes, I mean? Well, the chap that gets away is the chap that does his stuff and just walks off and waits for the other side to do theirs. See what I mean? If you put up a barrage everybody knows where you are. You think it's goin' to protect you, but it don't. It just draws attention to your whereabouts. If you must stick a knife in this chap's gizzard, stick it and then get out. And let the police get on the job. Don't start thinkin' about fingerprints and alibis. I've heard it said that the public knows too much. That's where the police score. They like the public to know a lot. However much they know the police know more. That's what they bank on. See what I mean? Just be simple. That's the end of the prologue," he added a little unexpectedly. "I always say my piece at the beginning, though I don't think any one believes it. Anyway, they don't take any notice; and if they did it probably wouldn't matter, because the chap who pulls in the criminal nine times out of ten isn't the police or even the beggar himself, but someone nobody's noticed, who hasn't really got a part in the picture at all, some hawker selling flowers or a woman exercising a dog. The fact is, murder's like practically everything else. It's nine-tenths of it luck. Now go ahead and tell me what the trouble is."

Colin, marshalling his facts with creditable lucidity, considering how deep were his fears, outlined the position.

"You must agree there's something damned odd about the whole thing," he wound up. "This girl was fit enough on Friday night. Why should she die suddenly and in this discreet fashion on Saturday?"

Crook picked up a thin red pencil and twisted it in his thick clever fingers.

"There is one answer that p'r'aps hasn't occurred to you," he suggested. "P'r'aps she never did go to this Mrs. Ponsonby."

"But she told me . . ."

"What the soldier said ain't evidence, my boy. She may have had her reasons for stringin' you along."

"But it doesn't make sense," protested Colin. "Why should she bother to make excuses to me? She could just have faded out."

"You might have gone and made inquiries at her doss house, see? As it was, she had you nicely muzzled."

"But where do you imagine she's gone?"

"Ever heard of the word that's engraved on every dame's heart? Romance, with a capital R."

"Ridiculous! If you mean she might have gone off with another

67

man. But why tell me about it? Apparently she didn't say a word to her boardinghouse or so the old witch in charge declares—she talked of money owing, too."

Crook took his hat gravely off and set it on the desk. This always indicated that he had reached the top note of interest.

"Tell me, old boy, where did you meet this girl?"

"In a teashop."

Crook nodded. "Oh, well, it has to be somewhere. But—any one introduce you?"

"We wouldn't be on nodding terms yet, if we'd waited."

"I get you. How long ago?"

"About seven weeks."

"H'm."

Colin stared at him. "But look here, Crook, there are some damned odd features to this. Why is the house suddenly shut up?"

"It mayn't have been so sudden as you think."

"But I tell you, I rang up on the Friday night and a woman's voice answered me and it wasn't Julia's. There was someone there then."

"That," allowed Crook ponderously, "is damned fishy."

"Look here," Colin was quick to press his advantage home, "you can make a few inquiries at any rate. How about this announcement in *The Times*? What sense was there in Julia doing that? Can't you trace the person who put it in? Doesn't *The Times* exercise any check?"

"Nothing that 'ud help much. This may have been handed in at any place that takes advertisements for *The Times*, that is to say at almost any of the big stores. I believe they generally ask if you're a relation, but they don't ask for any proof that it's a genuine death."

"That's a pity. Isn't it a crime to advertise a death that hasn't taken place?"

"I wouldn't say that, but it's a damn' silly thing to do."

"All the same, how about the funeral? If Julia is dead she must have been buried somewhere. Some doctor must have signed her certificate; an undertaker must have arranged about the coffin. Is it probable that a woman who didn't know of her existence twenty-four hours earlier should have gone to all that trouble? Besides, how about shifting the furniture? I tell you, that hall was as empty as a bankrupt's pocket."

"All right," said Crook soothingly, "all right. We'll get ahead for you. There's only one thing—I won't have any job of mine bungled by amateurs. When we're in a blind alley we'll knock down our own walls. Get me?"

"I get you," said Colin, and went away. He had to see his aunt, who was distraught and slightly feeble-minded, anyway. He was rather glad about this; it gave him something to do.

Crook often said he was fortunate as well as wise in having for his chief assistant a man called Bill Parsons who had spent what are commonly supposed to be the best years of life on the windy side of the law. "Honesty's all very well in its way, but it's like a hobble skirt," Crook liked to explain. "You may look grand and a treat to the neighbors, but you don't get far." Crook now put Bill on to the job of finding the doctor (if any) who had signed the certificate and the undertaker who had attended to the funeral. It was a pity, he felt, that there was no house agent's board up at the house in Henriques Square, so that he couldn't have a legal opportunity of going over the place.

"What's eating you?" asked Bill, inelegantly. "If you find you need to go over the house, you can go. Aren't I as good as a key that's been cut to measure?"

Crook nodded thoughtfully. "That wasn't it, Bill. What I meant was that if the lady had put the house into the hands of an agent she might have spilt a few beans and we could have gathered 'em up. However, you go ahead. We shall have our friend, Streak of Lightning, back again this evening."

Bill, wearing the disguise of an English gentleman, went in leisurely fashion to Henriques Square and hung about until a policeman, who looked as though he had come straight from Hollywood, came into sight. Then Bill ascended the steps of No. 30 and rang the bell. This, naturally, did not ring, but it would have made no difference if it had, since the house was empty of any one capable of opening the door. Then he knocked. He knocked several times in a rising crescendo until the policeman crossed the street to say mildly, "No use knocking, sir. The party's gone away."

Bill turned and limped down the steps. He owed that limp to the police, though the representative to whom he spoke would have found it difficult to believe that.

"Amazing how many of these houses are empty," he observed in a friendly way. "There are six boards up on this side of the square, and on the others . . ." His eye scanned the rows of houses.

"Some of these haven't had a tenant since the war began," the policeman confided. "All dashed off to their bolt-'oles in the country before the first warning went."

"I should have thought some of them might have bolted back by this time."

"Well, I dare say a few 'ave, but this lady, she only went off last week."

"I thought it must be very recent, because my wife heard from her only a few days ago. I happen to be in town on business and I thought I'd snatch the opportunity to call. Not much chance of meeting your in-laws these days."

The policeman said, with a suppressed grin, "It's not every gentleman that finds that much of an 'ardship. You should 'ave come last week, sir."

"When was it you said they went?"

"Tell you the truth, I didn't know they 'ad gone till I saw the furniture being moved out. The butler was looking after things and I 'ad a word with 'im. Lady's bin 'ere a long time, though of course she keeps goin' away for changes. 'E told me she 'adn't been too well and the doctor wanted 'er to get out of town."

"I suppose as soon as I get back I shall find my wife's heard," remarked Bill with glib mendacity. "Well, no sense hanging about, I suppose. You don't know where they went to?"

"Just the country that chap said. 'E was to follow on."

Bill considered a moment. "They had a bereavement here not long ago. That may have got on Mrs. Ponsonby's nerves."

The policeman looked surprised. "Did they, now? I 'adn't 'eard of that. Kept it very dark."

"People always do keep funerals dark, as far as possible."

"That ain't very far," the policeman objected. "Still, I'm not 'ere twenty-four hours a day. All the same, I'm surprised I missed it."

"And you said the furniture went out on Saturday."

"No, the lady went Saturday, so this butler chap told me. Suppose it's a matter of days before they put up a board. Not that there's much call for these big 'ouses just now. They mean a lot of work, and you can't get servants, they tell me. Munitions and so forth and all the young ones fancy themselves in uniform."

"You're the last person to blame 'em for that," grinned Bill, and went off, asking the policeman to oblige him by drinking his health at a more convenient moment.

The policeman said, "Thank you very much, sir," and Bill went back to Bloomsbury Square. The next phase of the inquiry could be better carried out by a woman, they decided.

When Colin came dashing in about six o'clock that evening, his work in connection with his paid job having detained him to this ridiculously late hour, they had quite a lot of news for him.

"Mrs. P. went off early Saturday morning. The cook and the housemaid in the house two doors away watched them go. They went in a long black car, probably hired, since both the women say Mrs. P.'s own was bright red. And they didn't know the chauffeur either. So that might be fishy if you looked at it that way."

"Did any one notice who went in the car?"

"Mrs. Ponsonby and the young lady."

"Ah!" Colin looked more intent than ever. "Would they recognize the young lady?"

"She was young and on the short side and dark."

"That's Julia," said Colin confidently.

"And she'd been with Mrs. Ponsonby about a week."

Colin swerved abruptly. "That," he said, speaking in a very careful voice, "must be a mistake."

"They don't seem to think so," murmured Crook. "That is to say, it wasn't just this one cook and housemaid who remembered her."

"Don't you see where that gets us? Something's happened to that first girl and Julia's taking her place."

"It could be," allowed Crook, thoughtfully. "It could be. That don't sound so good—from Julia's point of view, I mean."

"It means she's in the most desperate danger," said Colin.

71

"Well, no, not that exactly. If they've bumped off one girl they're not likely to try it a second time. After all, there are doctors and undertakers, as you reminded me this morning."

"But don't you see, Julia's a danger to them? She's only got to open her mouth and they're sunk."

"That's why they'll see she don't have the chance."

"Crook, stop playing the fool." Colin was so distressed that Crook overlooked the insult. "Haven't you the faintest idea where she may be now?"

"Not the faintest."

"How about the car? Can't you trace that?"

"Mrs. Ponsonby hired it from a company, saying she was going to motor about for a bit; she engaged it on what's called long-time service. She engaged it definitely for a month, plus chauffeur."

"Hasn't the chauffeur been in touch with his employers?"

"Be your age," Crook besought him. "Since when have hired chauffeurs started writing reassurin' letters? No, of course he hasn't."

"Still, you've got the number of the car. That ought to help."

"It 'ud help if we were the police, because then it could be circulated, but bein' only poor bloody laymen it don't get us as far as you might imagine. Once Mrs. P. is down in this one-horse valley, where she's presumably takin' care of your little bit, the car'll be laid up for a time. One thing, the fellow won't be sent back to town yet. That call of yours on the Friday will have put madam on her guard."

"What happened to the furniture?"

"Taken away by Atkinson's. Yes, we've been in touch with them, too. They had the order three days earlier, but were waiting for confirmation of the actual day. They got the confirmation on Friday just as they were closing at seven o'clock."

"It all fits," said Colin in agonized tones. "Well, what do you do now?"

"Wait till we've got a bit more information. There's the fact that no one in that very nosey part of the world remembers anything about a funeral. Besides, if the lovely Julia didn't die till Saturday she couldn't be buried from Henriques Square, because Mrs. P. had left the premises by nine o'clock."

"Have you tried the undertakers?"

"Give us a chance. What do you think we are? Hitler's Blitzkrieg? As a matter of fact, you ought to have seen Bill going the rounds of the undertakers, newspaper cutting in hand, representing himself as the father of the deceased and askin' for details."

Colin felt more than a little sick. "Did you learn anything?"

"No one, so far, will admit anything to do with the funeral. Besides, you're right, my boy, there's something fishy. Your young woman didn't reach Henriques Square till late on Friday, and she left it early Saturday morning. That don't give the undertaker a chance."

"Do you know where the notice was handed in?"

"A branch of W. H. Smith—the Mayfair one—that is, the one nearest Henriques Square. We've seen the girl who took it and she remembers it because it was so bald—no 'daughter of . . .' no details. She says frankly she thought it was a case of suicide, especially when she saw no letters and no flowers. It was brought in by an elderly man whom she took to be a servant."

"The butler," said Colin. "Which day was this?"

"First thing Tuesday morning. That was another thing that made her plump for suicide. It looked to her as though the family didn't mean to announce the news till after the funeral. If she died on Saturday, the funeral might easily take place on Tuesday."

"So the butler was in town on Tuesday, that is, yesterday. Of course, he may have joined madam by this time."

"There's the point about the other girl," said Crook slowly. "Supposin' there are two, what happened to the one who isn't Julia Ross?"

8

AT THE BIG HOUSE called Beverley and in its environs it was readily accepted that the young lady was "queer," and a big responsibility to her guardian. Mrs. Ponsonby had known very well what she was about when she engaged Alice to work in the house.

The amount of housework she did was negligible, and her slum-mocky ways were a thorn in Sparkes's prim flesh, but in other directions she accomplished more than a dozen better servants could have done. Indeed, Mrs. Ponsonby could have found no one better able to further her own ends.

The situation was pure jam for Alice. The youngest and weakest mentally of a large family she had always been "no-account" at home; she couldn't keep jobs, because employers wouldn't put up with her slovenly habits. Besides, she wasn't altogether honest. When she was given the post of maid-of-all-work at Beverley she whined at first, said it was ever such a big house and that dark, and she was frightened.

"Frightened of work, I suppose?" said her mother who had brought up a large family on a minute wage and had the cleanest house in the neighborhood. Alice was a throw-back, the only un-satisfactory child of nine.

"They won't be kind to me," whimpered Alice who spent most of her time trying to evade work of any sort.

"D'you want another taste of your dad's stick?" inquired Mrs. Reckitts unsympathetically.

Alice cringed and howled and went upstairs to pack her things in a straw Japanese basket. The only redeeming feature of the situation was that they certainly wouldn't keep her more than a week. By the time she had been there three days, however, all that was changed. For one thing, there was Ferrers. None of the local boys wanted anything to do with Alice; she was too much of a nuisance and not above following them home. And then her father made trouble. The two or three who'd had their bit of fun with her already had discovered that to their cost. So that the advent of a "London boy" entranced her. And besides Ferrers there was Julia. Julia was a source of persistent excitement to Alice's unde-veloped mind. That very first night she had tried to throw herself out of a window, and there had been other incidents since.

"You take care how you speak of the gentry, my girl," her mother warned her. "Rich is rich and poor's poor. They don't like to be told their own flesh and blood is daft." Country people, of course, looked at these matters differently. A lack of intelligence didn't unfit a man for earning a living. Plenty of laborers were "silly-like" but they earned as much as the Government allowed them all the same; and they meekly handed over their earnings when they got them, which was more than their sharper brothers would consent to do. Low mentality, hare lips, split palates, the country folk accepted all these with equanimity; they didn't try to shut up village idiots. It would only make them dafter, and the poor loons didn't do any harm, they averred. In that remote corner hardly any one had heard of eugenics; instead they believed in Fate and the Will of God, and would have been horrified at the notion of sterilizing the mentally unfit or putting them away. But people like Mrs. Ponsonby took a different view, as Mrs. Reckitts, who'd been in good service before her marriage, knew very well. To them any suggestion of lunacy carried shame. So now she warned her daughter to put a curb on her tongue.

"But, mam, I'm only telling you," said Alice in aggrieved tones. "She is daft. She keeps pretending she doesn't know when Mrs. Ponsonby speaks to her and says she's someone else and won't listen. And the very first morning she said what work was there for her to do, because she was being paid and she wanted to earn her keep."

"Pity you don't feel more like that," said Mrs. Reckitts grimly. "I suppose that would be enough for you to think she was daft."

"And then she put on a red dress and went out and teased the bull. Honest, she did. She must have crept through the hole in the hedge at the bottom of the garden. Mrs. Ponsonby was ever so upset. Said she'd told her to be careful and to stay in the garden. That bull's dangerous."

"All bulls are dangerous," said Mrs. Reckitts sweepingly. "Still, coming from London, p'r'aps she didn't know."

"Ever such a hullabaloo there was," continued Alice happily. "I was upstairs sweeping out a room—you never saw such huge rooms—when Sparkes came in and said, 'Have you seen the young lady?' Well, I hadn't, and then in Mrs. Ponsonby came and said, 'Sparkes, have you seen Miss Sheila?' Sparkes said, 'I was just asking the girl. Didn't she go into the garden?' Mrs. Ponsonby said, 'Yes, she had,' and she'd told her to rest, but she wasn't in the garden now. Sparkes said, 'Perhaps she'd gone for a walk in the fields,' and I said, 'She'd better mind the bull,' and Mrs. Ponsonby said, 'She was wearing a red dress and hat—oh, but she wouldn't be so foolish as that, because I warned her we were near a farm and she must be careful.' Then we looked out of the window and there she was, running like mad with the bull behind her. He nearly got her, too!" (Alice wound up regretfully.) "Only Jim Barber came rushing out with a fork and he got the bull away. A rare bait he was in. 'What d'you want to come teasing my bull for?' She was shaking all over and she kept on saying she didn't know there was a bull, and then she turned to Mrs. Ponsonby and said, 'But you knew, didn't you? Of course you did. That's why you gave me the red frock.' Mrs. Ponsonby took her inside, and Sparkes said they were ever so sorry, but the young lady had been ill and she didn't always know what she was saying. Jim went off saying that if the bull had got her she'd have known what the bull was saying all right. And inside she was making no end of a bobbery and saying it was a put-up job. You never heard such a noise."

"City folks are always daft," said Mrs. Reckitts.

"Oh, but there's more," declared Alice, proudly. "She says there's people moving about her room in the night; and when Mrs. Ponsonby says, 'Sheila,' she says, 'Who is Sheila? What have you done with Sheila?' Ferrers says when they go out in the car he's told off to keep an eye on her in case she tries to bolt out and do herself a mischief. Mrs. Ponsonby told him when she took him on that the young lady was queer and he mustn't mind, because she wouldn't want to do him any harm, only herself."

"Poor thing," said Mrs. Reckitts, indulgently. "That's the way your auntie was."

"I was telling her," said Alice, "and in the middle she said to me, 'Why are you saying this? Do you think I'm mad? But I'm not, of course, I'm not. It's just that they're keeping me here, they won't let me write to my friends . . .' But she does write. She sits about for hours, and when she's written and Mrs. Ponsonby says, 'Do you want Sparkes to post anything for you, dear?' she just sort of shrivels up and says 'No.' And presently I'll find the letters all torn into bits and thrown out of the window."

"I know her kind," said Mrs. Reckitts philosophically. "One of these days she'll be too clever for them, like your auntie was. The only way for that kind is to shut them up, and so she'll find out." The second she, of course, referred to Mrs. Ponsonby.

In the neighborhood Mrs. Ponsonby had made a good impression. She bought as much as possible locally, but naturally this was not a great deal, since the village consisted of some scattered cottages, a general shop and a butcher's. Still, the farm could supply fowls and eggs and there were vegetables to be had. So far no one had managed to make much out of Sparkes. She stalked about looking as though she had swallowed the poker, and didn't mix with the villagers. These were Mrs. Ponsonby's instructions.

"We don't want to overdo it, Sparkes," she said. "Alice is our best card to play here. She'll do enough talking for six. I shall get an occasional opportunity and shan't take it; that will convince them. You'd better keep your mouth shut, and whatever happens see that the girl never gets a chance to talk to any one but Alice. She can talk to her as much as she likes."

It was late in the evening. Julia had been shepherded to bed a long time ago. Mrs. Ponsonby and Sparkes sat in Mrs. Ponsonby's room. Mrs. Ponsonby had taken off the red wig that stood on a hat-rest on the dressing table. The hat-rest had come from a bazaar and represented a simpering young man. The foolish face under that red wig had a diabolical look; a stranger coming in quickly might have thought there were three conspirators whispering together in the lamplight. Sparkes put out her hand and took a cigarette from a box on the table.

"How long is this to go on?" she demanded.

"It won't do to be in too much of a hurry. We're getting exactly the effect we want. We must be prepared to wait another month, if necessary. Besides, there's the man who telephoned the night the girl came in. It won't be safe to forget him just yet. I don't mind admitting I was nervous in case he came round to the house the next morning. That's why I wouldn't have the furniture moved till Monday. But as he didn't ring up again or try to call I imagine we really needn't trouble much about him. I did think he might write to the girl, c/o myself, but if he had the letter would have been forwarded, and she's had nothing. I've always been careful to be about when the postman called. She hasn't had any opportunity to telephone, and I think Ferrers is to be trusted. He's too stupid to be a villain."

Sparkes looked less satisfied than her employer. "I don't like it," she said flatly. "I always said I'd draw the line at murder."

"Don't use such words," Mrs. Ponsonby admonished her sharply. "Now, I've got all this mapped out. Next week I'll take the girl into Shepley to see the doctor. If anything is going to happen a doctor's evidence is enormously useful. Luckily, she's getting so fey any one would think she was crazy. Don't try and rush things Sparkes. That would be fatal."

"What news from Peters?" Sparkes wanted to know.

"He says everything's quiet and satisfactory. As soon as we're out of this bit of trouble we can go back to town, though, of course, not to that house. But we can easily find a small furnished house somewhere convenient and take it on a wartime lease. Without my wig, no one's the least likely to recognize me, not if I take a little care. There are advantages, Sparkes, in having been an actress for part of your life."

Sparkes, still looking stern, stubbed out her cigarette and went upstairs to perform her nightly job of turning the screw a little more tightly on Julia's sanity. It wasn't much that she had to do, just open the door noiselessly and breathe on the girl's face; or move across the room with a limping step or tap on the shutters. Big effects were not necessary or even desirable; she was like an artist who gets his results by a multitude of minute, feathery touches. As she came up the dark stairs this evening, however, she was arrested by the sound of feet moving cautiously along the carpeted passage. Instantly she had flattened herself against the wall, scarcely breathing, so like a shadow you could have passed her without knowing she was there. The steps above her were almost noiseless, yet her trained ear warned her of the direction in which they were going. Julia's room was set at the end of a corridor, at whose farther end Mrs. Ponsonby slept. Opening out of Mrs. Ponsonby's room was a dressing room whose window gave over the road. It was towards this room that Julia was inch by inch edging her ill-fated way.

Sparkes did nothing to stop her, although already she had a notion of the girl's plan. It was so innocent, so futile, that she allowed herself to smile. She knew, from Ferrers, that Julia had already tried to persuade him to post a letter, but he hadn't had the wit to agree and bring it to Mrs. Ponsonby. He'd simply shaken his stupid handsome head and told her he was sorry, he couldn't, those were his orders.

Julia, unaware of the watcher on the stairs below, crept step by step towards the door of the dressing room. She had been lying awake for some hours, listening to the chime of the clock in the hall. It had struck eleven and half-past and twelve and half-past, and now it was about to strike one. She kept reminding herself that it was going to strike, so that she should be prepared for it. Each foot of the carpet seemed a mile, but she was so desperate by this time that she would have taken far more fantastic chances than actually she was taking now. During an outing she had contrived to pick up and secrete a large stone, by pretending that her shoe had become unfastened. As she stooped to trifle with the lace her hand closed surreptitiously round her prize. Sparkes who was her companion walked on, knowing that escape in such surroundings was impossible. Julia guessed it, too. All the members of the household had seen to it that she would instantly be recognized as the daft young lady from Beverley, who, of course, they could not help to get away. Julia hid the stone in her pocket and caught up with Sparkes who dawdled just ahead. After she went upstairs that evening, the girl wrote a desperate note on a slip of paper and tied it round the stone with a strip torn from her handkerchief.

"To Whoever Reads This—Please help me. I have been brought here under false pretenses and cannot get away. Please get in touch with Mr. Colin Bruce, Home Office, London, and Mrs. Mackie, Spencer House, Roland Street, Lancaster Gate, London. Julia Ross."

It was precisely the sort of note a deranged girl would write, but Julia did not think of this. She only felt it was her one chance of letting Colin know where she was. She printed the address at the foot of the letter, and then set out on her endless journey towards the dressing room. The window here would be open, and if she could evade detection she could fling the stone out and hope that it would be found by someone who took it seriously. When she actually stood inside the dressing room she was convinced that Sparkes was there also. She put out her hand in front of her, as though she would push the darkness back. At any instant she expected the hand to be gripped. But nothing happened. Closer and closer to the window she drew; now she had her hands on the sill. She leaned out into the starlit night, and pitched the stone into the road. She listened long enough to be certain it had cleared the grounds of the house, and began her nightmare journey back. By this time her breath sobbed in her throat, her heart pounded so that she had to pause and lean against the wall or she would have been overcome by dizziness. She wondered, if she were discovered, whether she could persuade her captors that she had only been to the bathroom. But as it happened, the contingency did not arise. When at length she reached her room she flung herself half-fainting across the bed.

"What is it, Sparkes?" Mrs. Ponsonby's voice came in the lowest of whispers.

Sparkes came downstairs. "It's all right, she's back. I was expecting something of the kind when I saw her take that big stone this morning. What she's done is to put a message round it and throw it out into the road. I'll just take a torch and see if we can find it."

"You must find it," said Mrs. Ponsonby sharply. "We've no idea what she may have said."

"Every one round here knows she's silly," returned Sparkes.

"It would be kismet if it was picked up by a stranger who started all sorts of inconvenient inquiries. It oughtn't to be hard to find, not if it's fallen in the road."

Sparkes fetched a torch and came cautiously out of the front door. In the road was a man with something in his hand that he had just picked up. He was a strayed reveller who, despite the war, had been to a dance at King's Sutton, the next village on the map, and was coming back distinctly the worse for wear. Sparkes had to act quickly. She thought it probable that the stranger was past reading, but he might put the stone in his pocket and unearth it several hours later and begin to jump to conclusions. Worse, he might show it to his friends, and Sparkes knew that they could none of them afford to have inquiries that might involve the police. So she walked up to the man and said, "Excuse me, did you just pick up something that fell out of the window?"

The man looked at her with drunken gravity. "Your window?"

"It's a little girl we have staying with us. She dropped it. . . ."

"Li'l girls shouldn't be up at this hour," he warned her, jocosely.

"Of course they shouldn't. Would you let me have what you've picked up?"

He looked down at the stone. "It's a letter," he said in blurred tones. "A letter—and it's not meant for you."

"I'm afraid the person for whom it is meant mustn't see it," explained Sparkes.

A gleam came into his prominent green eyes. "Tha' sort of a letter, is it? Live and let live, you know. Girls will be girls . . ."

For some minutes she thought it might come to an actual tussle between them; and all the time she was afraid someone else might come along. If curiosity began to stir among their neighbors, then the letter could as easily reach its destination. Fortunately, however —though not, of course, for Julia—the young man was far too drunk to be able to sustain any sort of argument, and after trying to tell Sparkes a bawdy story and forgetting its point, he yielded up the stone. Sparkes watched him stagger out of sight before she returned to the house. Julia slept on the house's blind side, and in any case her shutters were sealed. It was impossible that she should have heard any of the encounter.

"Did you get it?" asked Mrs. Ponsonby, as Sparkes reappeared.

"Only just in time," returned Sparkes, grimly. "Another minute and the man who'd picked it up would have put it in his pocket, and goodness only knows what mightn't have started."

She unknotted the strip of linen and spread out the paper. The two women read it in silence. Mrs. Ponsonby was the first to speak.

"Home Office," she said. "I don't like the sound of that, Sparkes. If she really has friends there, the sooner we get things settled the

81

better. I don't think I'll wait till next week for the doctor. I'll make it the day after tomorrow."

"At least it tells us who her friends are," Sparkes pointed out.

Mrs. Ponsonby nodded. "We must let Peters know. He's doing the London end of the business."

Before she went to bed Sparkes slipped out and replaced the stone on the road, hoping that no one would take a fancy to it before she and Julia went out next morning. As it happened, no one did. Sparkes, who missed nothing, saw the way the girl's eyes turned towards the road. She didn't say anything, but a new light burned in her eyes. It was hope and it stayed there all day. She was quite certain now that whoever had found the note would set in motion machinery to rescue her from this appalling house before it was to late.

9

DURING THE NEXT TWO DAYS Julia behaved more like a normal person than she had done since the arrival of the household at Beverley. She reminded herself frequently that it was absurd to count on getting a response to her melodramatic message, but actually that was what she did hope. She rehearsed a mental time-table forty times a day. Suppose X wrote to Colin and Mrs. Mackie the same day as he found the paper. The letters would reach London the day following, and Colin surely would come dashing down to rescue her. By this time her dependence on him was so great that she had forgotten the girl in Ireland and the fact that Colin himself had never showed more than the most casual friendliness towards her. As for Mrs. Mackie, though she hadn't cared much for Julia while they had been under the same roof, even she couldn't be so callous that she would disregard the message entirely. With these two strings to her bow, Julia felt she must somehow register a bull's-eye. Meanwhile, Mrs. Ponsonby had made the appointment with the doctor. It was for twelve noon on Thursday, May the ninth. She told Julia that the appointment was for herself but that they would both drive into Shepley.

"Such a lovely day," she said. "It'll do us both good."

That was breakfast-time.

At eleven-fifteen she was in her room putting on her hat and thinking, "He's had my letter. Will he come down right away? If so we might find him here when we get back. I hope it won't be very dangerous for him, but surely he'll realize what he's up against." Her hands shook so at the thought of seeing him again and all that seeing him might mean that she could hardly adjust her hat.

The door opened without ceremony and Sparkes came in. Julia was accustomed to this now; and she preferred this blatant entry to the soft sidling one, accompanied by a faint rapping after a minute or even two minutes' vigilance on the mat, that was Sparkes's other method.

"I'm just coming," she said quickly.

"Car's at the door," agreed Sparkes. "Oh, and here's something you must have dropped a day or two ago. I've been meaning to give it to you."

Julia looked down carelessly, saw the paper, couldn't believe the truth, stared, turned red, slowly turned as white as ashes. One hand came gropingly out towards it. Sparkes watched her like a snake.

"Don't keep Mrs. Ponsonby waiting," she said and went out again.

"That's done the trick," she assured her employer. "I knew it would. Much better than letting her know right away. Now you've got her just the way you want her to see the doctor."

About a minute later Julia came creeping down the stairs. The scrap of paper had been torn into minute shreds; her mind was still numb. It still didn't seem possible. When it did she might go into frenzies, create a scene, give any stranger good reason to believe her crazy. At the back of her mind she realized that and she clung desperately to self-control. Mrs. Ponsonby said nothing about the paper; she talked pleasantly about unimportant things and Julia thought her own thoughts. They were quite unpleasant and quite hopeless.

Sparkes, of course, was right. Had Julia been given twelve hours to recover from her shock she could have put up a bold front, but the blow had been too sudden. She felt as though the ground had

83

collapsed under her feet and she had fallen sickeningly through an abyss. At the doctor's she was put in the waiting room while Mrs. Ponsonby went to keep the appointment. Julia was sure that a word had been passed to the white-coated attendant to keep an eye on her. In any case, Ferrers stood outside, a stolid unimaginative figure, who wouldn't have any compunction in using violence, if necessary. Julia turned over the pages of The Bystander and The Sketch, looking at photographs of girls, plain and pretty, dressed in tweeds or evening coats, but all having one thing in common, that they were free. Nothing else mattered any more. She was surprised from her brooding by a male voice saying, almost in her ear, "Well, let's have the patient in," and rising awkwardly she found herself face to face with a fussy little man with a moustache and an Edwardian manner.

"Come along, dear," said Mrs. Ponsonby.

Julia stared. "But . . . I don't want a doctor—I—it was for you . . ."

Mrs. Ponsonby laid one hand on her arm. "Now, my dear, we mustn't have any more fuss over this. It's only a temporary condition and Dr. Turner is going to help to cure it. That's right, in here."

Before she could recover herself Julia had entered the consulting room, noting with dismay that Mrs. Ponsonby intended to remain during the interview. The doctor had seated himself and looked at her, a little patronizingly, as he did to all women, his fingertips together. Nerves, he told himself, that's all. He didn't believe in nerves as an illness. An ounce of smacking, where nerves are concerned, is worth a pound of coddling, was his belief. This girl now . . . the aunt had spoken of a tendency to instability. She didn't like to put it more strongly, poor thing. Of course, it was possible there was mental derangement, but, because he liked to avoid the unpleasant side of things, he decided to treat it as nerves pure and simple.

"Now," he said in a friendly way, "your aunt's been telling me you've been overdoing it and have had a bit of a breakdown. Like so many of you young ladies, I suppose, thinking the whole war depends on you."

"If I am run-down," said Julia, "it's because I was out of work for so long and didn't get enough to eat; and I had a bad operation for appendicitis . . ."

The doctor tutted and pshawed. "Bad operation—appendicitis," he said. "Why, that's nothing these days. Mustn't start making heavy weather over that. Now—I understand you're not sleeping very well. That's bad—in itself and as a symptom. However, it ought to be possible to put a stop to that."

"No one can be expected to sleep well if they can't be sure who's going to come in during the night," said Julia. The lack of grammar made the sentence sound like something out of *Alice Through the Looking-Glass*, and the doctor passed it off with scarcely a comment.

"Come, come. You mustn't take an occasional nightmare so seriously."

"People do come in," insisted Julia, her voice shaking with earnestness.

"Well, suppose they do." He decided to humor this tiresome patient a little. "If you're not well you shouldn't make heavy weather because people want to look after you."

"There's something else I'd like to know," Julia continued, "and that is if you think it's really a good thing to sleep with windows hermetically sealed, as mine are."

The doctor didn't bat an eyelash. Mrs. Ponsonby had made good use of her time.

"If it isn't possible to have windows open, you can always open the door instead," he pointed out. "That'll ensure a constant supply of fresh air through the room."

"But I can't sleep with an open door," objected Julia, quickly.

The doctor leaned back and smiled. "Really, Miss Campbell! Now I have quite a number of patients who can't sleep with it closed. It's all a matter of habit. Try sleeping with your door open for a few nights and you'll find you'll soon get used to it."

"I'm afraid my niece thinks we're in some dreadful plot to murder her while she's asleep," observed Mrs. Ponsonby tranquilly.

"I'm quite sure," flashed Julia, "you'd rather I murdered myself."

The doctor stood up and leaned over the girl, catching her by the wrists. "Now, Miss Campbell, this has got to stop," he assured her harshly. "What you're suffering from is a form of hysteria. You imagine yourself surrounded by enemies. Asylums are full of people like you and so are prisons. You appear to be making a number of quite unfounded charges against your aunt. What you have to realize is that you're in a bad state of health, and it's reacting on your mind. There's no earthly reason why you shouldn't pull yourself together and become a perfectly normal and useful member of society. The truth probably is that you've been burning the candle at both ends and you're a trifle unbalanced. Mind you," he added quickly, seeing the change that came over Julia's face at his words, "I don't say it's a serious condition—yet, but you know, you have to be your own doctor. No one but yourself can cure you, though naturally the rest of us will give you all the help we can."

"Can I see the doctor alone?" demanded Julia, but without much hope. Mrs. Ponsonby hesitated, but the doctor replied suavely, "Why not?" As he held the door open for Mrs. Ponsonby he whispered, "A very usual symptom. Nothing to be distressed about."

Mrs. Ponsonby went with obvious reluctance. As the door closed the doctor turned back to the desperate girl.

"Now, Miss Campbell, what is it? You know, you're making mountains out of molehills . . ."

"How can you say that?" burst from his unwilling patient. "You don't know anything of what I've gone through. Oh, I can see what you think—that I'm mad. That's what she meant you to believe. It's what she means every one to believe. Wherever we've gone she's prepared the ground. She's warned the chauffeur, the maid, the shops, every one. And of course they take her word, because they argue that she can't have any conceivable motive for pretending such a thing if it isn't true."

"Come, come," said the doctor in his maddening way. "That's a hopeful admission. After all, my dear young lady, if you can see that she has no motive . . ."

"Ah, but she has. I only said these others don't realize what that motive is."

"And what is it?"

Julia was brought to a sudden halt. "I—don't know. That's the frightful part of it. I don't know. If I did perhaps I could start taking measures. But I'm absolutely in the dark."

86

"In the circumstance, wouldn't it be more sensible to assume that you're wrong, that your aunt has no motive, that all this feeling on your part is due to the strain of your difficult journey after an illness?"

"You told me a moment ago that appendicitis couldn't be called an illness. Besides, you don't understand. Mrs. Ponsonby isn't my aunt. My name isn't Sheila Campbell. It's all part of some frightful plot. I'm Julia Ross, and she engaged me as her secretary-companion, and from the minute I entered her house appalling things have happened to me. She won't let me get in touch with my friends; she won't give me an instant's freedom. Oh, can't you see what her plan is? She means to go on and on until she's really driven me mad, and then nobody will believe a word I say."

The doctor's face hardened. "Now listen to me, Miss Campbell. Your aunt explained some of these hallucinations to me. They're all part of symptoms I should expect to find in the circumstances. You've managed to convince yourself that you're a victim of some mysterious persecution. Unless, of course, there's some motive no one's been able to unearth. After all, why should Mrs. Ponsonby want to assume responsibility for you? You admit, I suppose, that you're an expense to her as well as an anxiety?"

"Then let her get rid of me. That's all I ask."

"And who'd look after you?"

"I can look after myself. I've been doing it for years."

He frowned ominously. "You don't want me to sign an order, I suppose?"

Julia stared at him in horror. "But this isn't possible," she whispered. "Things like this can't happen. You've never seen me till today; you don't know anything about me but what that woman's told you; you haven't an atom of proof that I'm not the person I say I am . . ."

For answer Dr. Turner leaned forward and picked up Julia's bag that lay on his table. He flicked it open and from an inner pocket drew out her registration card.

"If you're not Sheila Campbell, how did this card come into your possession?"

87

"She stole my own, burnt it, I suppose, and put that one in its place."

"And where did she find this one?"

"I suppose that belongs to the real Sheila Campbell."

"Unhappy young lady! I wonder what she's doing without it."

"Perhaps she—doesn't need it any more. That's what I keep thinking . . ."

The doctor shut the bag with a snap and caught Julia by the shoulder.

"Now, listen," he said, "this has got to stop. Take my word, if you don't get a hold on yourself you'll find yourself in a police court or an asylum before you know where you are. You may thank your stars you've got some one as devoted as Mrs. Ponsonby to take care of you. It's obvious to me, as it would be to any medical man, that you're in a very bad state . . ."

"This bad state, as you call it, didn't begin till I went to Mrs. Ponsonby at the end of last month. I was perfectly all right until then, except that I wasn't getting enough to eat. If I were allowed to go away from her, go back to London, unmolested . . ."

"That's out of the question in your present condition," snapped Dr. Turner. "Your aunt has confided in me the true reason why it was necessary to barricade your windows. I've warned her, naturally, that she's assuming a heavy responsibility, but she wants to give you every chance . . ."

"To go completely over the edge," completed Julia, unwisely. "Oh, yes, I've realized that all along. Goodness knows why, unless there's money involved."

"I understood that you had no money," rejoined Dr. Turner, unpleasantly.

"I haven't, but perhaps the real Sheila Campbell has—or had."

Dr. Turner picked up a round ruler and turned it thoughtfully in his hands. "I feel it's only fair for me to warn you that I consider your condition extremely bad. On the other hand, I'm convinced that you can cure yourself, if you please. Of course, there's something behind all this, something you've not been frank enough to admit. A love affair, perhaps . . ."

At the words the hot color rushed into Julia's cheeks. They flamed

88

and flamed until she put her hands over them to hide them from the doctor's dispassionate curious gaze.

"So that's it? I wondered. This young man——"

"He doesn't think of me like that in the least," Julia exclaimed, in her haste to absolve Colin from possible blame. "Why, he's engaged to a girl in Ireland, he hardly knows I'm born."

"But it's not quite like that for you. You wouldn't, I take it, mind changing places with the girl in Ireland."

"Oh, it's ridiculous," began Julia, and stopped. Because it was absurd to deny the truth. It wasn't exactly the same as being jealous of a girl she'd never seen; but she knew now, if she'd never allowed her heart to acknowledge it before, that Colin was all her hope of happiness from now to the grave. Not just her security or a friend in trouble, but the joy women need, women like Julia anyhow.

The doctor was quick to seize his advantage. "Just as I supposed. Look here, young woman, what you've got to realize is that disappointment of some kind or another is part of every one's experience. Do you suppose you're the first to be crossed in love? Haven't you any pride? Or courage? Pull yourself together and have done with these suicidal tendencies. You don't kill a person by just pretending she doesn't exist and adopting a new name. You're Sheila Campbell and you've got to be Sheila Campbell, in essence, till the day of your death. Bite on that bullet and remember that your affairs are very small beer really. The country's at war; people are suffering worse disappointments than you every day of the week. Doesn't that mean anything to you?"

Desperately Julia played her last card. "Will you do one thing for me? Will you write to Colin? Will you tell him what's happened this morning, Mrs. Ponsonby's story and mine? Give him my address and then see what happens."

The doctor, however, had lost patience. "Certainly not. I wonder you haven't too much pride to go on pestering a man who isn't interested." He was thinking that he'd probably make any amount of trouble for himself by dragging this other fellow into it. He'd see Mrs. Ponsonby again, warn her to keep a strict eye on the girl and if there was no improvement, take her to see Chalmers in London. Chalmers worked miracles in cases like these. Of course,

ANTHONY GILBERT

if there was inherited instability an unfortunate love affair was just the thing to dot the i's and cross the t's. It was a pity, but he wasn't really very distressed. Young women in love bored him. All women in love bored him rather. He had a most affectionate wife and when he had a few minutes to spare he used to dream that he was suddenly a bachelor again. As for Colin, all his sympathies were with the young man. He certainly wasn't going to be the agency for bringing this difficult girl back into the fellow's life. He pished and pshawed and got rid of Julia and recalled Mrs. Ponsonby and told her his conclusions.

"A good deal of it's exhibitionism," he said. "She's got a kind of inferiority complex because this chap prefers some other woman, and since she can't accept the situation at face value—and plenty of women can't—she's got to work up a new one in which she figures as heroine."

Mrs. Ponsonby shook her head. "You don't understand even yet, Dr. Turner. There isn't any young man. There never was. There never has been. It's that that galls her so. She goes about imagining men are in love with her, and when they get engaged to someone else she feels she's been ill-used, betrayed, and she makes the most appalling accusations."

"Difficult when they get to that age," agreed Dr. Turner, thinking, It's not so very different from children playing Make-Believe. Only kids are easier to deal with. He thought if he were Julia's father he might see what drastic measures could accomplish, but that wasn't the kind of advice he could give to a client; he could only hope she might think of it for herself. He didn't believe she was mad, after all, though he agreed that in her present state she might well do herself some fatal mischief. He felt he must reiterate to Mrs. Ponsonby the necessity for keeping her under the strictest supervision.

As soon as the pair had left his house his secretary brought in a new patient and he forgot about them.

On the way back Julia indulged in the strongest mood of despair that had yet overtaken her. She thought, Perhaps a man who's been condemned to death for a murder he hasn't committed feels as I do. At first he can't believe he won't be acquitted; then the net draws tighter until he's forced to realize he's got to die. No amount of protesting is going to help him. The thing's been taken out of his hands. She didn't see what else she could do.

That night sleep was impossible. She lay turning from side to side, scarcely caring if any one did intrude on her privacy. Some plan she must make before her weary mind accepted defeat. She thought of various ways in which she could achieve contact with Colin, and when she had discarded one suggestion after another she began to consider whether she could not make her escape unaided. This, however, she knew she would not be permitted to do. Shortly before dawn an idea occurred to her that seemed slightly less hopeless than its predecessors. At all events she must act quickly. She was aware that Mrs. Ponsonby intended to spend very little more time in disposing of her pseudo-companion, though she could not be certain of the methods she would employ. After breakfast she got notepaper and a pen and wrote to Colin.

"DEAR COLIN (she wrote)—I have been trying for some time to get into touch with you, but it has seemed quite hopeless. This is my last hope and if this fails I am lost utterly. I don't mean just lost to you but lost to myself. You remember that night in Lyons I told you I was going as secretary-companion to a Mrs. Ponsonby at 30 Henriques Square; and I want you to know that I know it was you who telephoned me, when she pretended she had never heard of me. I meant to escape the next morning, but she was cleverer than I was, and she managed to smuggle me down here as her prisoner. Colin, don't think I'm mad. It's what she wants every one to think. She's taken me to see a doctor and told him that my real name is Sheila Campbell and says she has never heard of Julia Ross. I know that she either means to get me certified, which is one form of death, or else she is going to murder me and pretend I did it myself. Already she has made me put on a red dress and lured me into a field with a dangerous bull, and she tried to throw me out of a window and then said I was doing my utmost to commit suicide. I don't know what her next plan will be, but I know I shan't have to wait long. Colin, as soon as you get

91

this come down here, if possible bring someone with you. Get me away before it's too late. I would have written before but they never let me post any letters. I've thought of a way in which I can bamboozle her, if I'm lucky. Anyway, I'm so desperate I've got to take risks. And can you do anything to find out about the real Sheila Campbell? I know there was one because I have a card for identity."

Then followed some directions as to the general location of the house and the nature of its occupants.

With trembling hands Julia signed the letter, folded it and directed it to the only address she knew: "The Home Office, London." Stamping the envelope she put it into her bag.

Then she took a second sheet of paper and scribbled a desperate plea to Mrs. Mackie to get into touch with Colin at once. She declared it was a matter of life and death, adding that she was in great danger. "It's like some awful story in the Sunday papers," she wound up. This envelope she also addressed and stamped, but she concealed this one in the pocket of her dress. At lunch time she started to lay her pitiful, desperate plans.

"Are we—shall we be going out this afternoon, Mrs. Ponsonby?"

"Where do you want to go?"

"I just wondered if we'd be going for a drive."

"Not today," said Mrs. Ponsonby, but she said it quite kindly because Alice was in the room. "Tomorrow morning we're going into Shepley. I have some shopping to do that I didn't have time for yesterday. Why? Did you want to go out specially? You could go for a walk with Sparkes this afternoon."

"I—I'd rather stay in the garden. It's so hot for walking."

After lunch she got a deck-chair and put it up on the lawn. Below her the meadow fell away in fold after fold of beauty. This had been a perfect spring; the fruit blossom was almost over, yet in the distance the browning edges were invisible, and the trees looked like snow against the clear blue sky. The hawthorn was out, too, and the hedges foamed with cow parsley. It looked like a scene of the most perfect peace. Sometimes it came as a shock to realize that just across the Channel men were struggling for their country's life.

Little nations were being ruthlessly trodden underfoot and for the time being it seemed as though nothing was strong enough to withstand the fury of the oppressor. Julia lay there a long time, her heart beating furiously. She had left her bag on a chair in the morning room, with the letter inside it. Mrs. Ponsonby was far too clever not to realize how she had spent the morning; surely, surely she would examine the bag and find the letter. After that, everything depended on her reaction to that discovery. Julia compelled herself to remain in the garden from two o'clock until the bell rang for tea. Then she came in, snatched up her bag and vanished to her room to powder her nose. She would not at once examine the letter. She could never wholly rid herself of the belief that she was under perpetual supervision; once, indeed, she had cautiously and absurdly felt her way round the inner walls of her room in case there should be a spy-hole through which she could be observed by night as well as by day. Of course, she found nothing, but the suspicion remained. It was some time before she felt safe enough to remove the letter from her bag. After careful thought she felt convinced that the envelope had been steamed open. Late that night, when her hot milk was brought to her, she ungummed the flap for the second time. As she had anticipated, her letter had vanished. In its place was a sheet of blank paper. Julia calmly resealed the envelope and replaced it in her bag. Tomorrow her opportunity would come; she could scarcely sleep for thinking of it. Soon after breakfast they set out. Julia was unusually docile, Mrs. Ponsonby unusually talkative. Both were acting a part. Julia knew that she would be allowed to post the letter. How much Mrs. Ponsonby knew she could only guess.

"We're going for a nice long drive today," the elder lady observed as they settled themselves in the car. "Ferrers has been very clever with the petrol, and as it's such perfect weather and it's not human to expect it to last I've decided to take a really long trip. We'll take sandwiches and fruit and a thermos and enjoy ourselves."

She said all this in a soft sweet voice that oozed falsity. For an instant Julia's heart misgave her. She thought, "She's cleverer than I've imagined. Something's going to happen to me on this trip, something that will make my letter unimportant. And she'll make it look as though I was responsible." She might even be able to make the

93

fact of the blank sheet contribute to her theory of madness. Mrs. Ponsonby was certainly very casual and pleasant. Sparkes was being left behind and Julia found herself hoping fiercely that Ferrers wouldn't go very far away. She was convinced that Ferrers wasn't consciously in the plot; he really believed what he had been told and wasn't intelligent enough to question the facts. It would be quite in keeping with Mrs. Ponsonby's cunning to send Ferrers off to buy himself a drink and by the time he came back Julia would have thrown herself off a cliff or something equally dreadful.

"But I'm getting hysterical," Julia warned herself. "I've simply got to watch my step very, very carefully. Only why is she taking us all this way out?"

It was a long golden day in late spring; the car ran like a celestial chariot. In spite of herself an element of happiness arose in the girl's heart. By tonight she would have taken the first step towards freedom. Through the open window of the car buzzed a great golden bee, floating on a wind like silk. They ran through a number of small villages, not the witch-ridden villages of her first drive with Mrs. Ponsonby, through a fog-laden world, but the sort of cottages you see on films, with village greens and public houses and ploughed fields with horses clearly outlined against the sky.

"It's a wonderful day," she breathed and Mrs. Ponsonby smiled.

They stopped at one of the villages for tea. By this time Julia was getting despondent and anxious. Surely she was to have her opportunity of posting a letter. So far they had not approached a letter box. But as they came out of the car and entered the tea-shop she noticed with a leap of the heart a red-painted box in the wall. She was too far off to take advantage of it, but she decided as they came out to make her frantic bid for freedom. It meant so much to her that during the meal she felt sick with apprehension. The walls of the room began to bulge in on the little table in a dark corner that Mrs. Ponsonby had chosen. Shakily she laid down the little silver fork with which she had been breaking up a meringue.

"What is it?" asked Mrs. Ponsonby.

"Perhaps it was all that motoring in the sun," whispered Julia who really did look ill. "I feel rather sick."

Mrs. Ponsonby spoke to a waitress who obligingly conducted the girl to the ladies' cloak room. Here Julia hurriedly shot the bolt and leaned against the white painted wall while waves of nausea passed over her. If only she had managed to get rid of the letter before this, she was sure she would feel all right. She opened her bag and saw it there, slipped her hand into her pocket and felt the much more important one to Mrs. Mackie. If she didn't succeed today she would feel that the last vestige of hope was lost. Turning on the cold water tap she began to splash her forehead and wrists. Presently she felt better. For a moment she felt like the Julia Ross of a month ago who might have come to just such a tea-shop as this, knowing that all she had to do was settle the bill and walk out into the sunlight, without any fear for her life. She drew a long breath, touched up her face and walked back into the shop. Mrs. Ponsonby had risen and was coming towards her.

"I was afraid you had fainted, dear," she said.

"I'm sorry. Was I a long time?" Even to herself Julia's voice sounded strained and unfamiliar.

"Come back and finish your tea."

"I don't think . . ." began Julia uncertainly, but already Mrs. Ponsonby had her by the arm and was leading her towards her chair. Julia prepared to finish the meringue and was actually picking up her fork when a new thought struck her. Surely the position of the fork was different? She had left it half-turned on its side, the little prongs concealed in the thick foamy cream. Now it lay neatly along the edge of the square blue plate. Was it possible that Mrs. Ponsonby had tampered with the meringue? She was watching the girl with a peculiar smile. Breathlessly, Julia put down the fork. "I don't think I better," she whispered. "I still feel a bit bad."

"Then don't touch it," was Mrs. Ponsonby's cordial reply. "Just drink up your tea."

"Yes—thank you." But surely the woman was eyeing her with extraordinary solicitude. She even touched the handle of the cup. So that, thought Julia, is where the danger lies. Quickly she took up the cup and emptied it.

"That's cold. I'll get some fresh." She washed out the cup carefully in hot water and poured out a fresh brew. Mrs. Ponsonby watched her with a smile.

95

"Still the same old idea?" she said. "Afraid someone's trying to do you a mischief?"

Some people sitting at a nearby table overheard the words, as she had intended they should, and they turned to look at the girl to whom they were addressed. Julia stooped her head over the cup and sipped the tea. It might have been imagination but it seemed to her it had an oddly bitter taste. Mrs. Ponsonby still smiled; she never took her eyes off Julia's face. So perhaps it was the teapot and not the individual cup that had been tampered with. The woman was by no means unintelligent. She was foreseeing precisely what the girl would do. The cold tea was probably harmless, but suppose she had doctored the pot? The crime would never be traced to her. The tea-pot would be washed before the first symptoms made themselves apparent. Any doctor might have been forgiven for hesitating about Julia's sanity at that moment. Pretty soon it wouldn't be necessary for Mrs. Ponsonby to do her direct harm; she'd simply have to put ideas into the girl's head, and she would do the rest herself.

She swallowed a second mouthful, then put the cup down. "I don't think I am so very thirsty, and anyway this is rather strong. No, thank you, I don't want any more."

Mrs. Ponsonby produced her purse. "Go out and sit in the car," she suggested. "You'll feel better in the fresh air. I'm just coming."

Julia hurried out. Ferrers was seated at the wheel of the car, staring at nothing. It was quite easy to drop the two letters into the box before he became aware of her presence. As Julia turned towards the car something made her fling a lightning glance over her shoulder. Through the glass she could see Mrs. Ponsonby standing by the counter talking to the girl at the cash desk. There wasn't the slightest doubt that she had seen exactly what happened. Still, thought Julia, I've posted the letter. If only Mrs. Mackie acts at once; if only Colin isn't away. The time factor was all important, as she well knew.

She had impressed on the woman the necessity for not replying to the letter, so that she did not hope for any answer. For the next two days she was like a prisoner on the rack. Every time a bell rang or a foot sounded she stiffened, her ears alert. Somehow, she was convinced, Colin would rescue her—if only he came in time. During those two days Mrs. Ponsonby left her alone. It had become a habit of hers to wake spasmodically in the night, listening for the limping footstep that Sparkes affected after dark. But on each occasion the silence seemed as complete as death.

On the evening of the second day it happened. She was in her room preparing for dinner when she heard a voice call her name. Not the name that Mrs. Ponsonby had bestowed upon her but the name with which she had been familiar for three-and-twenty years.

"Julia! Julia Ross! Julia, are you there?"

For an instant she could scarcely believe her ears. There was a mutter of voices rising shrilly in the hall. She heard Mrs. Ponsonby say "Impossible, I tell you you're mistaken," and at that she seemed to regain power over her limbs. Rushing to the door she called, "I'm coming. I'm coming," and came helter-skelter to the top of the stairs. What stopped her she never knew. It might have been the sudden breathless silence that followed her cry. It might have been that mysterious sixth sense with which Providence has endowed women who need it as men do not, because of their inferior physical strength. Whatever it was, just as she reached the head of the stairs, she shot out her hand to clutch at the polished rail. It was quite dark here, for the corridor windows had been boarded up to comply with black-out regulations. As she felt the wood of the rail under her hand she flung herself violently backwards, maintaining her balance with difficulty.

"Colin!" she called, but fear choked the word in her throat. No one answered her. It was as though the whole house suddenly drew its breath and waited. Something had touched her on the shin and she stooped, groping vaguely, but before she could discover what it was Mrs. Ponsonby was hurrying up the stairs towards her. She shook as much as the girl herself, her ample bosom quivered, her fat little haunches trembled like jellies.

"What are you trying to do?" she panted. "Sheila, what is it this time?"

Julia felt as weak as a piece of chewed string. "He called—Colin. I heard him."

"You're crazy. I don't believe it's safe to keep you here. What was it you meant to do?"

Panic invaded Julia's mind. "Where is he?" she demanded in

97

helpless fury. "He was here, I know. What have you done with him? Oh, I believe you've killed him as you'd like to kill me."

Mrs. Ponsonby said in firm, controlled tones, "Go back to your room, Sheila. I'll bring you a sedative. Really, I don't know what we're to do with you. These delusions——"

Julia shrank from her touch, from her proximity, from the warmth of the breath she could feel upon her cheek. As she regained her room she sank down on the bed, the tears pouring down her face. She felt as though she could never stop crying, because hope was dead, because she was caught, and she'd never get away—never, never, never.

There was an odd sound going on in the passage outside. It broke through the girl's mood of despair, filling her with curiosity. She felt she must know what it was. She wasn't afraid that it might be part of a new plot against her, because she didn't feel her position could be worsened. Cautiously she opened the door a crack and peered out. At the stairhead a small lamp was burning; on the stairs knelt Sparkes tugging at something. Julia watched, full of perplexity. Suddenly the task, whatever it was, was accomplished. Sparkes stood up holding in her hand something that looked like a dead snake. Julia stared. Suddenly she understood, both the nature of Mrs. Ponsonby's plan for her and the reason that her instinct had issued that eleventh-hour warning. There had been a piece of cord stretched across the top of the stairs at about the level of her knee. Sparkes and Mrs. Ponsonby had cold-bloodedly placed it there. Then they had retreated to the hall and shouted her name, pretty confident of the result. What they hadn't counted on had been that sixth sense that had saved her. But it wouldn't go on doing that. One day it would fail and Mrs. Ponsonby would win. It wouldn't have been hard to make it look as though the girl had flung herself headlong down the stairs and, landing on the stone floor of the hall, she would probably have been killed outright. Even if she had only been injured, it might well have caused concussion, and by the time she returned to normality all the arrangements would have been made. Mrs. Ponsonby had plenty of witnesses—Sparkes, Ferrers, Alice, Dr. Turner. Even if

Colin did succeed in tracing her it would be easy to deny her existence. He'd never discover where she'd been concealed.

Sparkes brought her up a tray, since clearly she couldn't dine downstairs, and later Mrs. Ponsonby came in with hot milk in which she'd put some bromide. Julia took the glass without a word. She was not afraid of being poisoned in the house. Mrs. Ponsonby's anger had quite abated. Seated on the edge of Julia's bed she asked very gravely, "What was it you thought you heard? Come, Sheila, I must know."

"I heard someone call my name. You can call it an hallucination but we both know better."

The woman gently shook her head. "Have you ever stopped to wonder if you really are right? You're so confident, but suppose you have made a mistake? Suppose all this story of yours is a delusion? Wouldn't it be better to find it out quickly and face up to it? Remember, you can't prove a single one of your pretensions. There isn't a living person who would believe you. If you could make yourself accept the truth you'd be happier, because then you'd start the process of readjustment. You know I'll help you all I can."

"Please," said Julia with deadly earnestness, "will you go away?"

Mrs. Ponsonby rose. "Think over what I've said. It'll be worth your while. There's no happiness for you while you cling to this delusion about your second self."

She went quietly out, closing the door behind her.

Although she had not entirely succeeded in attaining her objective, Mrs. Ponsonby's seed began to sprout in Julia's mind. She didn't believe, of course, that she actually was Sheila Campbell, but she did begin to wonder whether her suspicions weren't a form of mania. Yet she redoubled her precaution, even while sometimes she railed at herself for folly. She was afraid to sleep, and after that first night Mrs. Ponsonby offered her no more tablets. She would prop herself up in the bed, listening for the sound of feet in the corridor. She kept away from windows, looked both ways before she crossed the street. She looked up in case something should fall from above, looked down for fear of some invisible menace designed to trip her. When she was alone in any of the sitting rooms she would stare unwinkingly at the painted eyes of the family portraits until presently they would move and roll, and then she would be justified in her suspicion that a human intelligence was concealed behind the frame. She shook out curtains, because they might conceal an enemy, kept away from windows because hands can come through the glass, and stared fixedly at doors, because sometimes they swung open as she approached and sometimes they shut noiselessly. Sometimes when she caught a handle and twisted it the door resisted her, yet when she did enter the room it was empty. These things, she knew, do not happen to normal people. They had never happened to her before. The change that had taken place in her could be dated from the time of her engagement by Mrs. Ponsonby. And unless Colin came soon he might save himself the trouble because what he'd find wouldn't be the Julia Ross he knew, but someone with her face and voice, but with someone else's mind that wouldn't know him and that he wouldn't recognize. The day that she began to think possibly Mrs. Ponsonby was right and Julia Ross and her history were no more than a dream, she was ruined beyond recall.

So, lying awake in the nights, she drew nearer and nearer to the abyss of madness.

10

COLIN BRUCE SLEPT with a telephone beside the bed. This was convenient personally as well as essential professionally. One morning early in May the telephone rang just before eight a.m. Colin, who had been extremely busy the night before and had not gotten to bed until four hours earlier, slept through the first peel and wakened with a jolt at the second. He had been dreaming of Julia and was still so much enmeshed by his dream that if he had heard her voice he would scarcely have been surprised. The speaker at the other end of the wire spoke in a whining tone that certain women seem to consider denotes refinement. It called him Mr. Bruce, pronouncing the name as though it were spelt Brewce.

"Yes?" he said hazily. "Colin Bruce speaking."

"This is Mrs. Mackie."

"Mrs. . . ?" For an instant he groped in the caves of memory. It meant nothing to him whatsoever.

The voice sharpened, sounding offended. "Mrs. Mackie. You did ask me to let you know if I should hear anything about a lodger of mine, Miss Ross. So, seeing what the post brought this morning . . ."

Colin sat bolt upright. "You mean, you've heard from her? Why didn't you say so at once?"

The voice intimated that not thus was its owner accustomed to being addressed.

"I'm sure I've been on the line long enough trying to wake you . . ."

"What does she say?"

"It's a very peculiar letter, very peculiar indeed. She says—but perhaps I'd better read it to you." She proceeded to do so, giving each word exactly equal weight.

"What's her address?" demanded Colin.

"Beverley, Kings Marlow. But the funny thing is the postmark says Martindale ever so clearly. That's funny, isn't it?"

"Oh, no," said Colin, vaguely. "There's probably quite a simple solution. Perhaps they were out for the day and she had to jump at the chance . . ."

"You don't mean you think she's been kidnapped?" Mrs. Mackie's voice throbbed with pleasure. Colin cursed himself for an impulsive fool.

"Not necessarily," he said. "But I'm not altogether happy about the position. And you see yourself from her letter . . ." It occurred to him that he was wasting his breath. "I'll be with you in a quarter of an hour," he promised.

Mr. Crook lived very snugly in Earl's Court; it suited him to perfection. Mayfair or Belgravia would have been ridiculous and pretentious; Hempstead and Golders Green were ruled out because so many of his dubious clients lived there. But about Earl's Court there is a sober respectability allied with thrift. This respectability delighted Crook; he said it tickled his sense of humor. He occupied one floor in one of those big houses built towards the end of the last century for well-to-do middle-class families. It had five floors and a steep basement and Crook said in his irreverent way it reeked of hopeful daughters and discreetly-soured spinsters. When Colin descended upon him that May morning Crook was disproving the idea that you can only do one thing at a time. Crook was doing three, anyhow. With his right hand he forked up mouthfuls of grilled sausage and bacon; with his left he held a telephone receiver to his ear; while his eyes were fixed on a letter that had come by that morning's post. Although he was talking and eating energetically, he seemed to be taking in all the salient points of his correspondence. When Colin broke in he gave him his attention, too, so that made four things, quite apart from what he was thinking, which no one could guess.

"My dear fellow, what are you driving at?" he bellowed down the telephone, with his mouth full. "Of course, we've got to tell the truth. It's ridiculous to hide it, anyway. Truth is just the sort of simple thing the police do find out. Besides, where would lawyers be if they didn't even have the truth to work on? The fact is, clients give them damned little as it is, and they expect Buckingham Palace out of a handful of mucky straw—and anyway what matters is how the judge hears the truth, and that's my job, not yours. Sit down and ring for coffee, if you want it (that was to Colin). What's that you say? Well, of course, I believe you're innocent. Haven't I proved that by agreeing to act for you? And don't you know that my clients are always innocent? Well, then, what more d'you want? The Kingdom of Heaven as well as Buckingham Palace?" He rang off abruptly. "If ever you commit a murder, Colin," he remarked, spearing yet another sausage and inviting his guest to do likewise, "don't go all sissy about it afterwards. After all, someone's got to commit murders, haven't they, or how about poor devils like me? We'd be lining up for the dole and being refused it as like as not. Well then, look on the bright side. Reflect that you're putting a job of honest work in another chap's way, so you're doing him a bit of good. And someone has to pay. That's the law of life."

"The someone being the corpse?" contributed Colin brilliantly.

"Right first time. That chap shouldn't have killed his man, though. He's gone all squeamish since. It isn't only he's afraid he'll hang. He's developing a conscience, beginning to wonder if perhaps it wasn't quite cricket. Well, what's your development? Found the lady?"

"We've had a letter from her. I've brought it round." He produced it. "Now then?"

"It's a letter," agreed Crook cautiously. "As to whether it's actually from her is another matter. But then, I don't know her writing."

Colin's face changed. "I don't either," he confessed, flatly. "Do you mean you think this may not be from her at all?"

"If you wanted to coax a man into a trap wouldn't this be the sort of a letter you'd write?"

"I dare say it would," Colin admitted. "But why should any one want to trap me?"

"Aren't you the only person who knows that the girl went to Mrs. Ponsonby's?"

"Then why not write to me direct?"

"That's one of the things I shall find out—naturally," returned Mr. Crook, with hauteur.

"I thought I'd better tell you I'm going down," continued Colin.

"I have heard nicer ways of telling a man you're taking your business away from him," Crook reflected aloud.

"What the devil . . . ?"

"Remember what I said at the start? No amateurs on the job. You go back to your own lay, whatever that may be and let Crook and Company go right ahead. After all," he nodded pleasantly, "they might get you in a trap, but they've got to get up the day before yesterday to catch Crook bending."

Mrs. Ponsonby and Julia had been for a drive. All the afternoon Mrs. Ponsonby had made a point of calling her Sheila; she chattered about a very nice place in the country, you really couldn't call it a nursing home, it was just a big house where a delightful woman took people who had had breakdowns and nursed them back to health in no time. She said, "How do you like the idea of that?" and Julia said, "I suppose, if you've had a nervous breakdown, you're past caring what any one does to you."

Mrs. Ponsonby tapped her hand with her fat little fingers—like a bunch of little jewelled sausages they were—and said, "That's not at all the right way of looking at it. It's a matter of getting you well," and had continued in this vein until they stopped at the green wooden gate of Beverley.

As she opened the front door Sparkes said instantly, "There's a gentleman here from London, madam. He's been waiting quite a time."

Mrs. Ponsonby's small features seemed to freeze. Her pupils shrank to slits in her relentless face. Julia was reminded of a sleeping python she had once seen in the zoo.

"I'm not expecting any one," she said sharply. "Did he give his name?"

"He said he was a lawyer."

Julia, who had shrunk back, fearing that the newcomer might be a neurologist called in to assist Mrs. Ponsonby with her plot, came quickly into the hall.

"Perhaps it was me he wanted," she suggested.

"Nonsense! You'd better go upstairs and lie down. You've been complaining of a headache."

"It was you he asked for, madam," Sparkes chimed in.

"It might be for me," Julia insisted, though without much hope behind her words.

"You're crazy." Something in the woman's contemptuous tone made Julia cry out in a loud voice, "Not so crazy as you'd like people to think."

"Well, well, well!" said a new voice. "That's interesting, isn't it?"

The three women turned abruptly. A fat, rather common-looking little man was standing in the doorway. He looked as though he'd be more at home on the race course yelling the odds or wearing a stiff white apron, garnished with a knife sharpener on a long steel chain, shouting the bargain prices of meat in some Saturday night market. He wasn't remotely what any of them thought a lawyer should be like.

"Mrs. Ponsonby?" said the stranger, taking advantage of the silence that greeted his appearance. "My name's Crook—Arthur Crook, the Criminals' Hope and the Judge's Despair. I'm here on behalf of a client who prefers to remain anonymous in connection with a young lady named Julia Ross."

"I said it was for me," exclaimed Julia. Her heart began to sing. Crook might be common, unimpressive, as vulgar as truffles or cow heels, but he represented the world from which she had been separated for some weeks.

Crook nodded thoughtfully. "So you're Julia. Well, you do the lad credit. I suppose you realize you're officially in the churchyard."

Mrs. Ponsonby here found her tongue. "This is absurd," she began, but Crook was not so easily silenced.

"Just the point I was coming to, lady," he agreed. "That's the first thing we've got to settle. If this lady is Miss Julia Ross, then what's the meaning of the obituary column notice?"

"I don't understand." Julia was staring.

"There was a notice in the *Times* to the effect that you were one more candidate for the churchyard mold. In fact, you died on the 27th ult."

"I knew you were a wicked woman," said Julia slowly, "but I didn't think even you would have done that."

"This is perfectly ridiculous." Mrs. Ponsonby took charge of the situation. "This young lady is my niece, Miss Sheila Campbell. Why she should imagine she is someone else I cannot pretend to understand, unless it is that she saw the name in a paper . . ."

"How could I, on Saturday?" broke in Julia. "We came down to this horrible house then."

"With you dyin' all the way?" applauded Crook.

"I am afraid I must ask you to leave my house," continued Mrs. Ponsonby. "Both my maid here and my butler, who is looking after my London house, will bear out in my statement."

"Sure they will," agreed Crook, cordially. "You mean the house you left unfurnished?"

"I fail to understand," Mrs. Ponsonby began, but once again Crook interrupted her. He had no manners. He always said that great men don't need them and small women, by which he meant those of Mrs. Ponsonby's moral calibre, don't understand them. They think them a sign of weakness.

"That's why I'm here. Now then, will you tell me why this young lady should call herself Julia Ross if that isn't her name?"

"Because she suffers from delusions. I have brought her down here, where it is very quiet, in order that she may have a chance of recovery. I don't know who sent you on this wild-goose chase . . ."

"My client. I told you. He thinks she's Julia Ross, too."

"How can he? Oh, I don't mean there isn't such a person and that he doesn't know her, I only mean that this girl is not her. Why, I challenge you to produce one single jot of evidence of identity."

"I wouldn't be much use to the sort of client I generally collect if I couldn't answer a simple one like that. You give me twenty-four hours and I'll have so many proofs that you'll wonder how you could ever have thought her your niece."

"This is most irregular," protested Mrs. Ponsonby. "I can only imagine that somehow my niece managed to get into touch with you and persuaded you to take part in this monstrous charade."

"How about the lady at the Victoria Agency who sent you a Miss Ross as prospective companion-help?"

"I certainly telephoned the Agency and certainly two or three girls came to see me, but they were quite unsatisfactory. There wasn't a Miss Ross among them."

"What happened to the companion?"

Julia could have sworn that the woman flinched; but in an instant she had made a magnificent recovery. "I don't understand."

"The one you phoned for."

"I had to let the Agency know that I was suddenly called out of town and therefore wouldn't be requiring any one just now. But my niece had been with me for some time before that."

"It isn't true," begged Julia. "Oh, surely you can help me."

"There's another interesting thing," Crook went on blandly, "and that is we can't find any record of Julia Ross's death. That's funny, ain't it? No doctor, no undertaker . . ."

"It's not a criminal offence to insert a notice in the obituary column by way of a practical joke," suggested Mrs. Ponsonby icily.

"You've said it, lady, but when the object of the notice don't find the joke amusing or even in good taste—well, how about it?"

While they talked Crook had been gradually moving backwards and by this time they were all in the room Sparkes called the library. It was a large dark room with square windows looking over a soaked dark green garden; trails of ivy smothered the glass; there were no books anywhere.

"I really fail to understand why you have come to see me on this matter," reiterated Mrs. Ponsonby.

"Because we received information that Miss Ross is a member of your household."

"And who told you that?"

Crook winked. "A little bird."

Mrs. Ponsonby was thinking hard. "The only explanation I can offer you is that my niece, whose mental condition gives grave cause for anxiety and who is under medical attention at the present time, has seen this notice of which you speak and has adopted the name— no, don't ask me why . . ."

"I wasn't going to," returned Crook, with a grin. "Even I know the answer to that one. But now you tell me something. How is it that she got information through to one of the two living people to whom the name meant anything? And if you can think up an answer to that one, I'll eat my hat with horse-radish sauce."

Mrs. Ponsonby was in a pretty desperate position; but she reminded herself that every scrap of evidence that could be brought into court would support her case. The momentary hesitation before her reply was so brief that Julia did not realize it existed.

"My niece may have met this Julia Ross somewhere, have known her history, and is now using the details for her own distraught ends I believe," she added slowly, "that you are sincere; you really believe this young woman is the person she pretends to be. How can I prove to you your mistake? I have her registration card, her clothes and brushes with her initials . . ."

"Her birth certificate?"

"Of course not."

"I haven't an iota of proof as to who I really am because these two have destroyed everything," broke in Julia in a frenzy, but Crook was no more moved by her distress than he had been by Mrs. Ponsonby's flat denials.

"Don't let that trouble you. I'm accustomed to providin' my own proofs. That's part of a lawyer's job, if you ask me. I can't stand these shilly-shallying white-livered chaps who wash their hands of a case

107

as soon as they come up against some insignificant little fact that, they think, cuts away the ground under their feet. A lawyer's job is to prove his client's case. That's what he's being paid for. He's no right to let a little matter like absence of proof stand in his way."

"Do whatever you think necessary," Mrs. Ponsonby encouraged him. She was white with anger and fear. "You will find yourself up against a blank wall, but perhaps you don't mind that."

"Never yet met a wall so blank I couldn't hammer a way through it," grinned Mr. Crook. "But p'raps you've never heard of dynamite."

"Dynamite?" she stared.

"That's my middle name. Arthur Dynamite Crook. You mention dynamite on any of my circuits (he liked using this expression though he wasn't, of course, a barrister), and you'll get a free drink anywhere." He nodded and stood up, taking a hard black bowler hat from the cushion beside him.

"Are you going?" stammered Julia, in dismay.

"Can't start laying the foundations too soon."

"But—what are you going to do?"

"You watch the papers. I tell you, the average man and woman in this country don't understand the power of the press. They're our real rulers. Hitler, Mussolini—where'd they be without the power of the press? You wait." He laid one thick finger on his big indomitable nose. "You've got a treat coming."

"I shall permit no pressman to disturb our privacy," rasped Mrs. Ponsonby.

"We shan't need your co-operation, lady," Crook assured her. "Oh, it's goin' to make a pretty story. Just the kind of thing the public likes best.

"In a lonely house in the country, shut away even from the echoes of daily life, is a beautiful young girl who, known as Sheila Campbell, protests that her real name is Julia Ross. That such a girl as Julia did exist is proved by the fact that her death was recently announced in the press, although no doctor can be discovered who signed her certificate and no undertaker who buried the body. What is the Julia Ross Mystery? Why does Mrs. Ponsonby, in whose charge the girl now is, declare that her real name is Sheila Campbell?

"And then, in caps, very black, so even a moron couldn't miss it:

"WHO IS SHEILA CAMPBELL?

After all," he reverted to his ordinary voice and turned to Mrs. Ponsonby, "even she must have a history. How long has she been living with you? Who are her parents? Why hasn't anyone heard of her until a few weeks ago? They didn't, you know, because we've found that her registration card's only just been issued. Well, well," he clapped on his hat, tilting it over one eye, "we'll meet again, Miss Ross. Just had to make certain you really did exist. When you know me a bit better you'll take off that anxious expression. Know my motto? CROOK ALWAYS GETS HIS MAN," He chuckled and walked out of the room.

After he had gone Mrs. Ponsonby said nothing to Julia; she didn't keep an eye on her the way she usually did; she seemed almost indifferent. Julia knew less then than she learned later. If she had known more she might have admired the way her enemy took that blow.

After a few minutes, still without speaking, she went out of the room and along the hall. Julia knew she was going to see Sparkes, who had shown Crook out, to discuss with her this new startling development. Julia had sometimes tried to talk to Sparkes, in an endeavor to discover the link between the two women, that seemed to her more intimate than is usual even when a servant has been in the same employment for many years. Sometimes she even suspected that Mrs. Ponsonby was afraid of Sparkes. And what, she asked herself, her mind occupied by a dozen trifles at once, had she meant when she said to Peters, "Remember my instructions. Carry them out to the letter." Surely, surely the insertion in the Times was part of those instructions; and the demobilization of the house in Henriques Square another. Yet the girl was still as far as ever from discovering the motive for this involved and dangerous plot. Tonight, however, she had a sense of security she had not known since she first heard Mrs. Ponsonby's name. However much the woman might hate her, that night at least she would do her no harm. She wouldn't dare. Crook might be an odd sort of lawyer, but he had the protruding jaw of a bulldog, that animal whose grip can never be loosed.

Throughout the rest of the evening Mrs. Ponsonby scarcely spoke; after dinner the oddly-assorted pair sat in the drawing room with books on their knees, but neither of them read much. Julia was wondering how soon it would be before help arrived, what had been simmering in Crook's active brain. Mrs. Ponsonby's thoughts followed the same road, but for a briefer period. She had more than speculation to employ her mind; she must make plans for the future and make them swiftly.

11

JULIA WENT TO SLEEP that night in a mood of comparative gaiety. That Mrs. Ponsonby would speedily seek some way to nullify Crook's efforts she was aware, but Crook looked like a sticker. As usual, she heard the key turn in her lock after she was in bed, but she refused to allow that fact to ruffle her nerves. When the house was quiet she slipped out and stuffed the lock with shreds of tissue paper; this would prevent the key being reinserted and guard her privacy until morning. This done, she slept. She was awakened by the sound of someone violently rattling the door handle. Sparkes' voice was calling.

"What have you done to your door?"

"Just a minute." She got up and with the aid of a hairpin slowly fished the bits of paper out of the lock.

"What new trick are you up to?" Sparkes was clearly rattled this morning; her tone of voice indicated that. She spoke like a nurse threatening her charge with severe penalties.

"It's because of the footsteps," returned Julia lightly. "I know you and Mrs. Ponsonby think I'm crazy because I hear steps in my room some nights, so I thought if I blocked the keyhole and I still heard the steps it would mean . . ." she paused.

"That you were crazy?" Sparkes spoke in grim tones.

"Actually, I suppose it would mean there was some other way into my room. However, I didn't hear anything. I think it's rather a good idea." She had been looking at Sparkes as she spoke and her eyes were puzzled. Surely there was something odd about her appearance, something out of the ordinary. After a minute or two she realized that this was because the woman, today, wore a dark overall over her dress instead of her usual cap and apron. Her head was bare; her hair, thick and springy like horsehair, was done up in a number of little curls on her neck, pinned in very close. She thought it strange she had never noticed that before.

Sparkes crossed to the windows and opened the shutters; the day outside looked like a clouded pearl; a thin silver mist lay over everything like a sparkling veil.

"What's the time?" exclaimed Julia. "My watch says half-past six and it doesn't seem to have stopped."

"Why should it?" asked Sparkes.

"You mean, it is only half-past six? Then what . . . ?"

"My instructions were to wake you at once. The car will be round at seven."

Julia dropped on to the edge of the bed, stupefied. "At seven? But—where are we going?"

"Just away."

"You mean for a drive? At this hour? But you don't, you mean for good."

"That's right," agreed Sparkes calmly. "Well, what are you looking like that for? You've never liked this house; you've always wanted to leave it. And now we're going."

Julia felt a roaring noise in her ears; she put her hands over them to shut it out; but it was in her brain and she couldn't get away from it.

"This," she heard herself say, "is because of Mr. Crook. But you can tell Mrs. Ponsonby I'm not coming."

"You heard what I said, didn't you—Miss Campbell?" repeated Sparkes. "And you better hurry, because madam doesn't like being kept waiting. And there's no sense your saying again that you're not coming, because you are, if we have to tie your hands and feet together and carry you in."

111

She was quite capable of putting her threat into action, nor would she hesitate to call upon Ferrers, if her own strength failed. Ferrers, actually, was as good a witness as Mrs. Ponsonby could have found anywhere. He had no mind at all, so when he was told that Julia was deranged he accepted the fact, because he hadn't any thinking apparatus with which to refute the suggestion. Everything he had ever heard Julia utter had been suspect before it was spoken; no court of law, not even Crook himself, could suggest that Ferrers was aware of the plot. Julia knew that; knew, too, that on this occasion at least she was worsted.

"I'm coming," she said woodenly. "Am I expected to be ready and packed within half an hour?"

"You won't have to bother about packing," replied Sparkes. "I did that last night before you came up."

"Where are we going? But I suppose you wouldn't tell me, even if you knew."

"So you may as well save your breath," concluded Sparkes, grimly. She stalked out of the room, saying she'd be up for the luggage in a quarter of an hour. Julia dressed as far as her petticoat, then slipped out of the room and leaned stealthily over the bannisters. It was possible, she thought, she might overhear something. Luck lay with her to some extent. Mrs. Ponsonby, already wearing her hat, with her gas mask slung round her fat little shoulders, was talking to Ferrers in the hall. Julia distinguished a few words. "Two hundred and fifty—can you manage it?" she heard Mrs. Ponsonby say. That puzzled her for a moment. It wasn't possible that the figure referred to cash. People like Ferrers don't have to be bought with large sums of money; they are perfectly prepared to acquiesce without argument, no matter how strange their instructions.

"He doesn't even think they are strange," thought Julia, and then realized that the two hundred and fifty must refer to mileage. "How does she get hold of all this petrol?" she wondered. "She may be as rich as Crœsus but there must be more to it than that." At that moment Mrs. Ponsonby looked upwards and instantly Julia melted into shadow. Even so she couldn't be sure she hadn't been seen.

"We're going somewhere two hundred and fifty miles away," she reflected. "Presumably she means to get there tonight, since we're starting so early. Now there are so few cars on the road you can make a good pace, and if we don't stop for meals—and I don't suppose we shall, because she won't want to leave any clues for Mr. Crook to pick up—we can do it easily. Ferrers drove well; he would certainly manage an average of thirty miles an hour."

Somehow she must contrive to leave a message for Crook. She hadn't much information for him, only that she would be somewhere about two hundred and fifty miles from Beverley. Possibly he could learn from some local person the direction they had taken. It seemed to Julia that unless she were very subtle the end of the thread that had been put into Crook's hand would be jerked away again before he realized his danger. (She had, of course, no previous experience with Crook or his methods.) Somehow she must ensure that when he next visited Beverley he should find some hint to guide his further search. How she was to leave any such message troubled her for some time. It would have to be in this room, she decided. Crook would be sure to come there when he found the nest empty. He would be able to identify the room because of Mrs. Ponsonby's admission that she had had the windows screwed up. Of course, there was the chance that Ferrers might be sent up to unscrew them, but Julia considered that a remote possibility. For one thing, there was so little time, and for another, those fastened windows were proof of the dangerous nature of her ward. Julia remembered that she had a pen in her bag and some slips of paper she had managed to secrete. After Ferrers had come upstairs for her case she would scribble a message and leave it in some place sufficiently prominent to attract Crook's attention. As she was putting on her jacket, Sparkes returned.

"I'm just coming," said Julia placatingly.

Sparkes made no reply; she snatched up the girl's hairbrush, sponge and nightgown and packed them into the bag that lay open on a chair. She closed the lid and snapped the locks. Then, to Julia's dismay, she swooped down on the girl's handbag.

"I'll take this down as well," she said.

"Oh—but I shall want that," exclaimed Julia.

"What for? I thought you were just coming down."

"My—my lipstick," she murmured.

113

"Take it out then."

"I'm perfectly able to carry my own bag," protested Julia.

"Madam's orders," intoned Sparkes. Julia took out the lipstick, wondering if she could secrete the pen at the same time; but Sparkes' eyes were fixed upon her, and she snatched at the bag giving the girl no opportunity. As soon as the door had closed behind her Julia searched frantically through the drawers of the dressing table for anything with which to write a message. But there was nothing—not an inch of pencil, not the back of an envelope. There wasn't even a burnt match. She felt frantic; she had no good reason for remaining up here; every instant she expected the door to burst open and Mrs. Ponsonby herself to appear. She took up the lipstick and began to paint her mouth. Then she paused. What a fool, she reflected. In her hand she had a perfectly good red pencil; all that she needed now was some surface on which to inscribe her message.

She looked round eagerly. The walls were covered with an intricate design of leaves and ribbon bows. Impossible to make any show there. But there was a long pier-glass in the wardrobe. Red would instantly attract the most casual attention. Hurriedly she moved across the room and began to write. She scrawled her name—Julia Ross—and then two hundred and fifty miles. And she added the number of the car XYZ 19001. Surely Crook would understand that. She was thickening the downstroke of the final figure when she stiffened and the lipstick all but fell from her hand. In the mirror before which she stood she now perceived a second form, a tall black figure with a round black straw hat on its springy curled hair, a figure with a white inscrutable face and thin lips slowly widening into a malicious grin. For the first time she really saw Sparkes as an individual. Hitherto she had seemed an appendage of Mrs. Ponsonby. Now she realized that the woman had an intense personal life of her own, with pleasures and ambitions. And there could be no doubt about the fact that the present situation pleased Sparkes very much indeed. Her lip curled with amusement. Then she began to laugh.

"Very funny," she said. "What a schoolgirl's trick, writing on mirrors."

114

Julia turned, white as death. "Why are you always spying on me?" she whispered. "I believe you're as bad as she is in your heart."

"That shows you're crazy," Sparkes continued, wrenching the lipstick from the girl's hand. "Writing silly messages that don't mean anything on a nice clean sheet of glass. Only mad people do that. Don't they? Don't they?"

Julia stared at her, panting with apprehension. Sparkes caught her wrist, holding it so tightly it seemed as though the bones must crack. "It doesn't mean anything, does it?" she insisted. "It's just a jumble of nonsense. Well?"

Mutely Julia nodded. Not that the woman would believe her, but what use was argument at that juncture? Besides, the bitterness of disappointment bereft her of speech. Sparkes let go her arm and, snatching up a towel, rubbed the glass clean.

"It's a good thing Mrs. Ponsonby didn't see that," she observed. "She wouldn't be a bit pleased. I can tell you, finding you make so free with her furniture. Of course, if it meant anything, that would be different, but since it doesn't . . ." She slipped the lipstick into her pocket.

"That's mine," said Julia, but without much spirit. Then she stuck out her hand. "That's mine," she repeated sharply, "and I want it."

"You shall have it when we're out of the house," Sparkes promised. "You might forget yourself and start scribbling on the walls next time, and walls aren't so easily cleaned off, are they?"

Julia almost ran from the room, ran from that sneering, triumphant voice and down to the hall.

"You've got ten minutes for your breakfast, Sheila," said Mrs. Ponsonby, as though moving out of a house at seven o'clock in the morning without notice was the most ordinary thing in the world.

"I only want a cup of tea," said Julia, her voice suddenly quiet again. At this stage she couldn't risk lending body to Mrs. Ponsonby's accusations of hysteria, melancholia and wild excitement.

The car glided away from the door of the mysterious house as the clock within chimed the hour. A fine rain, like a mesh of silk, hung between its occupants and the banks between which they drove; it was like being imprisoned in a bell of fine glass. Julia felt as though,

115

if she put out her hand, she would touch something smooth, glittering, infinitely brittle. It was so early that there was very little traffic on the roads. This, of course, was part of Mrs. Ponsonby's plan. Later there would be people whose attention might be drawn to the big black car and its occupants, but at this hour only workers were on the roads, and they were too much engrossed in their own affairs to spare a thought for strangers. In addition, Ferrers perpetually turned the car into the least frequented ways, where a less skillful chauffeur would have found it difficult to maneuvre a passage. The rain, slight though it was, kept pedestrians away from the roads, and they made a fine even pace. A small very noisy open roadster, painted bright scarlet and incredibly battered, roared after them for a time, until Ferrers drew into the side of the road and let it shoot past them. Now and again passers-by shot glances of admiration at the lovely machine as it slid by them, though few noticed the occupants. In any case, there was nothing noticeable about them; two elderly women and a girl, presumably the daughter of one. Quite soon, however, as the rain became more dense, they seemed to have the world to themselves. The rain was a nuisance; from Mrs. Ponsonby's point of view it was more, it was an impertinence, inasmuch as it delayed her speed. But, as she consoled herself, it did mean a lessening of traffic and even less likelihood of that common intruder, with the apposite name of Crook, discovering the road they had taken. Ferrers had been given instructions to travel by a circuitous route, sometimes indeed going a considerable distance out of his road. Whenever this happened Mrs. Ponsonby would tell him or Sparkes to get down and make some inquiry at a local shop, always for some place they had no intention of visiting. In this way any one trying to follow them up would indubitably be put on the wrong scent. They stopped the car in a byway at one o'clock and ate the lunch they had brought with them, and then Ferrers drove indefatigably on again. Eventually they reached their destination just before six, having made their journey in a little under eleven hours. Julia was so stiff she could hardly crawl down from the car. The waning light showed her the outlines of a tall bulky building, so effectually blacked out that it seemed to possess no character whatsoever until you were inside the door and saw that the plush-furnished lounge sparkled like the finale of a musical play. This was as vast a change from the dark solitude of Beverley as could well be imagined. At numbers of little tables well-dressed men and women were sitting with little colored drinks in front of them. The wireless was announcing the news in a heartily cultured voice; waiters ran up and down bringing more colored glasses to more guests. Several people glanced up as the three women entered the lounge, and instantly glanced down again. Two porters ran out to help Ferrers with the luggage. Mrs. Ponsonby went up to the clerk and explained that she had booked rooms by wire, thus disproving her own assertion to Julia that there was no telephone at Beverley. The clerk said, "Certainly, madam. Come this way, if you please. We were able to give you a suite on the first floor. Two bedrooms and a private sitting room."

"What about my maid?" demanded Mrs. Ponsonby. "I must have her close at hand. My niece is very delicate and may need help during the night."

A glance at Julia, drugged and exhausted by the long day, seemed to justify the description. It made no difference to the clerk, so long as the girl didn't actually die on the premises, but he mentally added half a guinea to the charges. He explained that Sparkes could be accommodated with a room on the same floor, but at the farther end of the passage.

The suite was large and excellently furnished, consisting of a private sitting room overlooking fields and a silver strip of river, a large bedroom allotted to Mrs. Ponsonby, and smaller one opening out of it for Julia. Through the open window of the sitting room came the scent of syringa, released and heightened by the rain. Julia suddenly threw back her head. That fragrance, so unexpectedly encountered at such a time, filled her with a new courage, reminding her of her youth when she had been a stranger to fear, and strenthening her determination not to lose heart, no matter what enemies might be arrayed against her.

Mrs. Ponsonby said briskly, "These will be quite satisfactory, thank you. No, we shall require nothing sent up to us. We shall dine at seven and I should like a word with the headwaiter in advance."

117

The clerk bowed himself out and Mrs. Ponsonby, turning to the girl, said pleasantly. "This is an improvement on Beverley, isn't it? You won't feel so shut up here, will you? And I think we are going to be comfortable. Now you'd better get unpacked and changed for dinner. You don't feel too tired to come down?"

"Oh, no," said Julia eagerly. "Indeed, I'm quite hungry."

She didn't trust this new affability any more than she had trusted the suspicion or threats Mrs. Ponsonby had lavished upon her, but she was racking her brain for some way of letting Crook know where she was. Mrs. Ponsonby was doubtless explaining the position to the hotel staff. Before her return there must be some opportunity. She was still pondering her chances when she became aware of the handle of her door slowly turning. It turned with a faint creak first in this direction, then in that. Then it remained still. Julia watched it, fascinated for an instant, then leaped forward. Most probably this was one more of Sparkes' tricks for upsetting her nerves. But there was no one there. Only on the mat lay a slip of paper. She stooped and picked it up. On it was printed neatly:

MISS JULIA ROSS. REMEMBER—CROOK ALWAYS GETS HIS MAN.

As she stood staring at the paper she heard the hooting of a motor horn outside. Automatically she crossed the room. In front of the hotel stood a battered little noisy roadster, painted bright red. There was a lumpy figure in the driving seat, but he didn't look up at her window even for a second before he put in the clutch and drove off.

By the time she had been at the Rosedale Hotel four days Julia was beginning to wonder whether she could have been mistaken in the identity of the driver. After all, she had only had the briefest of glimpses, and he hadn't even helped her by turning round. If it was indeed he who had scrawled the message she found on her doormat, he was being uncommonly leisurely in following up his case. And if it hadn't been his work, what assurance had she that he had any idea as to her whereabouts? That consideration led to a second. If the message was not the work of Crook, who could be responsible for it but Mrs. Ponsonby herself? That lady's behavior was giving Julia fresh cause for anxiety. At the Rosedale Hotel there was no question of her liberty being curtailed. Mrs. Ponsonby made it clear from the first that she could come and go as she pleased, provided she turned up punctually for meals and was there to accompany her employer whenever she was required. But no one now tried to enter her room at night. Indeed, Mrs. Ponsonby herself suggested a re-arrangement of the furnishings of the room to block effectually the communicating door, while the door opening on to the passage was fitted with a key that was kept on Julia's side. It was impossible for the girl to accept this apparent consideration at its face value. Whenever she went out she would glance stealthily this way and that to see whether she were being followed, but although once or twice she saw Sparkes in the distance she was never able to convince herself that the woman was deliberately spying on her.

The clientele of the Rosedale was for the most part elderly and sedately moneyed. There was a stout middle-aged Major whom Mrs. Ponsonby annexed almost from the first, offering him car drives or suggesting his making up a fourth for bridge during the long evenings. The hotel, while not being in a defined danger area, was nevertheless within sound of constant gunfire from the coast, and Mrs. Ponsonby would not allow Julia to go out after dinner. Sparkes was free from this embargo. The woman had a passion for the cinema, and night after night she vanished to one or other of the picture houses in the town. Once Julia caught sight of her walking with a soldier, and the discovery was a shock. They were talking amiably and vanished into a public house called The Bell and Bottle. Julia for the second time was forced to recognize Sparkes as a person apart from Mrs. Ponsonby. Perhaps, she reflected, this unpromising woman led a wild night life, concerning which Mrs. Ponsonby asked no questions.

She amused herself for a time constructing a background for her before she realized that, although she had been living with both women for some weeks, she knew nothing whatsoever about either. Nor had she gleaned any further information about the mysterious Sheila Campbell. In the evenings, while Mrs. Ponsonby played bridge or engaged the Major in conversation, Julia sat in the lounge reading or chatting desultorily to one of the quiet spinsters who are to be found in every hotel. One of these, a Miss Carpmael, a member of the Ball of Wool Brigade, whose symbol she wore on her thin bosom, took a shy liking to the solitary girl.

"I do hope this lovely air will soon set you up," she said one evening. "It's so very bracing here. You come from London, don't you?"

Julia agreed guardedly that she did.

"I suppose you had work there?"

"I've always earned my own living," Julia explained.

"Oh, yes? How sad!"

Julia looked startled. "It's much sadder not being able to earn it."

"Oh, yes—I didn't mean that. I was independent myself for a great many years. My dear father was so wise. Although it involved marrying again he insisted on my being given my freedom. Of course, I wasn't trained for anything very much, but I was fortunate to find work as a nursery governess, and one thing led to another, you know, and I was able to save, and I was so grateful." Her words were incoherent as she puzzled out a slipped stitch. "No, I meant living in London is so sad—so much noise and bustle and petrol fumes— and all those cats. So very difficult for the birds."

"There are people," Julia reminded her, "as well as cats and petrol fumes and all the rest."

"Oh, yes. Another horror, don't you think?"

Julia regarded her with amazement. "People? Oh, but I like them."

"But there are people in other places besides London. For instance, here. Now at night I really enjoy sitting in my quiet corner and watching life. If ever I were to be put into Who's Who, a contingency, of course, that will never arise," she laughed with girlish self-consciousness, "I should have to put down observing people, as my hobby. And really there are so many interesting people in this hotel. Major Gordon, for example."

"I don't really know him," Julia confessed. He was a paunchy rather aggressive man with a great sense of his own importance. From what Mrs. Ponsonby said he was a poor hand at cards, but she clung to him as one of the few unattached males in the hotel.

"Oh, he's had the most adventurous life. In ordinary times he'd be salmon fishing in Norway now. He went every year until the war prevented him. So original of him, I think. Most men just go for pleasure-cruises, don't they?"

Salmon fishing in Norway in May, thought Julia? Not likely. Probably he went to Weymouth or Brighton in the summer and lay about on marine parades and tried to pick up shopgirls. There weren't any shopgirls at the Rosedale, which explained Mrs. Ponsonby's easy conquest. He got a great deal more than he gave, which was an occasional glass of sherry or a cheap liqueur. Still, Mrs. Ponsonby appeared to be one of those people to whom any man is better than none. And, after all, he was in uniform.

"Your aunt," began Miss Carpmael, and Julia interrupted sharply, "She isn't my aunt. She's no relation at all."

Miss Carpmael looked astounded. "Dear, dear. I quite understood from her that you were her niece. But perhaps it's one of those unofficial relationships. I do admire her energy so much. Whenever I see her she's writing letters or sending telephone calls. I suppose she sits on a great many committees and does any amount of war work. I'm afraid my little effort is confined to this," and she waggled a khaki sock at Julia and screeched sedately.

Julia thought her a fool; well-meaning and kindly, no doubt, but a fool just the same. She hadn't yet realized that her father's permission to her to earn her own bread had had nothing altruistic behind it. It was obvious that she had been one of those gawky, sallow girls who, even at seventeen, are utterly without beauty or grace.

"And he married something young and plummy as soon as he'd pushed her out of the nest," Julia reflected. "Still, there's no sense in cold-shouldering her. If Mrs. Ponsonby sees us getting matey she may take her eye off me for a bit, and poor Miss Carpmael shouldn't be hard to shake off." She had no compunction whatever about using the poor harmless creature as a blind. Not even Mrs. Ponsonby, she thought, could suspect the neat little spinster of double dealing.

Julia now began to turn her thoughts in the direction of London. Once in town she could go direct to Crook's office; or she could return to Mrs. Mackie; and, of course, there was Colin. The desire for escape flamed like an incendiary bomb; her whole being was on fire with impatience. Yet she knew she could not afford to make a single mistake. Mrs. Ponsonby might appear to have relaxed her vigilance, but Julia was not foolish enough to suppose that she could walk out without any questions being asked. She laid her plans carefully, therefore, with Miss Carpmael as her involuntary accomplice.

Once get Mrs. Ponsonby to accept her fellow guest as harmless and she, Julia, would be allowed to go out with her, unwatched. Then it shouldn't be too hard to find some excuse, slip away and board a London train. Julia lived with the idea for several days and nights before she attempted to put it into action. Meanwhile Mrs. Ponsonby's mild flirtation with the major caused smiles on all hands. Certain female guests of longer duration were openly jealous. It was obvious that the purse-proud little man was an object of admiration to several rather withered old maids, all of whom looked as though they had been decorated whenever he spared them a word. To Julia it was pitiful, but rather horrible, too. She was smitten with the appalling thought that all these women had once been young and hopeful, like herself, and hadn't dreamed that a day would dawn when they would sit around a hotel lounge trying to score one off their next door neighbors.

"Perhaps I was as obvious as that over Colin," she thought guiltily.

Miss Carpmael was one of the major's most ardent admirers. One afternoon Julia, coming downstairs, having left Mrs. Ponsonby writing letters in her own room, found the two together in the lounge. The major was holding forth about the war.

"That chap Hitler'll find he's bitten off more than he can chew," he announced. "Fact is, he's never had a big adversary before. These little European states—Poland and Holland and so forth, they never had a chance. The British Empire's a very different pair of dancing pumps."

"Do you really think he'll try and invade us?" fluttered Miss Carpmael.

"He'll get the shock of his life, if he does. Not that we shall care. We're ready for him, you take my word."

Major Gordon was one of the first to join the Home Guard, the Local Defence Volunteers, as it was called at first. He said that this war wasn't only going to be fought by the youngsters, but that fellows with some experience of the beggars' tactics, chaps like himself who'd gone all through the last war, were going to have their chance. To Julia he sounded exactly like a major on the stage; it was difficult to see what Mrs. Ponsonby saw in him beyond his uniform.

Miss Carpmael looked disappointed when the girl appeared. It was clear that she was enjoying her little tête-à-tête. Nevertheless she kindly patted the chair beside her in invitation.

"Come and sit down here," she said. "You know, you're really looking better. Don't you think so, Major? Mrs. Ponsonby—it is funny that I quite understood she was your aunt—was telling me that you'd been quite ill and must take things easily, but this lovely weather really is setting you up."

The major had no interest in Julia whatsoever. He'd heard about her from Mrs. Ponsonby, one of these tiresome young women who had the vapors when they couldn't get some young nincompoop to fall in love with them. He wondered why so sensible a woman wanted to be bothered with a girl like that. He had his own views where the widow was concerned. She seemed to him the right sort of woman— realized that war was a man's business. She wasn't like a lot of these females who let you talk for a couple of minutes and then interrupted you to go in enormous detail into their potty little efforts. Rich, too. He'd been looking for a woman like that for years.

"What are you doing this afternoon, dear?" Miss Carpmael continued. "You ought to be out in this nice bright sun."

"I thought of going up to the library to get a book changed," Julia acknowledged. "I suppose there isn't anything I could do for you?"

"Well, actually, no. I do want some more wool, but it's rather a responsibility to ask someone else to match up a particular shade. It's very odd how the different bales come out different shades even though they're the same color number," she went on, obviously talking at the major. "You have to be very careful."

The major muttered something about an important letter and plunged through a glass door into the writing room. He sat down and began to scribble energetically.

"If you are going up to the town perhaps we could stroll up together," suggested Miss Carpmael. "I shall need that wool tonight. And if we start at once we shall be back in nice time for tea."

"We might even have tea out," suggested Julia, but Miss Carpmael said at once, "Oh, I think that would be a pity, seeing that tea is inclusive."

"I must just let Mrs. Ponsonby know where I am," said Julia quickly, jumping up again.

Mrs. Ponsonby looked at her keenly when she told her of her plan.

"You like being here, don't you, Sheila?" she said. "Better than at Beverley, I mean?"

"Oh, yes," said Julia. "It's much more open and there's more to do."

Mrs. Ponsonby's hand closed firmly on the girl's shoulder. "No tricks, mind," she said. "Don't abuse your liberty and you can have as much as you like. But if I find the delusions returning and you start telling foolish stories to strangers, I shall have to take steps."

Julia thought she knew exactly what a mouse feels like between the paws of an experienced cat. She felt that she had about as much chance of escaping as a pack of Messerschmitts with a brace of Spitfires on their tail. Nevertheless, she meant to make the effort, and the first step should be taken this afternoon. Briefly, her plan was this. She still had a pound note and a little change in her possession; she had looked up a railway table and saw that she could buy a ticket to London for nineteen shillings and fourpence. The balance of four shillings would pay for a cab to Crook's office. Once there she would turn the whole problem over to him, including its financial aspect. At the library, where she and Mrs. Ponsonby occasionally went to change books, was a booking office where tickets could be bought for theatres, coaches and railways. While Miss Carpmael matched her wool she would hurry on alone to the library and purchase a ticket. Then somehow tomorrow she must slip away up to the station. She had heard Mrs. Ponsonby say that she and the major were going for a drive immediately after lunch. Presumably Sparkes would be left in charge; but if, thought Julia, I can make a date with Miss Carpmael, Mrs. Ponsonby might give Sparkes the afternoon off, and that would be my opportunity.

"I won't do anything stupid," she heard herself promise Mrs. Ponsonby.

"Then go out by all means. I suppose you'll be back to tea?"

"Oh, yes, we shall."

Miss Carpmael was still in the lounge, surreptitiously watching the major through the glass. When she saw Julia she called out merrily, "What a streak of lightning! I must just finish turning this heel and then I'm ready." As she turned it she brought the conversation back to the major. It was really very nice having him here, she said, he was such an educated man, not a bit like so many army men who didn't care about anything but shop. He was devoted to music, for example. He and she had had such nice talks. "And," she whispered, "I believe he really admires Mrs. Ponsonby; I believe it's quite serious."

"Oh, I shouldn't think so," said Julia comfortingly.

"I always think these accidental romances are so charming," breathed Miss Carpmael. "Dear me, he's finished writing his letter."

She looked quickly down at her knitting, then, as the major came striding past in short fussy steps, she looked up and beamed.

"Writing a letter?" she inquired inanely.

The major lost step for a moment, paused, said, "Certainly, certainly," and went into the hall. Miss Carpmael turned her heel in the shortest time on record, bunched her knitting together, said to Julia, "Just a moment—must get a hat," and ran after the khaki-clad figure. The major was turning from the desk, the letter still in his hand.

"We're just going for a little stroll," she confided. "That pretty girl—so unfortunate . . ." Julia missed the rest, but it didn't matter. What she had heard was enough. So Mrs. Ponsonby had been spreading her stories here, too. After a moment, however, she decided it didn't matter. Any unexpected behavior on her part would be comfortably explained away by the fact that she was admittedly "peculiar." She thought the major gave her an odd glance as he passed her; probably Mrs. Ponsonby had been making good use of her time. Julia was learning the truth of the adage that the best, usually the only, form of defense is attack.

Miss Carpmael came down in one of those hats associated with good women from the country, a round black straw with a wreath of poppies and buttercups, and a good deal of fine feathery grass;

125

round her neck was a kind of feather wrap called a marabout with silky tassels; she carried cream-colored fabric gloves.

Everything went by clockwork. Miss Carpmael, anxiously matching electric blue wool, was quite glad for Julia to go on ahead to the library. By the time she had satisfied herself of a reasonably good match, Julia had bought the ticket and inquired the times of trains to town in the afternoon. When her elderly companion pushed the door open, she found the girl examining book titles. She said at once, "There was such a sweet book I read last month. I'm sure you'd love it. Let me see, what was it called? Oh, yes. *Across the Foam*. A really pretty book." But Julia disappointed her by taking out *The Grapes of Wrath*.

1 2

TEA WAS BEING SERVED in the hotel when Julia and Miss Carpmael returned. The major was having tea in splendid isolation at a little table in the corner; the other guests were dotted about in twos and threes. To the girl's relief, Mrs. Ponsonby was not yet down.

"Perhaps we might all have our tea together," suggested Miss Carpmael. "Do you think you should let Mrs. Ponsonby know that you've returned? Will she be anxious? Oh, here she comes. I think she's looking for you."

Mrs. Ponsonby came quickly through the lounge and, catching Julia by the arm, pulled her down on to a couch beside her.

"Where is it, dear?" she asked instantly.

"Where's what?" For an anguished second Julia believed the woman had the gift of second sight and knew of the existence of the railway ticket securely tucked away in her handbag.

"You know, dear." Mrs. Ponsonby raised her voice a little. "Come, tell me. I've looked everywhere and I can't find it, so now you must tell me."

"I don't understand," stammered Judia. She could feel the color running out of her face.

"Oh, come." Mrs. Ponsonby laughed a little; Julia was always most afraid of her when she laughed. "It's only a game. And you win.

You must have hidden it very cleverly, because I've looked everywhere and I can't find it."

Julia was aware of Miss Carpmael watching the pair of them in undisguised amazement. Mrs. Ponsonby saw it, too, and she turned at once.

"It's a game my niece and I play," she said. "She hides something and I have to find it. If I can't she wins."

She employed the tone used by responsible persons referring to a mentally deficient child. Miss Carpmael's thin fishlike mouth opened slowly.

"Oh—I see," she said. "How—how amusing!"

"It's a lie," whispered Julia. "It isn't a game at all." But Mrs. Ponsonby interrupted her sharply.

"Now, then, dear, you know it's a game. If I thought otherwise, I should have to take a very different view, shouldn't I? Now, then, tell me where it is—my emerald ring."

Julia was so much taken aback that she was incapable of replying at the moment. Vaguely she remembered the ring in question. It had been on Mrs. Ponsonby's finger on the night of their first meeting, but she had never seen it subsequently.

"Don't pretend you don't know what I'm talking about," prompted Mrs. Ponsonby, and Julia shook her bewildered head.

"I remember it of course. You were wearing it that night in Henriques Square. I remember thinking how like mine it was."

"Like yours?" Actually only Mrs. Ponsonby uttered the exclamation, but Miss Carpmael gave the impression that she also had spoken.

"Only, of course, mine was just paste."

"Pull yourself together, Sheila," admonished Mrs. Ponsonby in more dangerous tones. "What ring are you talking about?"

"My emerald paste."

Mrs. Ponsonby looked across to Miss Carpmael. "It's a delusion," she explained. "There was never a second ring."

"Yes, there was," said Julia dully.

"Then—where is it?"

"It's in my suitcase."

Mrs. Ponsonby shook her head. "Oh, no, I've looked there."

"I don't mean the case in my room. I mean my own suitcase, the one that got left behind and that I suppose now I'll never see again. There was a ring and a brooch and twin bracelets. A jeweller once told me that for color they were better than lots of really valuable stones."

Mrs. Ponsonby's small firm hand closed on the girl's arm. "And where is it now—no, not your ring. My ring—my—emerald—ring, Sheila? Is it in your bag?"

"No, no," said Julia, instinctively clutching the bag closer.

"Let me see."

"I tell you, it's not there."

Miss Carpmael bent over and in her turn gently held Julia by the arm.

"If it isn't there, my dear, you won't mind your aunt looking inside, will you?"

Quite how it happened Julia didn't know, but an instant later Miss Carpmael had taken the bag from her and had passed it to the older woman.

"I hate to do this," murmured Mrs. Ponsonby apologetically, "but you see, I daren't take risks. So long as it's only my things, well, it doesn't matter so much. I don't mean the ring isn't valuable, but —well, you quite understand. But one day the thing that disappeared might belong to someone else. It isn't fair to the girl to let things slide. I could get a certificate, of course . . ."

"No," said Julia in a slow dead voice, "that isn't true. No doctor would dare certify me as mad."

"I didn't say anything about madness."

"It's what you mean. It's what you've been trying to do ever since you tricked me into coming under your roof. And I'll tell you this. I didn't want to come; I knew it was dangerous, I knew it was wrong, I knew it would be better to go on being hungry, but I was being a fool, a coward, and so I made myself come . . ."

Mrs. Ponsonby exchanged a glance with the other woman and snapped open the bag. After a moment she said, "No, it isn't there, but I think I could make a good guess where it is now. So that's why you were so anxious to go out this afternoon."

"I don't know what you mean," stammered Julia.

For answer Mrs. Ponsonby took out the ticket to London and laid it on her knee.

"Where did this come from?"

"It's mine. I bought it—with my own money."

"And where did that money come from? You admitted to me that you were quite without means, and I've supplied you with none —I haven't dared. So how did you pay for this?"

"With money I'd saved—and hidden from you," panted the girl.

Mrs. Ponsonby shook her head. Miss Carpmael shook hers. Julia looked in a desperate hunted fashion from one to the other. Too late she realized what should, she supposed, have been apparent from the start. The little shrivelled spinster was another of Mrs. Ponsonby's tools. She hadn't been deceived about the library. Probably she had been peering through the glass when the ticket was being purchased; or else she had found a moment to inquire at the counter while Julia made her final leisurely selection of a book. In any case, the position was lost. Julia wasn't going to London. It seemed to her likely that she would die at the Rosedale Hotel. After this scene—and the woman had taken pains to ensure plenty of publicity—the lounge was full of curious eyes and whispering tongues by this time—no one would be surprised to hear that the distraught girl had committed suicide, taken an overdose of sleeping draught, say. Unbalanced—that's what their explanation would be, and Mrs. Ponsonby would tell the court how there had been two previous attempts by means of windows, with Ferrers and Sparkes to back her up. And so Mrs. Ponsonby would have achieved her objective. It was all written clearly, like the writing on the wall.

She lay back in her chair, utterly defeated now. Mrs. Ponsonby had removed the ticket and Miss Carpmael was making little sympathetic noises.

"Very sad," she chirruped. And, "Such a responsibility for you. Anything I can do . . . ?"

And Mrs. Ponsonby smiled her false capable smile and replied, "Too kind. If I may really call upon you in an emergency . . ."

And there was Miss Carpmael beaming, too, and saying eagerly, "Any time—so much leisure—only too happy to be of assistance . . ."

After that Julia was hustled upstairs and told she had better have dinner in bed. Down in the lounge they were chattering intently. The actual facts did not emerge, only it seemed obvious that the girl with Mrs. Ponsonby was a kleptomaniac, to give it a discreet name. The ladies all clutched their little embroidered bags as though they feared that, even from that distance, the creature could spirit away their funds; and when she came down again Mrs. Ponsonby found herself the recipient of many vague smiles and murmurs of sympathy. She satisfied no one's curiosity, and no one quite had the nerve to put a direct question. Still, they could speculate and surmise, and that filled in the time very nicely for a good many of them until the nine o'clock news. This was not cheering—news during May and the first part of June had a distinctly depressing tendency—and when the epilogue for the evening had been given—it took the form of yet another plea for the savings of the nation—most people were glad to switch on to the Forces programme that was giving part of a variety concert from a northern music hall.

Julia breakfasted in bed, too—Mrs. Ponsonby thought that was wise—and made no public appearance until midday. She found Mrs. Ponsonby and the major seated, with Miss Carpmael, at a joint table in the dining room, and she had scarcely taken her place when Mrs. Ponsonby said, "Such a treat for you, Sheila. Miss Carpmael has very kindly offered to take you for a drive this afternoon in her car."

Julia felt a stab of surprise. Miss Carpmael didn't look the sort of person who would know how to drive a car, much less own one. You'd have to put her down as the passenger who always occupies the back seat and twitters that it's the best seat of all. However, it seemed that the car really did exist, and that Miss Carpmael had very kindly offered to take charge of the tiresome Julia for the afternoon, so that Mrs. Ponsonby might keep her engagement with the fascinating major.

Miss Carpmael simpered and said, "Oh but it was a pleasure. And really, when you'd had a breakdown, it was so important to be in the open air." It was clear that Mrs. Ponsonby had her eating out of her hand. It was difficult to see what the woman hoped to get out of it, but probably she thought a rich widow a useful person to keep in with. She looked as poor as Job herself.

Julia agreed in colorless tones to whatever was suggested. She would never, she knew, forgive Miss Carpmael for her treachery of the previous afternoon. As for Crook, he'd let himself be very easily foiled; or else he had decided that there was neither money nor kudos in the case and was spending himself on more profitable clients.

Miss Carpmael was her usual fussy self as she backed the car out of the hotel garage. All the time she was looking over her shoulder and saying, "Are you quite sure it's safe?" regardless of the fact that she had a driving mirror and there was an attendant watching her. She almost drove Major Gordon crazy. It so happened that he couldn't get at Mrs. Ponsonby's car until the old maiden aunt was clear; and it had been arranged to leave Ferrers at home that afternoon, while the major drove.

Julia wondered if Mrs. Ponsonby really contemplated marriage. If so, surely she could have found someone more attractive than a fat dug-out major. She had had a fluttered whisper with Miss Carpmael over the coffee, after Julia had been sent upstairs to fetch her hat, and Miss Carpmael had beamed and nodded and said, "Of course" and "Naturally, I quite understand." Julia came to the despairing conclusion that even if she could contrive to murder Miss Carpmael it wouldn't help her much. She couldn't drive a car, the old soul probably hadn't the price of a ticket to London on her, and the police would be sure to interfere, and if she wasn't hanged she'd be shut up for life, which in some ways was worse.

Miss Carpmael was deliberately gay. She made it quite clear that she intended to forget that yesterday's scene ever happened. She talked a little about herself and tried to persuade Julia to do the same. Then she talked about Mrs. Ponsonby and what a beautiful car she had and how clever she was to be able to get hold of so much petrol.

"I notice that she goes out every day," she went on with a little laugh at her gossiping old-maidish ways. "Now I can only use my car on very special occasions."

"You call this a very special occasion?" inquired Julia with mild derision.

Miss Carpmael nodded emphatically. "Very special indeed," she said. "You don't know . . ." She trod on the accelerator and they suddenly shot forward.

The words and, even more, the tone in which they had been spoken, sent a new thought spinning into the morass of Julia's mind. She tried to drive it away but it insisted on coming back.

"And that," Julia told herself, "is more than I am going to do. That's what they were whispering about. No one could possibly suspect Miss Carpmael of being anything but what she appears on the surface. If there's a fatal accident while I'm driving with her, she might be censured, but that's the limit. Naturally Mrs. Ponsonby wouldn't take the risk. It might look queer. But Miss Carpmael . . ." and then she began to wonder if Mrs. Ponsonby could be right, and she was really going mad, because casual old spinsters you meet at hotels don't suddenly turn into murderers.

"But," said Julia's brain, ice-cold and ticking as steadily as a clock, "murderers do sometimes turn into casual old spinsters. And no one else would think of that. The man in the street has his own ideas of what a murderer looks like; he wears the brand of Cain on his forehead. They don't realize that he may quite easily be a middle-aged faded woman wearing a lace modesty vest with whalebone slips." Desperately Julia began to sustain her share of the conversation. It was improbable that Miss Carpmael knew she had been found out. Even now there was a slender chance of escape.

They had left the hotel at two-thirty. At a quarter past three they reached the town of Moreton and Miss Carpmael drew up her car in front of a bakery.

"It's rather early for tea," she said. "But they keep a particular kind of digestive biscuit here. I'm just going in to buy a packet."

She left the steering wheel and walked inside the shop. As soon as she was engaged in conversation with the proprietress Julia looked round, thinking, "This is my chance, the only one I'll ever get." What she was to do with it she couldn't imagine. She had seven-pence in coppers—Mrs. Ponsonby had removed the little stock of silver—and they were some distance from the station. Julia remembered their passing it on the right as they halted an instant at the top of the hill. It was at this moment that glancing down, she saw on the floor of the car the little red notecase.

For an instant she looked at it as though it had no real existence, was just a creation of her overwrought brain. Then that brain began to work at lightning speed. Picking up the case she found inside several notes, totalling eight pounds She abstracted three of these, worth fifty shillings and dropped the case back where she had found it. If Miss Carpmael missed it she would return to the car, and the odds were that she would stoop to retrieve it before she began looking for her charge. She might even stop to count what remained. In an instant Julia had opened the door of the car and scrambled out. At a stopping point a few yards ahead a tram was just drawing up, a tram with the magic word STATION on the front. Waving wildly Julia stumbled on board. The next five minutes seemed to her the longest she had ever passed; at every instant she expected the little green car to overtake them. But the miracle held. No car appeared, the tram drew up safely at the station, and the booking clerk announced that there was a through train to London, a fast one, in about ten minutes' time. Julia bought a ticket and retired to the waiting room that commanded the entrance to the station. One minute passed, two, three. The girl's heart beat so thickly she felt choked; mists moved in front of her eyes; when at last the roar of the approaching train sounded in her ears she found she could hardly stand. The train snorted to a halt. A few other people boarded it. Julia found a smoking compartment with no one in it. She took a corner seat and held up a paper she had had the forethought to buy to conceal her treacherously working face. If any one else got into the carriage she would probably be mistaken for the idiot Mrs. Ponsonby had done her best to make her. Up to the last second she could not believe herself safe. The guard held up his flag, a long whistle sounded, the train began to move. After a minute it gathered speed and vanished into a tunnel. When it emerged at the other end, one of the smoking carriages was occupied by a girl in a blue suit and no hat, who was crying as though she would never stop.

The train only paused twice between Moreton and London. At the first stop a mother with a child and its nurse got in; they gave

133

Julia one glance—she had calmed down before this and had got her face into some sort of order—and then ignored her. At the second stop two girls with hair hanging down to their shoulders swung open the door. They ignored Julia, the mother, the nurse and the child. Their conversation was rapid, confidential and entirely of the "So I said to him" type. At London all the passengers got out as quickly as possible. If Julia had been an escaping murderess and they had been asked for a description of her, not one of them could have supplied a single detail that would have been of use to the police. This is usually the case with people travelling together in trains, but the majority of murderers are too conceited to understand this. If they were not (Crook says) fewer murderers would be caught.

Paddington is not the most beautiful station in England, but Julia thought that Paradise itself would not wear a more heavenly aspect. She let all the other passengers alight, and then jumped out and made for a telephone booth. It had occurred to her that she didn't know Crook's address. There were only two Crooks called Arthur and one lived at Leytonstone, so she had very little trouble in identifying her man. Another minute and she was clear of the station and inside the taxi. Even then she could scarcely breathe until it had set her down at the address in Bloomsbury. There was a list of names in the hall that told her Crook lived at the top of the building; there was a lift with a notice "Lift out of order"; there were enormous flights of stone steps curving into the darkness. Julia caught the rail and started to climb.

Only when she was almost at the top did it occur to her that Crook might have gone for the day. It was a little after six o'clock, and for all she knew lawyers had hours like trade unionists. But luckily there is no trade union for lawyers, because Crook would not conceivably have kept its regulations. It was often ten o'clock at night before he switched off his light and stumped downstairs to look for supper. Supper was his favorite meal; he said he picked up more clients between ten o'clock and midnight than most lawyers during the daylight hours. Julia tapped nervously on a door bearing Crook's name and was instantly bidden to enter. She walked into a little room and found herself facing a tall ruin of a man with a handsome face distorted by the scar of a dishonorable wound, and a slight limp. He evinced no surprise at the sight of her.

"Miss Ross?" he said before she could speak. "Mr. Crook's expecting you," and he pointed to a door on the left.

Julia was so staggered by this reception that for an instant she didn't move. The tall man took a couple of steps across the floor.

"He's got a drink for you in there," he remarked, invitingly. "He thought you might need it."

Julia, her head whirling, moved blindly in the direction indicated. As she opened the second door she saw the squat, pugnacious figure she had last seen at the dark house called Beverley. Crook stood up as she came in.

"Train must have been on the dot," he said. "Well, well, so the curtain falls on the first act. I promise you the second won't be without excitement. This chapter's called 'Crook on the Warpath.' "

Julia must still have looked pretty dazed, for he pulled out a chair and produced a bottle and glasses.

"Thought about where you'll put up for the night?" he inquired casually.

Julia sat down. "How did you know I was coming?" she asked weakly.

Crook picked up a telegram from the table. "This came soon after you left Moreton," he replied.

Julia took the paper. It read:

Arriving London 5.59. Carpmael.

13

CROOK'S HAND PUSHED JULIA forcibly into a chair; then it returned to the desk and poured out a strong drink.

"Take that," he said, thrusting a glass towards the shaking figure. "And don't argue. You're going to need it, believe me, before you're through."

Julia tasted it. It was whisky that she detested. She was about to say so when she caught sight of Crook's face and changed her mind. She was still too much bewildered to be able to fit the details of this extraordinary situation together.

"Getting there?" asked Crook with a grin. "Here, I'll take that if you've finished with it. You ain't in royal circles now where I'm told you pitch the glass over your shoulder, so that no one else shall ever have a chance of using it. Feeling better? Then how about telling us your story?"

"But there's nothing to tell," protested Julia. "I just saw my chance and came to town. It's your turn to do the talking."

"You might make a note of that, Bill," remarked Crook seriously, "and then get her to sign it. It's not likely I'll ever hear another woman say that. By the way," he turned back to the startled Julia, "I don't think you know Bill Parsons, my right-hand man. Knows the law's backside as well as its face, and that's a useful accomplishment to a man of my profession."

The meaning of this was largely lost on Julia, and when Crook added, with another grin, that it must make the angels chuckle to see Bill working for justice, she smiled politely but still without understanding.

"You know what they say about converts," went on Crook, helpfully. "They're always more zealous than those who are born to the faith. You won't find a man in the whole of the Yard more anxious to see right vindicated than my friend, Bill."

The two men exchanged grins. Julia began to feel irritated. They were, she thought, treating her like a child. Nevertheless, afterwards it occurred to her that, in spite of his extraordinary appearance and his unprepossessing manner, she had never once doubted Crook's integrity. Integrity to herself, she meant. His code of legal ethics was his own and a great many men, hesitating between liberty and fourteen years hard labor, had reason to be grateful for that.

"I'm still in the dark," she complained. "Who is Miss Carpmael?"

Crook waved a large freckled hand. "Just part of the Arthur Crook service," he said. "Nice comedy actress lost when she went in for bein' a perfect lady. Though she's luckier than she'd have bin if she'd stuck to the stage. Ever thought of trying it?"

Julia shook her head. "I wouldn't be any good."

136

Crook clapped one hand to his forehead. "This is getting too much for me, Bill. There's a trick somewhere. The honest woman's a new one on me."

Julia painstakingly sorted her impressions. "Then Miss Carpmael wasn't really an ally of Mrs. Ponsonby, as I thought?"

"If you ever do secret service you take a leaf out of her book," Crook advised her. "The thing that wins wars ain't brute force, not even mechanical force. It's gettin' right into the enemy's line. You ask the Dutch. You ask the French. Cleverest thing Hitler ever did wasn't to build up an army of tanks but to create the Fifth Column. Oh yes, Miss Carpmael knows her onions. You have to hand it to her for that. She had her eye on that dame. A lot of people have for that matter, and Mrs. Ponsonby is beginning to realize it."

"Who were the other people?"

"Sheila Campbell, for one."

"Sheila Campbell!"

"You know, I'm not sure you were right when you said you'd be no good on the stage. That was a very nice inflection you got then. Yes, Sheila Campbell—poor girl."

"Then—is she dead?"

"As Bill will assure you, I only bet on certainties, but I'm prepared to risk my reputation, which is more than the crown jewels to me, that she won't come knocking at any one's door again. Y'see, it was her or Mrs. P., and Mrs. P., very sensibly decided she'd like to go on living."

"But what did Sheila Campbell want from Mrs. Ponsonby? I suppose there was money involved . . ."

"That's one way of putting it. But—hullo, wasn't that a bell? That'll be our man."

Bill Parsons lounged out into the passage and returned a moment later with a tall fair young man with a lock of hair falling into his eyes.

"Colin!" The cry broke incredulously from Julia and she started to her feet.

Colin saluted in a friendly way and accepted Crook's offer of a drink.

"So you've arrived safely. How did you leave our friend?"

"You mean?"

"The scourge of the Secret Service."

Light broke over the girl. "You don't mean Mrs. Ponsonby was a spy."

"She gets going slowly, this girl," grinned Crook. "Hold it, honey, hold it."

"But it doesn't seem possible. I mean, she doesn't look that kind."

"All spies aren't replicas of Mati Hari," Colin reminded her gently. "Yes, she's a spy all right, and Sheila Campbell got on her tail. And Mrs. P. tumbled to it, so—exit Sheila Campbell."

"And she knew you knew about Sheila Campbell, so she tried to pretend I was Sheila Campbell and then when I was dead or mad there'd be a perfectly logical explanation and no one would worry about the real Sheila . . ."

"Old Uncle Tom Cobley and all," broke in Crook. "You're getting there."

"Slowly," agreed Julia. "Why did she want a second Sheila, though? Couldn't she just announce that the first one had left her?"

"It wasn't so simple," Colin told her. "Sheila Campbell was abroad when the war broke out doing secret service work. Information was seeping through to the enemy by a channel we couldn't trace, until Sheila traced it, that is. Mrs. Ponsonby kept up that big house at Henriques Square and it was noticed that she was perpetually advertising for servants, saying she'd take refugees. Well, that in itself wasn't necessarily suspicious, only no refugee ever was engaged. The only servants were a married couple or so it was generally supposed, and they didn't change. And yet the refugees kept coming and Mrs. Ponsonby saw them, and she went on saying she couldn't get servants. That started the ball rolling; eventually Sheila wormed her way into the household by assuming the rôle of another spy. She could speak several languages and she had a good deal of information that was invaluable to Mrs. Ponsonby. It was a tremendous risk, because the instant she was suspected she was done for. She knew that. Also, they were three to one, for the married couple were in it, too, of course. Well, the luck didn't hold. It's never safe to count on it, and it may be that they had their doubts from the first. After all, two can play poker, and this time Sheila lost. So, of course, she had to be put out."

"And what did they do?" Julia's voice was very low.

"We don't know yet."

"That's one of the things Mrs. Ponsonby must have meant when she said to Peters, 'Remember all my instructions.' Do you mean, you think perhaps Sheila was still there when I went to see Mrs. Ponsonby?—Oh no!"

"It could be," acknowledged Crook, "it could be."

"And now?"

"That's what we've got to find out," said Colin. He looked rather white.

"We?"

"Sure," agreed Crook. "You wouldn't go back on us after all we've done for you. A place in the ranks awaits you, each man has his part to play. It's a real female lead, too," he added.

"And as dangerous as hell," added Colin. "You'll realize that a woman who's bumped off one girl isn't going to be too delicate when it comes to the second. She knows we suspect foul play, even if we can't prove it yet."

"Why on earth did she engage me at all?" demanded Julia. "Why couldn't she just give out that her secretary had left her at very short notice? That's what she told me—that she'd gone to nurse a sick mother."

"It seems that the news of Mrs. P. having a secretary got about. Someone saw the girl in the hall or something, and, telephoning a couple of days later to ask the old ghoul to lunch, she added, 'Bring your pretty secretary with you.' Mrs. Ponsonby said, on the spur of the moment that 'the pretty secretary was down with 'flu, and the doctor wouldn't let her out.' Actually, no doctor ever visited the house. Well, that's what you'd expect if the girl had already been done for. But having made that first mistake, Mrs. Ponsonby was committed to it. Oh what a tangled web we weave and so on. She couldn't say the girl had left because in a place like the Square you can always corroborate a thing like that. If questions had been asked it might seem funny that no taxi had taken away her luggage, and no luggage had been seen to leave the house. Besides, it was necessary for the lady's plans that Sheila Campbell should die in an above-board manner. That meant gettin' a substitute Sheila, and she picked on you."

"No wonder she asked me so many odd questions about next-of-kin and wedding prospects. She decided I was the ideal substitute, I suppose. I wonder if Sheila was anything like me to look at."

"She wasn't takin' any more chances," Crook assured her. "She whisked you out of sight the next day. I dare say she told the friend you'd been ordered convalescence—or more likely she beat it before questions could be asked. Anyway, she meant to make a good job of it this time. Y'know," his voice became reflective, "that woman had bad luck. You can't say she didn't work, but the cards were against her. Your phone call that night," he nodded to Colin, "must have given her the jitters. That warned her she hadn't any too much time." He turned casually to Bill Parsons. "What's the matter, Bill? Keeping the rest of the beer to bathe in?"

Bill filled up the three tankards and Crook set his gratefully to his lips. When he set it down again, it was empty.

"D'you know who, they say, make the best G-men?" he inquired of his audience. "Ploughboys who've been too stupid to learn anything. That means they've nothing to unlearn. It's these clever chaps who end in the pen. They want to put so much over that they go round layin' clues and buyin' witnesses, whereas if they'd take a chance they might get off scot-free. Suppose, f'r instance, Mrs. P. had said boldly that Miss Campbell had walked out on her? The girl friend might have thought it meant the secretary couldn't stand the job, but what would that have mattered? But Mrs. P. probably saw the police on her track, her confederates questioned, taxi drivers cross-examined, notices in the papers . . ."

"You have to admit it would have been damned unpleasant for her if any of that had happened," deprecated Colin.

"It's news to me that the Home Office wet-nurses its small fry that way," retorted Crook. "Still it's not for me to complain. If it wasn't for these crashing errors, chaps like me would soon be out of a job. People talk of lawyers and counsel hangin' criminals; that ain't so. Every chap that goes to the gallows signs his own death warrant. The perfect crime would happen much more often if a fellow simply jabbed or smothered his victim and then went on with his usual job. But he's so keen to be overlooked that he makes a regular spoor leading to his hidin'-place. Still, all that's just the parsley round the dish. What we've got to do is act, and act damn' fast. You know what the lady's like—she don't stop at nothing. When Miss Carpmael gets back, as she's certainly done by now, and tells how you pulled the wool over her eyes, there's going to be a shimozzle that'll make Joe Louis' latest look like a bun-fight."

"You mean," suggested Julia, "she may suspect Miss Carpmael?"

Crook treated her to an enormous wink. "It could be, Sherlock Holmes, it could be."

"Why didn't Miss Carpmael come up to town by the same train, and miss all the trouble?"

Crook stared at her. Bill stared. Colin stared. Crook was the first to speak. "I goggled, he goggled, we goggled all three. You ask me to believe you're a workin'-girl and then pass me that one? Why, the dame's got her job, hasn't she? Miss Julia Ross ain't the only pebble on the national beach, not by a long chalk, and don't you forget it."

Julia colored furiously. "You mean, she's still after Mrs. Ponsonby? Of course, I'm only an incident."

"Oh well." Crook grinned generously. "It's these separate incidents that make the story." And Colin broke in, "As a matter of fact, Julia, to be honest with you we had lost sight of her for the time being. It was your letter to Mrs. Mackie that put us back on her track. You see, until then we hadn't understood where Sheila Campbell came in. After you handed us that tip we could go right ahead. Now we've got to find Sheila Campbell."

"And I can help?"

"You're the one person who can at the moment. You see, it's likely there's only one man in London who knows where she is, and you're the only person who can positively identify him for us."

"Peters!" exclaimed Julia.

"Exactly."

"But you don't know that he is in London still."

"I'd make a safe bet on it. Of course, he's in touch with Mrs. P., they're working the thing together. We can't do much more till we've run him to earth. That's where you come in."

Julia thought for a moment. "You mean, I'm to be a—what do they call that thing?—a decoy duck."

"The girl's coming along," ejaculated Crook with approval.

"But why don't you get in the police?" suggested Julia, reasonably.

"The police?" The three men spoke with such unanimity it sounded like a rehearsed chorus.

Colin stooped to explain the position. "We don't want the police in on this if it can be helped," he told her. "Mrs. Ponsonby in a prison cell is precious little use to us. We belieive she's rather an important person, and we know she has accomplices. Sparkes and Peters are two; there may be others. Miss Carpmael's keeping an eye on the two women, but we want to get our claws on Peters. It's a marvellous chance for you, if you can see it that way."

Julia drew a long breath. She had hoped, when she escaped from Mrs. Ponsonby, to know a spell of safety, but with Colin's eyes meeting hers so eagerly, without a shadow of doubt, only one answer was possible.

"Of course I see it that way. You must tell me what I'm to do, and if I can, I'll do it."

"You can do it all right," said Colin soberly. "But we can't force you. It will be damned dangerous."

Julia suddenly laughed. "I've just discovered something."

"And that is?"

"There's a big difference between danger you're pushed into and danger that you choose for yourself. Besides, I shan't be in it alone now."

"Good girl," applauded Colin, but Crook chose to look offended.

"You haven't been in it alone for a long time," he pointed out. "You've had me to back you, and I should like to know what more you want."

14

AFTER A TIME certain practical objections began to occur to Julia.

"About Peters," she said. "You say I'm to help to find him, but

I've no more idea than you have where he is. How do I set about looking for him?"

"You don't, sugar." Crook had recovered his usual imperturbability. "You just let him find you."

"I see. Or do I?"

"Sure you see," Crook agreed cheerfully. "By tomorrow—or at least the day after—Peters will know you've cut the cable that bound you to Mrs. Ponsonby, and he'll have his instructions, which are roughly the same as he got where that other poor girl was concerned. Well, it stands to reason he can't move till he knows where you are. Mrs. P. will guess you'd come to London like a homing pigeon, but London's a biggish place. You might stay hidden in an air raid shelter for a month, and we'd be no further on than we were before. So all you have to do is to make yourself as conspicuous as you can. And that oughtn't to be too difficult."

"You mean, he mustn't guess there's someone going around with me."

"I mean, there won't be any one going around with you. That's the chance you have to take. But we shan't be far behind."

"No," agreed Julia with a little ghostly smile. "I hope you won't be—too far behind." She tried to look casual and efficient, but in her heart she doubted whether she was really the stuff of which heroines are made. In her mind she saw herself again in the hands of Mrs. Ponsonby and her crew, and this time she knew she could anticipate no mercy. They had, almost certainly, done Sheila Campbell to death, and they were not likely to hesitate at a second murder. She looked up to find Colin watching her intently; his hand closed warmly over hers.

"We wouldn't ask such a thing of you," he urged, "but you're simply indispensable. There's absolutely no one else."

"That bein' the case we might exchange a few ideas as to the whereabouts of the missin' lady. Mind you, by the time she's found she won't be fit for any kingdom but the kingdom of heaven—I'll stake my davy on that—but equally till she's found we can't hope to pull in our men, and I'd hate to lose my family crest." He caught Julia's eyes and winked. She remembered the arrogant little figure standing in the doorway at Beverley. Crook always gets his man, he'd

143

said. She believed that was true, and she recognized, as well, that he really didn't mind how many other lives were jeopardized so long as he was eventually successful.

"Do you think she might still be in the house?" she suggested hesitantly.

"You're new to this game," said Crook, kindly. "It's never any too safe leaving corpses about in unoccupied premises. It's asking for trouble. You never know who mayn't break in—or Adolf the Armageddonist might stage a mock raid and hit a house by accident—or the police might find themselves short of a job and take a fancy to look over the premises. There's nothing so nosey as a good man, and the police are naturally the best men in the state." He chuckled vulgarly. "You take my word. Or ask Bill here. He'll tell you the same as me."

Bill had hardly spoken since the conclave began. He was a man with a great gift of silence and perhaps the most dangerous of the three.

"Anyway," Crook continued, "in wartime only a chap qualifying for the booby-can would leave a big house empty of everything but a corpse. The authorities have a lot more power now than they had twelve months ago. They might come down on the owners or tenants of the house for refugees or evacuees or even for the troops, and you know what people are like. If they open a cupboard and a body falls out there's goin' to be a spot of bother, and it ain't going to be exactly healthy for the chap that left the body lying about. Besides, it's untidy. I hate loose ends to a case, and any enterprisin' criminal, particularly if he's a murderer, feels the way I do."

"Then why not have left the furniture where it was?" demanded Julia, sensibly. "Peters could have kept up appearances by acting as caretaker. No one could commandeer the house if he said the owners were simply away on holiday and would be back in a week or two."

"Ah, but that wouldn't work any longer. It was all right before you dragged the boy friend into it. Who was Peters that any one should notice him? What did you say he was like? A white fox. Well, well, I dare say he's not the only one. But once the authorities had the low-down on him it wouldn't be safe for him to stand out in the open. He had to go to ground; and there wasn't any one else he could put into the house in Henriques Square, not, that is, so long as there was a body in it. So the house had to be dismantled. And if the body was there, as very likely it was, that had to be disposed of, too."

Julia stared at him in horror. "Do you mean, you think the body may be in storage somewhere inside a wardrobe or something?"

"It could be," said Crook, "though, mind you, I don't say it is. Still, with a war on, there are lots of less likely places. Well, think for yourself. It ain't so easy to get rid of a body as amateurs suppose. In real life people don't switch on death-rays or drop corpses in convenient tanks of acid or crystallize them and use them as sofas or prayin'-stools. They have to find some simpler way. And there aren't so many as you might think. This wasn't a house with the river comin' up to the back lawn, so that Peters could ease the body over after dark—and even if he did, it 'ud come up somewhere and questions would be asked. He didn't live near a sewer full of eels, like a chap I read about in a crime book the other day; there wasn't the right kind of garden for buryin' it—all gravel, and anyway neighbors are so nosey—they have a way of talking if they look out after dinner and see a chap puttin' a body in the ground. Freedom went out when the police came in and that's a fact. You can't very easily burn a body, and it takes a lot of nerve and medical knowledge to slice it up with the bacon knife and bury a bit here and a bit there. Thanks to the I.R.A. you can't even shove a parcel in the cloakroom of a railway station without havin' to open it for inspection first . . ." Besides, Peters had to remember the time factor. The sooner he got out of that house, the better it would be for him. And, since we've agreed he couldn't leave the body behind, he had in a sense to take it with him."

"Yes," breathed Julia. "I begin to see. You remember what Chesterton said about the wise men and the leaf, that he'd hide it in a forest among a thousand other leaves. Of course, the best place would be a mortuary . . ."

"Now you're gettin' poetical," Crook objected. "No, no, you stick to the furniture depository. With a bit of luck no one would open that cupboard till the body was beyond recognition anyway. That's what they're counting on, of course."

145

Yes, thought Julia to herself, and the next body may be mine and Mrs. Ponsonby will see to it that it isn't found until it's unrecognizable—a jolly prospect. She said uncertainly, "Of course it might occur to the removers that the sideboard or whatever it was was particularly heavy."

"What d'you think they're bein' paid for? Their job is to shift furniture and no questions asked. Anyway, on the law of averages, the numbers of bodies found in wardrobes must be less than point five per cent. No, no, it was a fine scheme, and if you hadn't upset the apple-cart the odds are it 'ud have gone through. You can't take up a profession like Mrs. Ponsonby's without runnin' some risk, and I don't doubt she finds the game worth the candle."

"And of course," put in Colin casually, "it needn't have been the wardrobe."

For a reason none of the three men could fathom these simple words suddenly threw Julia into a violent fit of trembling; she shook until it seemed as though she might shake herself to pieces.

When at length she spoke her voice sounded foreign even to herself. "Might it—could it—have been an ottoman?" she whispered.

Crook looked surprised that so emotional a mountain should produce so minute a mouse.

"Well, it might. In fact, it 'ud be a lot better, provided there was one handy. Pack it tight with women's gear with the body like a sort of mummy in the middle—what's up now?"

For Julia had pressed her hands over her eyes and was shaking her head at him.

"Oh, don't," she whispered. "You see—I sat on the ottoman while Mrs. Ponsonby told me about the job. She—told me to sit there."

Crook looked alert and pleased. "Be sure to mention that when you write up the story for the Sunday press," he advised her. "That's a marvellous touch. Now then, we can't have any more hysterics. They're not going to help."

Julia stood up. "I suppose I'm tired or something," she confessed. "You don't want me to start as the human silhouette tonight, do you?"

"It wouldn't be any use. Peters don't know about you yet. Miss

Carpmael wouldn't get back to the hotel till after your train arrived, for fear Mrs. P. should flag the station master at Paddington. She might send a wire, but even so he'd barely get in by now. No, no, you have a good night's rest and begin in earnest in the morning."

It occurred to Julia that she had nowhere to go unless she returned to Spencer House; but when she made this suggestion both Crook and Colin vetoed it at once.

"We don't want any amateurs bunglin' our trail," the lawyer explained. "The minute you appear they'll start lookin' for squalls. They'll come after you as heavy-footed as an elephant, and glory only knows when we'll nail our man. No, you choose somewhere fresh. I'll tell you a place. You'll need some cash, too, won't you?"

"I've hardly a penny," Julia confessed. Crook put some notes on the table. Julia stared. "Are those all for me?"

"You just tell us when you need more. No, don't thank me. That ain't goin' to come out of my pocket. This is the Government's money for jam, and they'll probably ask for a receipt. Now, don't leave this address without lettin' us know, and if you do discover anythin' give us the word at once—never mind if it's dangerous. Got that?"

Julia said she had and turned to go. Crook surprised her by offering his hand. He held hers for an instant, then said, turning to Colin, "If ever I get landed with a dame she's got horners and a red nose for a dead cert. You young chaps pick up all the lookers."

"I suppose he's slightly mad," hazarded Julia, as she and Colin went out to look for dinner. He wouldn't come with her to her room. Crook said it was better not. He had made all the necessary arrangements by telephone.

"Who? Crook? We could do with a bit more of that sort of mania. No, no, he's just an enthusiast."

"But what does he get out of it? I mean, he's not in the Secret Service, is he?"

"You'll never see Crook taking his orders from any other man. No he's what's known as a free lance."

"And—who pays him for his trouble?"

"In a sense, you do—by giving him the sort of case he adores. You see, Crook's line is disreputable high-fliers. He's got no conscience except towards his clients. You remember the chap who said that what mattered about evidence was the way it was arranged? That's Crook's viewpoint, too. All the bad hats who ought, by rights, to swing or anyhow get fourteen years are so grateful for their liberty they'll put up anything he asks without a whimper. They know that freedom's priceless, and Crook knows it, too. You'd be surprised if you saw some of the checks he gets from the most unexpected quarters. It isn't that what he does for them costs all that, but they've got to cover his non-profitable cases—like this one. He explained it all to me once. It's perfectly logical. Just Harley Street all over again. Crook says he's following the governmental prejudice for robbing the rich to give to the poor. I don't know which particular criminal is franking you . . ."

"You mean, he really enjoys all this? It's a game to him? But then he's not risking much . . ."

Colin shook his head. "Don't you believe it. He's risking more than any of us. No man can be as successful as he is, particularly in his line, without creating an army of men who'd like to see him under the sod. I believe he's worth any amount to the chap who, by fair means or foul, gets him down. But that's what he enjoys. He's a gambler to his finger tips."

"And I don't believe I am," said Julia slowly. "Isn't that contemptible?"

"You're the kingpin of the situation," said Colin simply. "I'm not afraid you're going to let us down. It's no longer just a personal affair."

Julia said nothing. She marvelled at the obtuseness of the man, though it was something to realize that she hadn't showed her hand as obviously as she had feared. But after a minute she felt his hand close round her arm and his voice said, "How about the pictures on our night out? Heaven knows when we may get another."

It was, perhaps, unfortunate that the picture they chose was a full-blooded gangster film, with a lovely heroine perpetually on the verge of being murdered and always escaping by the skin of her teeth. Colin thought it would calm Julia's fears to see how many chances of winning she possessed, but its actual result was to make

148

her see how many possibilities there were she hadn't so much as considered hitherto, because she hadn't known that they existed.

The next three days were a nightmare. Julia had supposed that her earlier experiences would have hardened her to anything that might follow, but there at least the danger had been localized. She had known who were her enemies, and, roughly speaking, the direction from which they would strike. But back in London, exhibiting herself for fourteen hours a day, never knowing if she had been recognized, whether the man on the escalator behind her was an enemy or the stranger he appeared to be, scarcely daring to turn her head or pause to re-tie a shoelace, suspicious even of taxi-drivers or elderly ladies who asked her if she was sure that hadn't been a siren—this took desperate toll of nerves already keyed to the uttermost. Nor did she see anything of Colin. It was generally agreed that it was best for them not to meet. Julia understood that, too. Colin in his own way was quite an important person. He mustn't be subjected to an undue amount of risk and her company definitely spelt danger. She would not even telephone to him during the long evenings in her combined furnished room, lest a spy tap the wires. But she had her moments of feeling that, if Peters was to get her in the end, she might as well be taken now and have done with it.

"It's possible, though difficult, to be on your guard against two women," she reflected. "It's impossible when it's a whole city. Besides, he may be disguised; he'd make quite a passable woman."

In her lonely hours, and they were many, she would wonder how on earth she was to pass on her information before Peters blockaded the move. Colin was showing considerable respect for her intelligence, but when she expressed her doubts of her own abilities he had only repeated, "I'm not afraid you'll let us down."

On the fourth morning she had a line from Colin. "Lunch at the Ivy one-fifteen sharp," it said. After so official a summons Julia felt she should have anticipated Crook's attendance at the party but when she came through the door and saw him sitting with Colin her heart plunged with disappointment. Colin, however, made it clear at once that this was a purely professional appointment.

"How are you feeling, sugar?" Crook asked in airy tones.

"Weakening," said Julia flatly. "How long do you think this is going on?"

"We're not makin' the runnin'," Crook told her reprovingly. "Though we do our best."

"Do you mean, you've found . . . ?" she paused, her eyes fixed on that red determined face.

"The ottoman? Sure."

"And was there anything inside it?"

Crook nodded. His little pigs' eyes never faltered.

"You mean . . . ?" Once again horror paralyzed her tongue.

"I mean, it was cram bang full of rugs and quilts and flotsam and jetsam, but not one single body, if you'll believe me."

Julia gave a little gasp of relief. Crook looked at her in surprise.

"I'm sorry, of course, for your sake," Julia explained. "I suppose it means starting again from the beginning, but I can't help being thankful to know that when I sat twisting the fringe on that ottoman there wasn't, after all, a dead body inside."

"Say all that again," Crook told her in so strange a voice that she was startled.

She repeated her words verbatim.

"Holy smoke!" ejaculated Crook, and he turned to Colin. "You see where that gets us."

"Yes," agreed Colin, and his voice, too, had a strange ring.

"I don't understand," whispered Julia.

"I'll say you don't," agreed Crook. "Listen here and get this. *There's no fringe on the ottoman we found in the warehouse.*"

15

INSTANTLY EVERY ONE BEGAN to talk at once. Colin wanted to be reassured that Julia had made no mistake; Crook reiterated the fact that there was no fringe on the ottoman at the warehouse, Julia shouted above them both that she wasn't mistaken and that there had been a fringe on the ottoman in Mrs. Ponsonby's parlor.

"I remember twisting it into a silken rope," she explained. "You know how it is when you're nervous—you hang on to the slightest thing, and I can still feel the rather tangly threads between my fingers."

"Take your davy on that?" demanded Crook, when some sort of order was restored.

"Yes," declared Julia, unhesitatingly.

"Then you see where that gets us? No, don't tell her, Bruce. Let her figure it out for herself."

"I'm not such a fool as you imagine," exclaimed Julia hotly. "I see perfectly. It means that there are two ottomans, and the important one is the one you haven't found."

"Couldn't be more nastily put," agreed Crook. "Still, that's where you come in."

"What am I supposed to do?"

"Identify the ottoman, of course. You're the only one of us who can."

"Then—have you found it?"

"Not yet."

"Have you any idea where it is?"

"I couldn't be certain, but I'd say it was being offered for sale somewhere. Y'see, when I find myself involved in a job like this I try to put myself in the other chap's place. Now, supposing I were Peters, with a body to get rid of and assumin' that body's in an ottoman, what would I do? First of all, I've got to get the ottoman removed. We know it wasn't in the house on Monday when the furniture was shifted, and it was there on Friday night because you were sittin' on it, so it looks as though it was taken away on the Saturday. I'd say it wasn't the only thing that was taken away, either. Well, work it out for yourself. If a man—a little man that works with a horse and cart, a small greengrocer, say, who does a bit of furniture shifting in his spare time—if he's asked to take an ottoman to a new address, he's likely to remember it when he's asked. He might even remember what it looked like. But if he's asked to take an ottoman and various other things, then the ottoman won't make the same impression on him. No, no, I think you'll find Peters was quite fly enough to think of that. Saturday afternoon's a good time to get hold of a horse and cart or even a little van. I don't think he'd be likely to employ a local man, but on the other hand he wouldn't go too far. It wouldn't be worth the chap's while. No, no, the obvious answer is that he'd employ a man from the other end, that is from the district to which the stuff was bein' taken. Otherwise, someone might smell a rat. These little men don't bother to make an inventory of the stuff they remove, not as a rule, and in any case they'd probably write down an ottoman as a bed or a sofa. Well, then, friend Peters havin' got his body shifted, he's got to dispose of it."

"And have you any idea where it is?"

"Not the least," rejoined Crook calmly. "Well, if we knew all the answers at the beginning, where would the fun be?"

"And then," Colin wound up neatly, "just to make all the ends tidy, Peters gets rid of the couch in case any connection is traced between it and Mrs. Ponsonby."

"You don't think," suggested Julia timidly, "that the body could still be in the ottoman? In some unused flat, say, that he's filled with furniture?"

"I doubt it," said Crook seriously. "Keepin' a body on the premises is always risky. You can explain away a lot of things, but a body isn't one of them, specially when it's the body of a young lady the police are looking for. I've known a good many men try, but I've never known one really convince the police that the corpse was as much of a surprise to him as it was to the officer in charge. No, I fancy he disposed of it all right, and as soon as he could."

"I suppose he'd go to a second-hand dealer," Julia suggested.

"Seems reasonable, don't it?"

"Then all you have to do is to trace the dealer," Julia began and stopped at the howl of laughter that broke from the two men.

"Listen to the girl," exclaimed Crook, admiringly. "Quite right, honey. All I've got to do is to find the ottoman and learn the name of the man who sold it. Of course he mightn't have given his real name, and he mightn't even have sold it himself, but that's no matter. It's bound to be at a second-hand store or in an auctioneer's gallery or even stored somewhere. There's the chance it's already been resold, but all I've got to do now is to run it to earth. Well, come to that, I shall, of course," he added cheerfully, "only—don't make the mistake of thinkin' it's child's play, will you?"

They parted soon after that, Colin to return to his work and Crook to drive up west in a taxi, a huge cigar in his mouth, his hat over one eye, his legs crossed jauntily. As the cab drove off he removed the cigar and leaned out of the window to remark confidentially to Julia that she must be sure to let him know if she came across the ottoman anywhere, and of course if she got any fresh ideas as to the body itself, well, she knew his number. Julia, flushing angrily, turned towards a bus stop. She resented Crook's manner, and she felt forlorn at Colin's whole-hearted desertion. For the hundredth time she thought of the girl in Ireland whom he meant to marry; she even forgot about Peters and her own danger until a roar from the driver of a private car sent her hastily back to the pavement whence she had strayed during her reverie. As she boarded the bus she thought what a sell it would be for Crook if she happened to be the person who found the ottoman.

Nothing happened that evening. Julia found herself pounced upon by a Miss Pettifer, a middle-aged woman who liked to talk about her youth and how she'd had her own horse to ride and had studied painting in Italy under a celebrated master, and had never expected to be poor and live in a pension, but it didn't matter really, because people were so interesting in themselves, and thrilling things were happening all the time, weren't they? Julia said yes, indeed, and wondered if the lady's eyes would pop out of her head if she knew how her listener had spent the last six weeks, but she decided that most likely she wouldn't believe it, and wouldn't be interested anyway. So instead she asked if Miss Pettifer knew of a good shop for getting second-hand divan beds. Miss Pettifer said, "Setting up on your own, are you? I'm sure you're wise."

Julia said she was thinking about it, and Miss Pettifer said heartily, "Be sure of your own mind, won't you? I'm always so thankful I wasn't rash when I was your age. So many of my contemporaries never stopped to think and they've been so—miserable." And then she added acutely that she noticed Julia didn't wear a ring.

Her meaning was unmistakable, but Julia didn't mind; it was clear that Miss Pettifer's life had been a disappointed one for all her boasts and vaunted conquests. She spoke of two or three likely places in Kings Road and another in Camden Town and another woman who had overheard added more addresses. Julia carefully noted them all and spent the next two days looking at second-hand divans and ottomans. She became so much engrossed in this that she forgot Peters for hours at a stretch. During those two days she saw so many ottoman-beds that her brain began to reel. She calculated that there were innumerable second-hand shops in London, that the bed might have been dispatched to a relative in the country, donated to a fund for providing refugees with furniture, even been chopped to pieces.

It was on the evening of the second day that she thought of the advertisement.

The idea came to her with all the brilliance of a revelation. Even Crook, she thought, for all his vaunted powers, might seek for this one particular bit of furniture for six months without success; and when, long afterwards, he said explosively, "But what damned cheek you amateurs have! If I'd wanted the thing advertised I could have done it myself" she found herself faltering, "I thought perhaps it hadn't occurred to you."

The stupendous insolence of this saved her. Crook tipped back his head and broke into a roar of laughter that might have been mistaken for the warning voice of the A.A. guns.

"You win," he said, simply. "I thought I knew all the answers, but that one's beyond me."

The advertisement, framed by Julia, appeared in the Bazaar and Mart at the end of the week, two days after she had posted the slip to the editorial offices. It announced that the advertiser was anxious to trace a box ottoman (minutely described down to the fringe and the burn that had attracted her attention on that Friday evening) and gave a box number for replies. She even chanced the date of its disposal, naming that particular week end. What explanation she should offer should the ottoman's present owner answer the advertisement she did not think. In any case, he would probably be only too pleased at the opportunity of making a handsome profit on the deal.

She was surprised at the numbers of replies she received. It appeared that innumerable box ottomans all covered in a specific material, had been disposed of during the three days in question. Julia, who had intended to take any reply that came to Crook to be vetted by him, now perceived that she might be making herself a laughingstock. Besides, her mettle was being tested. As Crook had assured her, no one but herself could positively identify the ottoman; therefore, she decided, she must go the rounds and cancel all the non-starters.

Eventually she ran it to earth in a shop in Fulham Road. So blurred were the eyes of her mind by the number of ottomans she had seen that she could scarcely believe her luck when the shopman showed her the identical one she had sat on in Henriques Square. Now that it was under her eyes she had no doubt at all. The tangled fringe had been neatly combed smooth, there had even been an effort to darn the burnt place in the cover; but the distinctive pattern, even the shattered spring that had exasperated her in Henriques Square, all these proclaimed it the end of the search. Intoxicated by this measure of success, she proceeded to hammer a few nails into her coffin.

"I'm so glad to have run it to earth," she explained. "It ought never to have been sold."

"Come from your house?" asked the man, shrewdly appraising the situation and wondering what was the top figure he could demand.

"Yes. It belonged to a relative who was getting rid of some of her stuff before going down to the country. I wanted this and by mistake it was sold with some other things. I don't know whether you bought the rest . . ."

"Bed, two chairs and a wardrobe," said the man smartly. "Like to see them?"

Julia hesitated. It wasn't likely that she would recognize any separate piece from the house in Henriques Square; nevertheless she resolved not to miss the smallest opportunity so she agreed to look over the other sticks that had been disposed of at the same time. As she had anticipated, she recognized none of them, though she had too much sense to say as much.

"No," she told the man. "It's really the ottoman I wanted. I

155

know it's not perfect, that spring must be repaired, but it's got years of wear in it." And she asked the price.

The shopman watched her keenly as he replied, "Five pounds."

"That's a good deal," said she dubiously.

"It's worth a lot to you," he told her in cheerful tones.

Julia shot him a sharp look, but he was smiling with the pleasure of a man about to conclude a stiff bargain.

"Have to make our profits while we can," he went on. "This war's not made things any easier for us. So many people leaving London, no one wanting furniture much . . ."

"I quite see," Julia agreed. "Well, I certainly would like that ottoman. It has—associations. My aunt would never have let Peters have it if she'd known I wanted it."

"Peters?" repeated the man. "It was a party of quite another name that sold it to me. You're sure this is the right one?"

"Quite certain. Well, he may not have done the actual selling himself—I dare say you wouldn't remember him particularly—a tallish man with a thin white face."

Her companion shook his head. "I wouldn't know anyway. I was asked to send a chap to look at some stuff and he advised me to give a price for it and there it is. I don't do that part of the job myself," he added, indulgently.

Julia felt a sense of power rising within her; it gave her a slightly dizzy feeling, drowning her sense of danger. In her mind's eye she saw Crook's large derisive face telling her to be sure and let him know if she found the ottoman or Peters. She thought exultantly that this very night she might be able to tell him the whereabouts of both.

"Did you have to fetch it from very far?" she asked, in the most casual tone she could manage.

"Earl's Court. No, not far. Well, these days it's not worth a man's while spending a lot of petrol fetching in stuff he may not sell for six months."

"So that's where he is? My aunt was wondering. You have a sense of responsibility towards servants who've been in your employ for years," she went on. "I'd like to look him up, if you remember the actual address."

"I could get it for you," said the man, obligingly.

Julia's excitement rose like a wave. Poor Julia! She knew nothing of a conversation that had taken place not many hours earlier between Purvis and a tall man with a thin white face looking rather like a fox.

"Tell her anything she wants to know," the visitor had said. "It's jake by me."

The man came back with the address scribbled on a slip of paper. "151 Radnor Road, Earl's Court Avenue. You know the way, miss?"

"Oh, yes," lied Julia, who had never heard of the street in question. "Well, thank you very much. Now, about the ottoman. I can't pay for it this evening because I haven't got enough money with me, but I'll give you two pounds on account and come round in the morning. Will that be all right?"

"That's all right. I'll give you a receipt. There'll be a small charge for delivery. Can't afford to be like the big shops and deliver free, not with petrol the price it is now."

Julia was certain that the man was taking advantage of her eagerness to obtain the ottoman. Moreover, she thought she detected in his voice a note she disliked, something a shade too familiar, a shade patronizing. She stiffened as she replied that she would call in the morning and make a final arrangement.

"Could I have the name and address, miss?"

Julia gave her name, but said that the ottoman would not be sent to the hotel where she was at present staying. The man, however, pressed for this address and Julia gave it to him, seeing no reason, beyond a faintly instinctive distaste, why she should withhold it. As she waited for the receipt, exultation rose again. Any sense of peril she might have experienced earlier had vanished. She had now all the information that Crook wanted; the thrill of the chase was upon her. Under everything else was the sense that Colin must admit her coolness and initiative. As soon as she left the shop she would telephone to Crook. She looked round and saw a telephone standing on a side table.

"I might ask permission to use that," she reflected. "It's almost six o'clock, and Crook might be going home. It would certainly save time."

Then her resolve flickered. The man might smell a rat, think that something was up—as it certainly was. Julia knew vaguely that there is a large section of the community that detests all thought of police interference. There was sure to be a telephone booth or a post office near at hand. Keep your head, she counselled herself. You don't want to take any chances now when you're nearly home.

On such trifling decisions as these do lives and destinies hang.

There was a taxi cruising about in the streets where a thin drizzle of rain had begun to fall. Fulham Road had a deserted appearance. Shops were darkened and there were many unoccupied. Julia looked at the second chance Fate was offering her in the shape of the cab. If she had obeyed her first impulse and jumped into it and telephoned from her hotel, a whole chapter of danger and despair need never have been written. But she shook her head at the driver as he slowed down still further by the curb and moved his hand as if to open the door.

She wouldn't telephone from the hotel, she decided. The instrument stood on a bracket in the hall, and any one coming or going could overhear one side at least of a conversation. The place was one enormous ear, always listening for scraps of gossip and conjecture. Nor, she thought, would she go into a post office, where the booths stood cheek by jowl and an attentive person in the next cubicle could overhear much of what you were saying. The measure of success attending her efforts defeated her sense of proportion. She let the cab go by, hurried past a post office and turned into a narrow entry in which was situated a tall red box like an upended coffin. She went quickly over the damp cobbles, about a hundred yards down the alley, and pulled open the door. As she took down the receiver and pushed two coppers into the slot a wave of pure joy swept over her.

The telephone provided the first disappointment by giving out the busy signal. Impatiently Julia pushed Button B and the pennies came back with a hollow rattle. No one else was waiting, so she controlled herself for a minute and tried again with the same result. By this time the darkness of a wet evening was closing rapidly over the city. Although it was June a bank of dark cloud obscured the sky; the leaves dripped forlornly; hardly any one went past the end of the alley. Only now and then came the sound of footsteps hurrying homeward. A sudden sense of danger caught Julia by the throat. She realized that no one knew where she was, that she was now a definite menace to the people who had got rid of Sheila Campbell, that, just as a miracle had happened to her, so a similar miracle might happen to Peters. In her dismay at this thought she dropped one of the precious pennies and had to grovel for it on the dusty floor. Now she had begun to tremble. The gathering fog and mist were oppressive. She wished she had taken the cab and driven back to the well-populated and lighted hotel.

"I'll try it once more," she decided, dialing the number for the third time. And now all went well. She heard the familiar double ring and her heart clamored with impatience for a reply. It rang several times however before a voice—not Crook's—said "Hullo."

"Mr. Crook?" said Julia, quickly. "This is Julia Ross here. It's very urgent. Tell him I've found them both."

"Hold on a minute," said Bill Parson's easy voice.

Julia shifted in the box; she had been facing down the alley, now she turned and looked towards the high road . . .

"Hullo!" bellowed Crook. "That you, Julia? Hullo!"

But no one answered him. The black microphone in the booth dangled at the full length of its cord, swinging idly to and fro like something hanged and dead. Pressed against the back of the fantastic coffin, a white-faced girl stared, incredulous and aghast, at a whiter face pressed against the outer glass. The thin colorless lips parted, the pallid fox mask gleamed with malice and delight.

"Where the hell are you?" yelled Crook, but the receiver, swaying limply, could make no reply.

The fox face withdrew a little, a hand like a hooded claw rose out of the mist and pulled open the door of the booth.

"Good evening, Miss Ross," said Peters.

"There's no reply," said Crook sharply, dropping the telephone and shouting to Bill. "What did she say to you?"

"That she'd found the ottoman and Peters."

"These damned amateurs!" exploded Crook, ungratefully. "On my sam, I believe they think they're the original Sons of God. The professional knows he's a man of limitations, but the amateur's like the looking-glass dog. Wants to be judge and jury. And now she's got herself into a jam and we shall be expected to haul her out—and heaven knows whether we can do it in the time."

Bill knew his chief well enough to realize that this storm of fury denoted genuine anxiety for Julia. If, as seemed probable, it was Peters or Peters' agent who had interrupted the telephone call, then her life was probably in grave danger. The information she had gleaned made her a peril to the spies, and a man who had contrived to conceal one body might prove equally astute with a second. All Crook could do for the moment was attempt to trace the call, but he knew this was a pretty hopeless line of country. Automatic telephones made it even more difficult than of yore, and tracing local calls in the London area was never easy. It was Bill who suggested sending for Colin, and the first piece of luck they had was that Colin was instantly available. He came rushing round in a taxi, saying, "What the hell's that girl been up to? And why the hell weren't you there to stop her?"

Crook calmed him down a little, and proceeded to repeat his remarks about amateurs. Colin consigned him to hell.

"She's only done what you asked her to do, hasn't she? You wanted this chap found and she's found him. Well, what she's done on her own, surely the three of us can do together."

On Crook's suggestion they went round to Julia's hotel-boarding-house. They were interviewed by Miss Tweedale in person, who told them that Julia had gone out a considerable time ago and had not yet returned.

"Did she send any message?"

"No, I think not."

"Did you expect her back to dinner?"

"She didn't say."

A lady in saxe-blue cotton velveteen, who was turning the corner of the stairs, said in refined tones, "Excuse me, were you speaking of Miss Ross? I know she intends to be in to dinner because we have a little engagement afterwards to play bezique. She should be in by now—it's getting on towards seven o'clock."

"You a friend of hers?" inquired Crook in what he believed to be a gracious voice.

"I like to think she regards me as a friend," intoned Miss Pettifer. "She seems a nice girl, though a little reckless."

"What—at bezique?"

"Actually I meant with her own life. She was speaking of setting up for herself without any—er—very firm foundation."

"What d'you mean by setting up?"

"She spoke of buying an ottoman."

Crook let out a great guffaw of laughter. "If she was setting up in your sense it wouldn't be an ottoman she was after." Then he sobered. "Did she ever get it?"

"I gave her the names of two or three reliable second-hand stores, but I did see that she had put an advertisement in the Bazaar and Mart. I don't know what the result was."

"We could have told her," Crook remarked grimly to his companions. "Of course, the girl's cuckoo. I've always said it was crazy to work with a jane. They're too damned individual, always want to do things off their own bat and scoop the credit. Of course Peters got wind of this ad and then all the fat was in the fire."

Bill spoke in his usual languid drawl. "It seems to have brought home the bacon in this particular case, though. I mean, she spotted the ottoman."

"So she did. I wander if she left any clues behind her." He took Miss Tweedale a little into his confidence and obtained permission to examine the missing girl's room. In a bureau drawer he found the copy of Bazaar and Mart with the advertisement scored in blue chalk, and also a batch of letters that had arrived in reply. It was obvious that Julia had a methodical mind. She had made a list of the addresses of her correspondents, and had pinned this to the letters. Against a number of these Julia had set a large blue cross, "indicatin' they're no bon," reflected Crook. "Conclusion is that the right chap is one of the others. Well, that maps things out for us. We've just got to go round till we strike it lucky. We know one of these fellows has the ottoman. She's not likely to have tried to bring it away, so it'll still be on the premises. Now it's all a matter of time. We don't know how much we have, but we've got to see to it that it's enough."

His brow was heavy with displeasure as he climbed into his noisy little red roadster and took the wheel. At this hour the various shops would be closing for the day, but it was fortunate that the majority of proprietors lived over their premises. Of these, however, some were out and some remarkably long-winded, so that it was after eight o'clock when they at length ran the couch to earth.

Crook had been banging for some time on the locked front door before it was cautiously opened from within and an indignant face thrust forth.

"What do you want?"

"Home Office inquiries," said Crook, nodding towards Colin and Bill, both of whom looked the part to perfection.

The man was obviously shaken. "Home Office? You've got nothing on me."

"Perhaps we could discuss this better inside," suggested Colin suavely, and the four of them flowed into the shabby little passage.

The man was painfully distressed. "Look here," he said, "what's all this about, getting a chap up at this hour of the night? I don't know anything about the Home Office . . ."

"You'll learn," said Crook, simply.

Colin produced the copy of the *Bazaar and Mart*. "You answered an advertisement in this a few days ago about an ottoman, didn't you?"

"Well, s'pose I did? That's all right. You're not trying to tell me that was a code or something? Go on, it was all right. The young lady said so."

"Which young lady?"

"The one that came this afternoon. Why, there's not another of them, is there? This one seemed to recognize the ottoman, said it belonged to her aunt—though I must say," he added reluctantly, "she didn't seem to know the gentleman's name."

"Which gentleman?"

"The one that sold the couch in the first place."

"And you told her?"

"Well—yes, I did. I did right, didn't I? The gentleman himself told me to answer questions."

"And after she'd gone perhaps you got into touch with the gentleman?"

"I never. Well, he didn't say anything about it. How was I to know? And what are you getting at anyway? There wasn't any harm in buying the couch, I suppose, or in selling it when I got the chance?"

"Did the lady leave her name?"

"Yes. She said she'd come in tomorrow and pay the balance. She hadn't got the money with her, so she gave me a deposit and I reserved the couch for her."

"We'd like to see it."

The man put up a feeble bluster of defense. "Look here, this is all very irregular. I don't know who you are or what you want or what this is all about . . ."

"If you called it murder you wouldn't be far out," Crook assured him, crisply.

"Murder!" The man's eyes started from his head. "Coo, I never dreamed . . ."

"You're not asked to dream. Where's that couch?"

Still muttering, the man led them from the back premises into the showroom.

"Daren't put on a light," he said. "The wardens was round a day or two back complaining about the black-out. They don't stop to think what it's like having to cover windows that size. Still, I've got a torch." He led the way between solid blocks of shadow that proved to be cupboards and chairs, followed by Bill Parsons, who moved like a cat. Colin was less skillful and barked his shin against a tallboy, while Crook picked a careful clumsy way round the obstacles in his path. Seen in the light of the torch, the ottoman had an eerie appearance. Of the four men standing round it, three thought chiefly of a girl who had occupied it not so long ago, but Colin's main anxiety was for Julia. The torch threw little circles and arcs of light on their surroundings; the wind came through the open door and caused draperies to stir faintly, so that the place seemed alive with ghosts. The four men, remarkably like ghosts themselves, stood round the couch.

"Four angels round my bed," exploded Crook, suddenly, and Purvis, the proprietor, looked at him in a shocked manner.

"I never saw the chap that sold me this till after I'd bought it," he volunteered.

163

"How did you come to see him then?"

"He brought in a copy of the *Bazaar* and said, 'If a young lady should come inquiring about that ottoman I've reason to believe it's the one she wants. Tell her anything she wants to know. It'll be all right.' Well, I told him, it may be all right for you but I don't half like the sound of it. I thought it might be a matter of stolen goods, see? But he promised me it was all right. 'If I'd anything to hide I wouldn't go ahead and tell you to answer questions, would I?' he asked me."

"And what time did the lady come?"

"Just before six it must have been. She knew the ottoman right away, and then she asked me who sold it to me, and did I know his address, as he was a servant of her aunt (I think she said) and she wanted to look him up."

Bill spoke in his usual dry drawl. "And you swallowed that? An ostrich would have nothing on you."

Purvis looked distressed. "I hope I've done nothing I shouldn't, sir," he said uncomfortably.

"You're in luck that we found you this evening," was Bill's uncompromising retort. "What was the address you gave the girl?"

"151 Radnor Road, Earl's Court Avenue."

"That'll do to be going on with," said Bill. "What was this chap like?"

Purvis's suspicions lifted their heads again. "Meaning that you don't know him yourselves?"

"Do we look the sort of people who know murderers?"

"I couldn't know it was anything like that," exploded Purvis. "He didn't look like anything of the sort. I couldn't guess."

"That's where you chaps always go wrong," remarked Crook. "You expect a murderer to wear the brand of Cain, whatever that may be. Believe me, I've a closer acquaintance with murderers than you have," he nodded confidentially to the startled furniture dealer, "and I tell you as far as appearances go any one of us might qualify for the rope necktie."

"He was an ordinary looking sort of man," Purvis told him uneasily. "Thinnish, dressed in black . . ."

"A bit like a white fox?" suggested Colin.

"Well, sir, perhaps that does sound a bit like him. Do you mean, that this is going to be a matter for the police?"

"It won't be my fault if it is. Why should we do their work for them? Though as a matter of fact," he added in an off-hand voice, "we may let them have the dry bread when we've licked the butter off it. By the way, in the unlikely contingency of our Mr.—by the way, what name did he give?"

"Robinson."

"If he should turn up again you don't remember this visit. See?"

"I don't like it," burst out the man, "this sort of thing has never happened to me before. I've never been mixed up with the police. I've been here twenty years."

"No reason why you shouldn't be here another twenty," Crook told him indulgently. "If you listen to us, that is. On the other hand, there's no sense in not tellin' you that our Mr. Robinson won't be feelin' very friendly to you when he realizes we're on his tail, so you take my tip and lie low for a bit."

Purvis looked horrified as well he might. "And—how long is this going on?" he demanded, dry-lipped.

"We're quick movers," Crook assured him cheerfully. "The matter's bound to be settled one way or the other in the course of the next couple of days. If anything fresh turns up, here's my number. Now hop back and finish your night's sleep."

The three men left the premises in Fulham Road and jammed themselves anew into the disreputable little red car.

"It's to be hoped our friend, Purvis, isn't watching from an upper window," observed Colin, "or he'll get a queer idea of the equipment of the Secret Service. He'd expect a Rolls-Bentley at least."

"You amateurs would give away the show with parsley round the dish," returned Crook inelegantly. "Even in these cynical days a Rolls-Bentley gets an eyeful in this part of London, whereas in Caliban we shall just be taken for three cruising cads and no one will give a tinker's curse where we go or what we do."

Colin was silent for a minute or two, then he said, "You aren't expecting to find Peters on the premises, are you? I mean, it's altogether too simple."

"How you chaps love complications," groaned Crook. "I tell you

165

till my tongue falls out that the successful crime is the simple crime. That's why in the end I shall get Peters, because I understand the simple mind. No, of course I don't expect to find him at Radnor Road. But I'll bet you anything you like I shall find Sheila Campbell there."

16

RADNOR ROAD PROVED TO BE a terrace of rather mean little houses, two stories above a shallow basement, with small stony front gardens and battered green iron gates. No. 151 was an end house. In appearance it differed little from its neighbors; long lace curtains with elaborate patterns of cupids, urns and branching lilies almost obscured the windows. On the ground floor a collection of pot plants was visible; in the basement red plush curtains were drawn closely together, completely hiding the interior of the room from the curious passer-by. The brilliant moonlight made it possible for a close observer to note these details. It was also largely responsible for the fact that the street was practically empty. Only under a lamppost a couple were locked together oblivious of the world, and a large red cat jumped hurriedly from gutter to pavement as the small red car tooled by. From behind a few windows came the sound of radio music, a clear voice from a ground floor room ran through the stillness of the street. From No. 151 there came no sound at all.

"No one living there now," remarked Crook, thoughtfully. "Blinds not drawn, no lights visible. How about it, Bill? Think you can manage it?"

"They never bother with foolproof locks on houses like these," returned Bill dryly. "Nothing worth taking. I've known a few mean thieves in my time, but never one that sank this low."

While Bill turned his delicate attention to the matter of effecting an entry Colin stood a little apart from his companions, staring down the street. The silver light illumined great masses of cloud that floated tranquilly above the houses; leaves moved in the wind. The whole neighborhood seemed wrapped in peace. Yet the very silence had an intimidating effect. It was as though the houses themselves watched and listened; in a moment of fantastic imagination he could almost see them lean towards the trio standing as quiet as the rest of the world on that undistinguished doorstep. Colin was struck with the thought of the immensity of the city; thousands upon thousands of little boxes, each with its inhabitants reading or dozing or listening to the radio; but in one little box Julia would be, and perhaps Peters would be there, too, and both would be waiting. The thought was more than Colin could endure. Julia's danger increased with every instant; the very efforts they were making on her behalf accentuated her peril. If Crook should prove right, if the body of Sheila Campbell was behind these locked doors, then Peters could have no option but to dispose of the second girl who threatened his security, with the same mystery and despatch as before. Colin turned quickly at the thought.

"What's wrong with the door?"

Bill was dusting his hands together; they were long fine artist's hands, Colin noticed.

"Bolted on the inside," he returned dryly. "We must try the back way."

The alternative entrance proved to be a green wooden door set in the side wall. This was fastened but the lock presented no difficulties to the enterprising Bill. Within three minutes the invaders found themselves in a little London garden consisting of a gravel square bordered by the usual smutty laurels and privet bushes.

"Look for a window," said Bill coolly. "If this chap's any use he'll have bolted the back door, too, and made his getaway by the window. If I'm right that means a lot less trouble for us; not even a pane to smash."

He was right; a little skillful application of something Bill took from his pocket and the window of the back parlor gaped open and the three streamed in. The interior of the house presented an odd appearance. In each room there were curtains at the window, but, with the exception of the table of potted plants in the front of the house, there was no furniture whatsoever.

"Simple, my dear Watson," said Crook. "He never intended to live here; no one was going to live here, but he had to give an

167

impression that the house was inhabited. I guess he told the chap that brought his sticks from Henriques Square that the rest of the stuff hadn't arrived, and the fellow that removed them that everything else had gone ahead to the new address. He wouldn't expect Purvis to come snooping, since the chap would naturally suppose the place was empty. If he'd been a bit brighter Purvis would have smelt a rat when Peters told him not to try and withhold the address. Of course he never intended the girl to get here. But then come to that, he never expected us to get here either."

There was nothing in the hall, not so much as a rug. In the front parlor was the table of ferns and flowering plants, the latter drooping sadly. On the mantelpiece were a few advertisements—an appeal for funds for refugees from the Lord Mayor, a receipted bill for a ton of coal, a pamphlet regarding air raid dangers, and a leaflet from a local mission, headed: The wicked shall be turned into hell.

Crook glanced through them and turned towards the stairs. As he had anticipated, the upper rooms also were unfurnished. He snapped open cupboards, inspected the miniature attics, then made his way into the basement. This consisted of the kitchen premises and a morning room, the window of which they had seen from the street closely shrouded by the plush curtains.

"This is where the body should be," he remarked. "Otherwise why draw the curtains?"

"To prevent the world in general realizing that the room was quite empty," suggested Colin.

Crook took the suggestion in good part. "It could be," he acknowledged. "It could be. Then where's the girl? She's here somewhere; otherwise, what's the sense in keeping the house? He didn't put up those curtains just to satisfy the curiosity of Purvis's carrier."

They began the search afresh, this time in yet greater detail. The kitchen range was their first objective, but this was cold and rusty and it seemed clear that it had not been used for a considerable time. Cooking had been done by the last tenant on an old-fashioned gas cooker; that was thick with grease and dirt. When Crook held an experimental match to the oven burners he found that one side refused to light.

"This place has stood empty for some time," he remarked. "The agent could tell us more about that in the morning. That makes it all the more certain that Peters took the place as a sepulchre for Sheila Campbell. Only—where the heck is she?"

On the face of it there seemed few places where she could be hidden. It was when the three men stood together in the bedroom on the second floor that the hideous truth occurred to Crook.

"We're pretty good jays," he remarked in his candid fashion. "On my sam, we don't deserve to catch our bird. I've just remembered something."

"And that is?"

"The receipted account for coal in the room downstairs. If no one's lived here for some time and cooking's done by gas why does any one want a ton of coal?"

It was an instant before the implication reached Colin's intelligence and when it did so he shrank for a moment from the obvious corollary. Bill remained unmoved. He simply nodded his head and agreed.

"I guess you're right, Crook. So we'd better get ahead and prove it."

He was the least touched of the three as he led the little procession down to the cellar. But not even Crook, who had known him for years, had ever seen Bill shaken out of his normal languid calm. As a criminal, he had employed Crook to pull the noses of the police; as an honest man he had played Crook's game loyally, yet the essential man remained a stranger. Crook had once said of him that he was sometimes tempted to believe that Providence had experimented with a robot creation and that Bill was the result of the experiment. The fact that there was no one else like him implied that he had proved too much even for Providence.

The cellar was small, narrow and pitch dark. The coal lay heaped in a kind of pyramid in the middle of the floor.

"You're right, Crook," asserted Bill. "Coal never falls like that when it's shot through a locker. This has been assisted to make this nice pretty pattern."

There was a shovel leaning against the wall, and it was Bill who took it up and began carefully yet energetically to clear away the coal. After a very short time Crook's surmise was proved correct when a human hand was revealed. Colin, looking pretty green, leaned against the wall, ruining his well-cut suit, while the other two men speedily uncovered the dreadful secret of the missing girl.

"You have to hand it to Peters that he knows his onions," said Crook, after a time, drawing a blackened hand across his forehead. "Who the heck's going to say how that girl died?"

"Who," asked Colin in a sick voice, "is going to identify that as Sheila Campbell?"

"That's not our business. You chaps employed the girl—you'll have to get on with the job. H'm. It seems I spoke without the book tonight. We've got to get the police in on this right away, if we don't want to find ourselves accessories after the crime."

"We're going to have our work cut out telling our story anyway," Bill reminded him. "A jealous crowd, the police. They like to handle a story right from the title page, not have it thrown at them at, say, Chapter Five."

"I'm not here to oblige the police," returned Crook energetically. "They ought to be damn' grateful to us for doin' their spade-work for them."

The appositeness of the expression shocked Colin. He couldn't forget, as the others apparently could, that at this instant Julia Ross was at the mercy of the man who was responsible for the horror in the cellar.

"It's a good thing none of us are married men," remarked Crook in his irrelevant way as they left 151 Radnor Road.

"You've said it," agreed Bill, laconically.

Colin looked baffled. "You think it's going to be like that?" he suggested.

Bill grinned. "He thinks you mean 'Three corpses lay on the shining sands,'" he explained to Crook.

"He don't know us very well, does he, Bill?" Crook hadn't turned a hair. Even the gruesome discovery in the cellar and the knowledge that at this very moment they might be on the track of a second, equally repulsive murder, failed to affect his equilibrium. "No, no, what I had in mind is the fact that I've never yet met a man who could explain a night's absence in a fashion that his wife would accept. And that is going to be an all night job, if the police know anything about it. Well, be your age, man," he added impatiently. "Put yourself in the copper's shoes. We walk into the station and admit we have broken into another chap's premises without his or police permission and have found a body there. When we're asked how we suppose it got into the cellar we say a fellow called Peters rented the house particularly for the corpse's benefit. Do we know Peters? Well, not exactly. Can we tell them where he is now? Same again. What about the lady—perhaps she's a friend of ours. We couldn't quite say that. Any proof that Peters put her there? Well, no. Well, devil take it, any witnesses? There is one, but the odds are that before she can get as far as the witness stand she'll be in the same state as the deceased. Not so hot, eh?"

"There are the agents through whom the house was taken," suggested Colin without much enthusiasm.

"I'll be ready to bet a barrel of beer they've never heard of any Mr. Peters. And if they have, still we've got to contact him, and we've got to do it quick. That's our one hope."

"That and Julia," Colin amended. "After all, he probably won't expect us to be on his track before morning at the earliest. There may be information he wants from Julia, and if I know that girl she won't open up. She's got guts, Julia has."

"Long may she keep them," ejaculated Crook piously. "You take my tip, old boy, and stick to the straight and narrow paths of virtue. Peters ain't no fool. It's not likely he's going to keep that girl for a mascot. And what can she tell him, come to that? That Crook's on his tail. That's all, and that's the very thing that'll urge him to put out her light quicker than anything."

"There's a chap at headquarters called Ponsonby. I know him a bit. He'd be quicker than the ordinary police. I could ring him . . ."

Crook put a restraining hand on his arm. "Remember what I told you right from the start? Crook's running this job and he don't like having his cards arranged by any amateur. You leave this to your big-hearted Uncle Arthur. Ponsonby can have his beauty sleep. There's a beggar called Field. He'll come across for me if the thing's put to him right. It's now or never. You do get that. Unless we contact our man this evening we'll be singing, 'Now the laborer's task is o'er,'

171

for little Julia Ross within the week. Ah, that's what I was looking for." He espied a red telephone booth and doubled for it.

"If we had the remotest idea where Peters was now we might be able to do something," muttered Colin desperately to Bill, who had drawn out his case and was lighting yet another of his perpetual cigarettes. "But we're completely in the dark."

Bill snapped his lighter shut—it was a gold one and when it came into Bill's possession nine years earlier it had had someone else's initials engraved upon it—and asked in his habitually casual voice, "Ever heard of the Merseyside pearls?"

"I don't think so. What have they got to do with this?"

"I'm telling you. Merseyside was one of these chaps that believe the world owes him a living and sees to it that he gets it, what's more. When he was well on in the forties he wanted a change so he thought he'd see what virtue could do for him. And believe me, most Chicago gangsters are curly-headed babies compared with that fellow. He got himself engaged to a real peach and gave a stag party the night before the wedding. His present to the bride was the famous Merseyside pearls. He took 'em down to the party in the tail coat of his dress suit, if you'll believe me, and dragged 'em out as though they were a row of beads and handed 'em round. The party broke up soon after midnight and about four in the morning a cop found Merseyside as stiff as the ten Commandments on his own doorsteps—minus the pearls. There was no end of a rush here and there looking for them—they ranked second with the crown jewels— and it wasn't till well after the funeral and the grass beginning to grow again on the grave that some simple-minded chap thought of looking into the tail coat of the corpse's dress suit. And there they were, as snug as a bug in a rug. It turned out it was the fellow's own butler who'd done him in—the man had a grudge against his lordship on account of the way he'd exercised his *droit de seigneur* on the chap's daughter—and after the police had gone through the place with a tooth-comb Burton just slipped the pearls back—see? Case of the dog returning to its own vomit. Now do you know where we're going?"

Before Colin could reply the sturdy hunched figure of Crook reappeared.

"These formalists, even the best of them, take a lot of convincing," he observed. "Still, I fancy the odds are laid now." He inserted himself into the driving wheel of the little car much as a knife is inserted into an oyster. "I feel kind of bad not letting Cummings in on this," he went on. Cummings was the editor of the *Record*, London's most anecdotal daily paper and one of its most widely read; he was also Crook's very good friend, never sparing the long bow when the occasion appeared to demand it. "But it wouldn't have been safe. No one can tell me anything about the value of publicity, but I've seen the other side of the medal too. Once the press are in on this I wouldn't give a sucked orange for Julia's chances. We can't do anything for that poor girl in the cellar—she's gone to the pretty angels anyway, but we're Julia's only hope."

"Where are we going now?" Colin wanted to know as the car took a corner too sharply for comfort.

"When you're huntin' a rat, the safest bet is his own hole."

"Just what I've been telling him," drawled Bill.

"So now we're off hell-for-leather for No. 30 Henriques Square."

17

ALTHOUGH IT WAS NO MORE than eight o'clock the night was already very dark. A light fog had moved inland from the river, lying low, so that above the mist the sky could be seen, like a sable cloth twinkling with points of silver that did nothing to lighten the gloom of the almost empty streets. A good night for old Nasty, one man called to another at a street corner. The public houses showed chinks of light, and the sound of robust voices came from within; but outside everything was unusually quiet. The chug-chug of Crook's fantastic little car split up the silence as a flung stone will splinter glass, but he himself seemed impervious to it.

"Captain Hook's crocodile," exclaimed Colin suddenly, breaking a long pause. "That's what your car reminds me of, Crook. You hear it before you see it."

"But not long before," retorted Crook in unwontedly grim tones. He took another corner.

173

"How do you reckon Peters fixed it?" inquired Bill meditatively. "You can't so easily walk into a public call-box and yank out a dame in broad daylight. Or did he represent himself as a doctor and pretend she'd fainted?"

"Doctors' cars have a way of being recognized," Crook reminded him. "Specially these days when we all wear labels."

"Got her away in a taxi p'r'aps?"

"To an empty house? Think again, Bill."

"The driver could be in it."

"You bet your immortal soul he was in it."

"So that's two of them," Colin joined in thoughtfully. "Probably both armed."

"Not necessarily—not two of them, I mean."

Bill got his meaning now. "So that's the size of it. If the chap was made up as a taxi-driver the jane mightn't tumble till it was too late . . ."

"But even so he could hardly leave an empty taxi standing for two hours outside an empty house," Colin protested. "Even if he parked it opposite No. 28 it 'ud attract attention."

"I don't suppose he'd need to leave it all that time," Crook countered grimly. "You've not had much experience of murder, have you, Colin? Not as much as Peters anyway. Experts don't need long. No, his job is goin' to be gettin' rid of the corpse. It ain't so good these days leavin' it litterin' about in an empty house. Suppose the Government takes a looksee on behalf of the poor Belgians, say, and they find a body there—well, they're goin' to ask questions, aren't they? And that won't be too healthy for our Mr. Peters."

"So long as he doesn't realize we've been to Radnor Road we have a chance," Colin insisted. "I'm banking on that."

"The trouble about my profession," Crook assured the world at large, "is that you don't only have to do your own job—you have to waste a lot of time undoin' your clients' mistakes."

A final turn took them into the Square and they chugged gently up to No. 30. Here a surprise awaited even the phlegmatic Crook, jolting him out of his normal imperturbability. There was a motor vehicle standing by the curb, but it wasn't a taxi, it was a police car.

"Nice work," grunted Crook, drawing up behind it. "We're giving the neighbors a treat tonight. Ah well, it's probably the first time the police have put one over Arthur Crook. They'd better make a note of it in their records."

He got out and proceeded to lock his car in the most intricate fashion. He behaved, thought Colin, as though every thief in London had designs on the little monstrosity. Bill strolled forward and inspected the car in front.

"No one keeping guard," he reported an instant later. "Presumably they're all inside."

"Waiting for us," agreed Crook, importantly. "What's up, Colin? Can't you establish contact?"

From his position on the doorstep Colin returned in surly tones, "They probably think we're journalists. However, I'll have another shot." He lifted the great knocker again. This time he was more successful. He at least established the fact that the house was not deserted.

"We're bein' inspected from above," announced Crook after a moment. "Lord knows what they expect to be able to see on a night like this."

"They may think we're part of the gang," suggested Colin, seriously.

Crook grinned. "And virtue is so distinctive they can see from that height that we ain't? You're a daisy, Colin. Look out, here they come."

Footsteps could be distinctly heard descending the uncarpeted stairs, and a minute later the front door was opened by a tall sergeant of police. The hall behind him was black with shadow. The sergeant carried a shaded torch in his hand that he tilted cautiously upwards.

"Congratulations!" said Crook, in heartfelt tones. "I'm the chap who rang you up. I'll do the honors. That torch of yours ain't so hot. Mr. Bruce—Mr. Parsons—(you'd be too young, I suppose, to remember him—professionally, I mean)—and my name's Crook. We've come to make inquiries about Miss Ross."

The sergeant seemed quite unimpressed by this handsome admission.

"Why should you think she's here?" he inquired.

175

"Why else are you here?" asked Crook, simply. "Are you the chap that took my call?"

The sergeant stepped back a few paces, letting them all in. "The super wants to see you," he acknowledged. "Wait in here, will you?" He opened the door of a room on the right. "Sorry it's all so dark," he apologized. "The shutters are still up and the current's cut off."

Crook put his hand in his pocket and brought out something that looked like a large propelling pencil. He pressed a switch and a wan pale-blue light sprang up.

"Arthur Crook, the human glow-worm," he announced. "I think the hall will do for us. I don't suppose it'll be for long."

The sergeant, who didn't appear to think much of Crook's breezy manners, said O.K. and went to the top of the basement stairs. They heard him call to someone, and then he ran quickly down.

"Cellar Crime No. 2?" wondered Crook, aloud.

"He can't have had time to fill up the cellar since five-thirty," protested Colin. "God, Crook, you don't think . . ."

"I think we've got a hell of a long evening in front of us," Crook interrupted him. "I wish to heaven we'd remembered to bring some beer. I always do my best on beer. Some fellows," he went on chattily, "do their damnedest on gin, and I even knew one beggar who preferred lime juice. But he worked on a rum sort of lay anyhow."

"He didn't say a word about Julia," broke in Colin jerkily. "I wonder if they have got her. I should have asked . . ."

"He'd have referred you to the super. That's army discipline—civil division."

Colin moved away to the head of the stairs, and stood listening. After an instant he came back to Crook's side.

"I can't hear a sound," he said sharply. "They're not talking—I don't believe there's any one down there. We've been done, Crook. *That fellow wasn't a sergeant at all. It was Peters himself.*"

"You're telling me," said Crook, politely. "Let's go down and push our own inquiries, shall we?"

They waited another moment. The street was very still. They heard a solitary step on the pavement, a passing taxi sounded its horn, a radio from the house opposite blared softly. Crook seemed to come to a decision.

"Yes," he repeated, "let's go."

Bill flashed on a powerful torch and the three men made their way down the steep stairs into the basement. The door of the great kitchen stood open, and a single glance assured the searchers that the room was empty. The scullery door was shut; as Bill wrenched it open a faintly musty air, redolent of graveyards, came out to meet them. There were few hiding places here. When they had flung wide the door of the larder and uncovered the great dusty copper they came back into the passage. The coal cellar stood at the further end, and this door, they discovered, was locked.

"Mr. Parsons, forward," said Crook, standing aside and Bill, limping a little, came between them and, stooping, flashed his torch on the lock. The key was lying on the floor at their feet. Bill glanced at it. It was twisted out of its proper shape, and refused to fit when they tried it.

"Smashed the lock on his way out," said Bill. "That may mean something or it may just be a trick to hold us up." He flashed his torch again, and this time it was Colin who stooped with a smothered exclamation.

"Look at this," he exclaimed. He held out his hand, palm upwards, and all three men stared at a little trinket shaped like a pink flower.

"One of Julia's earrings," Colin told them. "I remember her showing them to me one night in Lyons. Well, that proves she's been here tonight. She was wearing them the evening she came up from Moreton and she's not likely to have paid a visit here between that day and this. That means she's in the cellar at this moment."

Crook looked questioningly at Bill. "How about it?" he asked.

"Might be," returned Bill noncommittally. "That jars me a bit. I was going to shoot our way in, but he may have figured we'd do just that and have planted the dame where she'll get a bellyful of lead." He drew a revolver from his pocket and regarded it wistfully. "Better not, perhaps," he agreed, and dropping on his knees he got to work.

Crook opened the back door and went up the tradesmen's steps. "Police car's gone as clean as a whistle," he announced on his return. "But he hasn't slit our tires, as I'd have expected. Didn't like to spare the time, maybe."

He turned to Bill. "How's it coming along?"

"This chap knows his onions." Bill straightened his tall form, and Crook doubled up his short one and bent to inspect the lock, looking rather like a small elephant in brown tweed.

"You've said it," he agreed. He took another weapon from his pocket, a strip of fine steel, and inserted it into the lock. Both men watched him, Colin sweating with apprehension of what the cellar door might conceal, Crook with professional interest. Bill manipulated his steel with the skill of a surgeon at the operating table.

"Hold everything!" he said, suddenly. "Shine your torches this way, will you?"

There was a click, a tremor, and Bill suddenly hurled himself against the door. Crook lent the weight of his short powerful body, and the door began to yield under the strain.

"Look out!" Crook exclaimed. "There are probably steps, and we shan't be much use to dear Julia or any one else minus our faces."

Between the three of them they wrenched the door open; as Crook had prophesied there were four steep, stone steps leading into a huge dark cellar, patterned with coal dust and a little heap of coal in one corner. There was about enough there, Crook calculated, to conceal a medium-sized rabbit. And that was all.

"Nobody, no time bomb, no nothing," commented Crook. "Well, he's made us look pretty silly, which was doubtless his intention. So what?"

No one had answered him when from the great silent house above them the telephone began to ring.

It rang with that peculiar forlorn clarity of telephones in empty houses. The bell came shrilling down the stairs like some insistent suppliant who refuses to take "no" for an answer. Its clamor was so unexpected that Colin felt it was as though a dead man had suddenly opened his mouth in urgent speech. Crook brushed past him, taking the steep flight of the basement stairs at an unexpectedly rapid pace. Colin came leaping up behind him.

"It must be Mrs. Ponsonby," he panted. "No one else would dream of trying to get Peters here. They wouldn't know."

"It could be that or a wrong number," agreed Crook, not without malice, turning the head of the stairs and moving towards the room where Julia had first attempted to defy her tyrant. The old-fashioned instrument stood on the dusty boards. Crook stooped down and put the receiver to his ear.

"Hullo! Yes. Yes, I know. I get you. That's what I said. Don't go to sleep on the job. We'll be seeing you." He slammed the receiver back on to its rest and turned back to the speechless Colin.

"This is where we have to step on the gas," he remarked. He hauled his great turnip of a watch out of his pocket. "Forty minutes we took getting that door open. We got here at 8.10. It's 8.50 now. Forty minutes on to that—call it forty-five—that makes it 9.35. That's grand. We're in clover." He nodded cheerfully to the unsmiling Colin and ran down the stairs to the hall. The front door stood open. Bill was already in the driving-seat. Crook jumped in beside him, barely giving Colin a chance to scramble over the side; Bill set her going. The fog had increased during the past half-hour. Bill was a first-class driver, but even so they didn't reach their destination in the forty-five minutes Crook had allowed. It was a quarter to ten when the car drew up in front of a public house called the Railway Inn, set back from a rather lonely road by a little paved yard. Colin had existed during the first half of the journey in silence; neither of his companions, of both of whom he stood in some awe, seemed to remember his existence. It seemed ironical that he should have by far the greatest stake in the proceedings—for what, he thought, was Crook's reputation compared with the love he bore to Julia?—and be so comparatively unimportant in this matter of her possible rescue that it would have made practically no difference if he hadn't been there at all. At the end of twenty minutes he burst into the explosive speech of desperation.

"Tell me something, Crook. You were expecting that 'phone call?"

"Of course I was expecting it."

"So you knew the line hadn't been disconnected?"

"Well, of course, I knew it hadn't. How could I have gotten in touch with Peters in the first place if there hadn't been a 'phone working?"

Colin's face was almost invisible in the darkness; nevertheless his bewilderment was obvious to both his companions.

179

"You mean, you'd already telephoned him?"

"You heard me tell him so. I'm the chap that rang you, I said, when he let us in. Suffering Pete! D'you think at my age and with my reputation I've got time to go chasing wild geese that mayn't be there at all? Of course I knew Peters was at Henriques Square. That's why we went round. I knew that if that bell tinkled he wouldn't be able to resist answering. You see, there was always the chance it might be Mrs. Ponsonby. If it wasn't he could always say wrong number, as in fact he did. It was a bad moment for him when we assembled on the doorstep. He couldn't be sure if I really had called him up, or if I was deceived and took him for the chap he was pretendin' to be. He had to take a chance and he's come down on the wrong side of the fence. That's all."

"And you know where he is now?"

"D'you remember, when we were waiting in the hall, hearing a taxi hoot? Well, that was our man tellin' us the coast was clear. He was followin' Peters, while we took the lining out of No. 30 Henriques Square. And he'll hold him till we arrive, what's more."

"And—Julia?" Colin could scarcely frame the word.

Crook leaned over and put a friendly hand on the young man's arm.

"Don't ask for more than one miracle at a time," he warned him. "We're all goin' to be able to answer that question pretty soon."

Colin fell silent again and the car ran on into the darkness. It had hardly come to a halt outside the Inn when Bill tooted lightly, and the door of the private bar swung open and a man came out. He crossed to the car and leaned confidentially in through the driver's window.

"You're all right till closing time," he said. "Fellow don't mean to make a move till then. Ferreman's inside keeping him busy, with instructions to hang on like the three-toed crab till you arrive. Better put the car where she won't be seen too easy," he added. "That is, if he'd know her again."

"The Scourge of the Roads," said Crook fondly, as Bill began to back into a narrow path. The three men alighted and all four of them stood in a patch of shadow, talking in whispers.

"Has he said anything?" Crook wanted to know.

"Given us all the works without so much as opening his mouth." the police officer assured him. "See the name of that pub? Well, the railway line runs at the back, about a quarter of a mile down hill. There's no station here, only a halt that's hardly ever used. They use this line after dark for the heavy goods traffic. It joins up with Charminster about twelve miles on. There's a train at ten-twenty, and there won't be a soul aboard her but her fireman and driver. They won't be looking out for fun and games at this hour of the night, specially on a thick night like this. I don't say that if they felt the wheels bump over something they mightn't stop, but if they want to ask questions it won't be of our Mr. Peters, because he won't be there. The vanishing rabbit won't be in it with him."

"It's not a new idea," conceded Crook, "but it brings home the bacon every time. It's the simplicity of it that counts for its beauty. But for us," he seemed to be addressing himself particularly to the horror-stricken Colin, "there'd have been neat little paras. in tomorrow's afternoon editions—Girl's Body Found on Line. It's a black night and it's getting blacker every instant we stand here. You couldn't blame a driver for not seeing something lying across the line which hasn't any right to be there. And when he found the girl I'll stake my davy he'd have found the handbag beside her, showin' that she was a Miss Sheila Campbell of London. As soon as that news became public property our Mrs. Ponsonby would have stepped into the limelight with her highly interestin' story of the girl who didn't know her own name, and had already made three attempts to take her own life. And she'd have a trail of witnesses to back up her yarn, what's more."

"There's always our version," Colin reminded him.

"Don't make me laugh," begged Crook. "Who, outside a lunatic asylum, is goin' to listen to us? You come into court, say, and tell the boys, 'That girl isn't Sheila Campbell. This girl is Julia Ross.' Well, that's a matter of opinion without proof, and what proof have you got? How long have you known this girl? Four months. Where did you meet her? In a Lyons' teashop. Have you any corroborative evidence of her identity?"

"Mrs. Mackie," Colin reminded him unhesitatingly.

"And what's Mrs. Mackie's proof more than your own? A girl

comes to her hostel, gives her name as Julia Ross. She never gets any letters; she never gets any telephone calls. The identity card in her bag is marked Sheila Campbell; all her belongings, hair brushes, undies, everything, is embossed S.C. Evidence is offered that she's unbalanced, suffers from hallucinations, has to be watched night and day. Mrs. P. will have everything docketed and a witness at every turn. You wouldn't stand an earthly."

"How about Julia's employers in Edinburgh? She was in one job for four years."

Crook's hand came out and nipped the young man's arm. "Steady on!" he reminded him. "You forget that our friend employs rather wholesale methods when it comes to covering a girl's identity. You said yourself no one would dare swear to Sheila Campbell. D'you think, with the rope dangling just above his head, Peters is goin' to be any more careless when it comes to the next girl?"

Colin hesitated before he put his next question. "Do you think she's dead already?"

"I'm pretty sure she's not. M.O.'s are a cagey lot. They can pretty well swear to the cause of death these days. If a girl's been strangled, never mind what a railway engine may do at a later stage, your competent M.O.'s, and of course when they're attached to the police there ain't any other kind, will tie on the right label, you can bet your shirt on that. No, no, she's hidden somewhere convenient and conveniently unconscious."

"Then why the hell aren't we doing something?" demanded Colin, furiously.

"Because we've got to wait for this chap to give us a lead."

"He couldn't have hit on a better spot," put in the policeman who was dressed as a taxi-driver.

"Hit nothing," returned Crook, contemptuously. "Our friend's laid his plans with the utmost care. He can't afford to be casual and he knows it. He's waiting his time till the pub shuts. On a night like this there won't be much hanging about, and when they divide up no one will come this way—no houses near the track. He can come down looking like a shadow in a world of shadows, and he'll no more be seen than you notice a particular leaf in a forest. The train goes by at ten-twenty, you say?" The other nodded. "It could hardly be better from his point of view. There's a convenient curve just there; the driver will have done Peters' job for him before he has a chance to realize what's going on. That means the girl must be hidden somewhere close by. There are clumps of bushes and little pits all over the place. She may be in any one of them."

"If we all got going we might locate her before this devil turns up," exclaimed Colin. "Anyway, if he sees lights he'll steer clear of the neighborhood."

"Precisely why we've got to hold our hands. This fellow's the country's enemy as well as yours, Colin. Texts ain't much in my line, but at a time like this you have to see things in the broad—greatest good for the greatest number—you know. We've got to get this chap red-handed. We haven't got enough proof if we don't. The police are here, and they're the kind of witnesses that get believed. What are you and me if it comes to a court of law, old boy? Interested parties, that's what we are. The Police are different; they're like Cæsar's wife, above suspicion. That's so, isn't it?"

"I get your meaning, Mr. Crook," said the man in guarded tones. It was obvious that he had met the dynamic little lawyer before.

"Why on earth did Peters waste all this time?" demanded Colin who was like a jack-in-the-box and couldn't keep still. "He had the girl before six. If he brought her here direct why not finish the job right away?"

Crook looked at him pityingly. "And you're one of the chaps paid by the government to help to win the war. Peters would have looked a nice kind of fool dumping a girl on the line in broad daylight. Besides, these goods trains don't run till late when all passenger traffic's off this part of the line. I don't suppose he meant to get down here till after the pub closed, but we smoked him out of Henriques Square, and he didn't know we were going to follow him here. Besides, haven't you noticed that chaps who make good in pubs never get suspected of murder? I daresay he has a very waggish way with him in the parlor. Probably a darts champion. People will forgive a darts champion practically everything."

There was another brief pause. Then Crook said sharply, "Hold your horses. It's zero hour," and the four men melted into a patch of shadow behind the Railway Inn.

The night was so quiet that they could hear the clock in the public bar striking ten; then the voice of the barman—"Time, gentlemen, time. Time, please." And after that the doors of the house swung open and men began to emerge. There were not very many of them; on such a night men were more inclined to stay at home, and those there did not linger. Footsteps could be heard moving down the road. The seconds passed, each rigid with apprehension. Even Crook's pulses were beating faster than usual. Time was like a trap, its teeth closing inexorably on the men who composed this grim incident. A minute passed; the footsteps now sounded very far away. Another minute ticked past, and still their man gave no sign. Colin held his wrist watch to his ear. It seemed to be ticking like a time bomb. At every second he waited for an explosion; and nothing happened. He felt Crook's hand touch his arm.

"Over the top," said Crook. "Look there. 'Ware hounds."

Out of the darkness before them slid a streak, as black as the night and seeming part of it. Peters came down the difficult slope without switching on the torch in his hand. His feet felt their way carefully. Presently the light might have to be shown, but as yet he was still too near the road. Behind him were the barred doors and shuttered windows of the law-abiding world. In front lay the worst part of his ordeal. Like a shape of doom he made his way towards the invisible track.

"Now?" whispered Colin, in an agony of suspense.

"It all depends on me," Crook reminded him. "One slip, one stumble, and we lose not only game but rubber. No, stay put for another minute. It's too dangerous."

Colin's whole body ached and throbbed. He strained his eyes into the darkness, but now he could perceive nothing. He was tortured by the belief that the criminal had escaped them, that even now he might contrive to put his horrible plan into practice before they could stop him. Not all Crook's whispered adjurations about the patriotic aspect of the affair could move him now. He was a man desperately in love, chancing everything on a second of time. He started as he thought he heard a cry borne on the wind, but it sounded only in his own anguished brain. The darkness was absolute, hope was half dead. The pressure on his arm relaxed.

"Good man!" said Crook, and all four began to move forward like a horde of ghosts. Colin, alone, would never have discovered the track the hunted man had followed, but Bill, who had the nose of a bloodhound and the sight of a cat in the dark, never faltered. Suddenly a pin point of light flashed out for a second and vanished again, but it was the signal for which they had all been waiting. Now they must separate to encircle the killer. All along this irregular track patches of bramble and shrub flung their inky shadows on the ground, but Peters paused by none of these. Another minute and they realized his objective. Round a turn of the track, hidden from the inn, was an unused demolition center, a scurry of flotsam and jetsam, ancient masonry, rotting boards, sheets of rusty tin for which, so far, the authorities had found no use. A little tumbledown shed stood at the far end of the disused yard, so remote, so desolate that on this dark evening a man might hide his life's treasure there and be reasonably certain of finding it intact by morning.

"I daresay the kids muck about there in the daytime," Crook reflected. "Peters probably didn't leave her here too early, but he didn't dare keep her in the car in case he was stopped. But that explains why he stopped at the pub. If by some stroke of ill luck the body had been discovered he'd have picked up the story at the local and could have made his getaway. Now then—he's gone inside."

The glow of the torch vanished. But still Crook wouldn't let them rush forward with cries of accusation to surround the guilty man. Even now Peters might bluff his way out of the situation. If he said he had heard a sound and come down to investigate—it was a slim chance, but men of his calibre take slim chances as they take their daily bread. And in that case, thought Crook wryly, it might not prove too easy to explain their own presence in this abandoned spot at such an hour. Crook, as he frequently remarked, had a reputation to maintain. It cannot be said that the police loved him, but they respected him far above the average law-abiding layman. If anything should go wrong now Crook would find himself in an extremely awkward position, not only as regards the present but in the future. When your clientele is composed largely of men who, in a just community, could not hope for their freedom, a single mistake may bring your whole castle of days down about your ears. Everything, there-

fore, depended upon perfect timing. And the same, of course, held
good for Peters.

As he thought this their quarry came out of the hut, bearing something carefully in his arms. His burden made neither movement nor
sound. Moving like a panther Crook digressed in the direction of
the line.

Peters stood stock still for an instant and then took a step forward
in a silence that was more pregnant than a roll of drums.

18

THERE WAS NOT A GLEAM of light anywhere. The darkness
was like a blanket. As the doomed man pressed his way forward he
felt as though at each step he was plunging through a jungle, where
lurked all manner of traps to trip him up. He was aware of sounds
inaudible to normal ears, glimpsed shadows that changed their shape
and vanished before he could identify them. He knew these symptoms of old. They denoted the fact that he had now reached the
very peak of danger. He spared one thought for the three men who
had followed him to Henriques Square. Had they yet forced the cellar door and if so, what had they made of what they found there?
Were they perhaps groping amid the coal and dust for some non-
existent trap, a time fuse, say, or some additional clue to the girl's
presence in the building? He remembered with satisfaction the little
bauble he had found clinging to the cuff of his coat and the instant
use to which he had put it. Its presence on the floor—always assuming that they discovered it—would suggest that the girl was or had
been on the premises. Even if Crook, that human vulture, should
later pick up the trail it would avail him nothing. The girl would
be dead and the case ended, as that other girl had died before she
was able to tell what she knew. It would be a relief when this part of
the job was done and he could assure Mrs. Ponsonby of their security
for this time at least. He shivered a little, recalling that pitiless
woman. The female of the species was always the most desperate,
he thought; a Chicago gangster he had once known had told him

that the gangs headed by a woman, of which there were several in the States, were the most cruel, the hardest to stamp out. Mrs. Ponsonby would have made her fortune over there, he thought. Pity was a word she couldn't even spell; this girl was lucky to have got away when she had. After all, she hadn't suffered much. The drug he had given her had resulted in a coma like death, and death itself would have overtaken her before she dreamed of its approach. Why, dozens of civilians died most miserably, in far greater agony from "natural causes" every week of the year. For a moment horror shook him. In his bones he was afraid of Mrs. Ponsonby, from whom until the day of his own death, there would never be any escape. It hadn't been Peters' hands that sent Sheila Campbell down into the dark.

He shifted the weight in his arms a little, so that he caught a glimpse of the luminous watch on his wrist. Three minutes to go, he thought. He shook the cuff back into place. Of course, there wasn't anyone within half a mile, but these luminous dials glowed like neon lights in the dark, so it seemed to him. He didn't realize how valuable that instinctive gesture had been to the men who were on his track.

Suddenly he stiffened. His forehead was clammy. The girl in his arms was a more dead weight than before. Somewhere—he was certain of it—someone was breathing! He shook off his fear, but it returned like an old man of the sea, clawing at his heart. He knew these moments of tension. Every time they came he thought, "This is the end! I've made that fatal slip they say every criminal makes sooner or later." He stood dead still. The darkness was full of eyes. There were stealthy movements all around . . .

Far away he heard the rumble of the approaching train. Now for it. He galvanized his stiff limbs into action.

Horror of horrors! There was someone besides himself moving through the blanket of the dark. A dead leaf rustled, a stone slipped; the rumble increased to a roar. Half a minute to go, registered his brain, half a minute to go. He took a desperate step forward. Now he could see the lights of the train. The track here followed a winding route. The golden eye seemed closed again; there were no lights, of course, on the long jolting caterpillar of trucks.

No lights! His blood chilled, he felt as though in his brain some-

187

thing was moving like a wheel. Why, there were lights all round him, lights coming nearer, shutting him off from the track, lights between him and the darkened road he had so lately left. It had happened, as, in his heart, he had always known it would happen one day. He couldn't as yet put his finger on the fatal flaw that had be-trayed him; that knowledge was to come. But already he could read the future. He couldn't even make the quick getaway he had always promised himself—the tablet hurriedly conveyed to the mouth, the police defeated in the hour of their triumph. And ironically enough it was the girl he had sought to destroy who was now destroying him.

The train came roaring round the bend. The driver felt no jolt, had no need to slacken his pace. His fireman said indignantly, "Beats me what the police are up to in places like this. See all those lights? They'd be a beacon to every bomber in Berlin."

"Ah!" said the driver solemnly, a portentous Tory and a member of the Silent Column, that he had thought of before even Mr. Churchill had made it (briefly) famous. "Quislings, that's what they are, you mark my words. Quislings!" an observation that was rather lost on his companion, who preferred darts to politics and believed vaguely that Quislings were a kind of herring preserved in tomato sauce.

The train had been swallowed up by the darkness, with a final swirl of sparks, and now the lights of which the driver had so greatly disapproved were coming nearer. Peters had a revolver in his pocket, but it was no use to him. By the time he had set the girl down and reached for it someone else's gun would have spoken. His one hope was to hang on to the girl; they wouldn't fire so long as he kept her in his arms.

The lights flashed upwards, blinding him. Someone sprang; he felt his burden wrenched out of his hold. Then his arms were gripped and twisted behind him. An unrecognizable voice close at hand was saying over and over again, "She's breathing still. Oh God, oh God!"

Now they were all marching back to the road. He waited for some-one to speak but no one did. That silence was like a form of torture. Not until they were past the demolition dump and straining up the steep uneven slope to the roadway did a voice observe, in drawling unfamiliar accents, "We're showing one hell of a lot of light. I don't know what the police can be thinking of."

"Now's your chance to ask them," returned another voice, brisk vulgar, assured. "You're not likely to see so many of them in a bunch together for a long time." Then, at last, someone addressed him direct. "Damned thoughtful of you to bring that police car along, Peters," it said. "A nice touch, my boy, a nice touch."

In the private room she had engaged at the Rosedale Hotel, Mrs. Ponsonby was setting out one of her innumerable patiences, while Sparkes sat beside her knitting pull-overs in Air Force blue for the men of the Merchant Navy. As Mrs. Ponsonby's hands flashed over the cards, so her tongue poured out a torrent of invective, supposition and comment regarding the third member of their team.

"I can't make it out, Sparkes," she said. "What's Peters up to? He ought to have settled that girl's hash by this time. Doesn't he realize that every additional day she's at liberty increases our danger? I've been expecting to hear from him. If there's nothing in the next twenty-four hours we'd better slip away from here."

As though in reply to her remark the telephone rang. The reception clerk's voice informed her that a gentleman was waiting in the hall.

"Did he give his name?"

"Mr. Peters, madam."

Mrs. Ponsonby's face darkened with rage. "The fool!" she said, "coming down here in that open way. Tell him to come up," she told the clerk imperiously.

But when the door opened it wasn't Peters who came in but a man whom she had never seen before. He was so commonplace in his appearance that it would have been difficult to recognize in him one of the most notable personalities at Scotland Yard. His name was Field.

"Mrs. Ponsonby? I have a message for you from Peters."

Mrs. Ponsonby was no fool; she might not know Field's name, but she was in no doubt at all as to his errand. In any case Field didn't leave her for long in the dark.

He had his men with him and had already explained the position to the horrified proprietor of the hotel. Not long afterwards both women left the premises in the company of Field and one of his men. The others stayed behind to examine the apartment.

19

AND NOW AT LAST it was all over, the horror, the danger and the fear, the long delays, the questions, the examinations and cross-examinations, the awful ordeal of standing up in the witness-box to a withering fire of ridicule and disbelief from McFadden, the counsel for the defense, the nightmares, the suspense. The trial had been delayed for some time, firstly in order to enable Julia to recover sufficiently to play her part of chief witness, and secondly because McFadden, that cunning fox, realized the extreme peril to his client of allowing this trial to be heard during the momentous month of June 1940. It was, perhaps, the bitterest June any of them had ever known. Each day the British people opened its papers or turned on its wireless with a sinking heart, and each day they learned of further defeat and disappointment, of withdrawal and of final capitulation. The authorities, while giving the accused every benefit allowed to them by law, could find no adequate reason for further delay, and Crook pressed his advantage home. The three prisoners were standing their trial for the murder of Sheila Campbell and, if the police could have had their way, the miscreants' other activities would have been passed over. But Crook had no intention of permitting anything of the kind.

The whole affair was unusual in as much as no direct evidence was available. There were no servants, no neighbors, no relatives even, to urge the case for the prosecution. Even the identification of the corpse found in the cellar at 151 Radnor Road presented exceptional difficulties. The police were handicapped by the fact that her disappearance had never been reported, and all three prisoners denied any knowledge of her manner of death. Peters had been discreet enough up to a point. The house had been leased through a third party who, it was proved, had no knowledge of the use to which it would be put, and it was difficult to show any connection between this person and the accused. It followed, therefore, that the chief witness was Julia herself. Mrs. Ponsonby stuck to it throughout that Julia was in reality the girl for whose death she had been put on trial. She told her story with great force and vigor, and with a disarming simplicity. She swore that only one girl had ever been under her roof, and that girl was now giving evidence against her. She marshalled her witnesses methodically. Crook, who was attending the trial on Julia's behalf and wouldn't have missed it anyway, didn't mind giving her her head for a time. There would come a moment when not all her apparent veracity, her coolness of head, would serve her. There was no getting away from the evidence of the police where Peters was concerned. McFadden, of course, knew this; he was acting only for Mrs. Ponsonby, and had seen to it that Sparkes also should be reasonably represented. But he had drawn the line utterly at Peters. Peters had got to be sacrificed anyhow. Mrs. Ponsonby's one chance lay in abandoning her one-time partner, in allowing it to be supposed that he was running a private vendetta against the girl. It might be that the court would be satisfied to accept that situation.

Nevertheless, the question of the attempted murder of Julia Ross was not the matter laid before it. It was concerned only with the murder of Sheila Campbell. It was contended by the defense, first that the girl before them was Miss Campbell and alternatively, that she had represented herself as such in applying for the position of secretary-companion to Mrs. Ponsonby. Mrs. Hurst of the Victoria Employment Agency was called, but her evidence proved to be purely negative. She admitted that she had given Mrs. Ponsonby's address to a Miss Ross, but she could not swear that the girl in the box was the one who had come to her office.

McFadden, who cultivated a smooth sarcastic manner, had floored many a nervous witness by his habit of inquiring, "And what, X, do you imagine was the prisoner's motive for behaving in the manner you have adduced?"

This frequently sent witnesses into hysterics; they lost their heads, floundered, added and subtracted to the sum of their original evidence, and finally left the box utterly discredited in the eyes of the jury. Julia, however, met all such inquiries by a simple, "I don't know, I wasn't in Mrs. Ponsonby's confidence."

"Come, come, Miss—er—Ross, you must have formed some theory that would account for such extraordinary conduct. Will you tell the court . . . ?"

But Julia shook her head. She had been well schooled by Crook. "Whatever you do, don't get yourself dragged into an argument with the chap," he had warned her. "Arguing's his profession; in fact, with him it's a vocation. You wouldn't stand an earthly. It 'ud be like the star of Little Puddleton Women Institute standing up beside (and here he named London's most famous actress). Just stick to what I tell you. I don't know. That's all you've got to say. I don't know. Go to sleep from now to the day of the trial repeating that, and don't forget it when you get into the box."

And so "I don't know," said Julia stubbornly. McFadden put the question in a different form. Now Crook's classic answer was inapplicable, but Julia met the situation by replying, "I can't remember. Everything went blank."

"Now, Miss Ross," McFadden sounded exasperated, "you can't expect the court to accept that."

The judge suddenly intervened. "Why not, Mr. McFadden? The witness has told you she doesn't know, she can't remember, everything was a blank. If that was the case a minute ago she isn't likely to have had a revelation since. She has replied to the best of her ability to your question. Continue, please."

Altogether Julia proved to be a witness of whom (he told her afterwards) Crook felt justifiably proud. "If all amateurs were like you, the pros would have to look to their laurels," he said. "Their trouble generally is that they can't resist introducing a little bit of business they think will go down well with the court. It's their one chance of publicity and they want to shine."

Julia didn't want to shine. She wanted to get away from the limelight, the horror, the insecurity she had known, and find peace. Of the patriotic side of the position she thought little. Counsel for the prosecution, however, in the person of Mr. Dickens Forrester, K.C., intended that this aspect should be stressed to the uttermost. England's ears were ringing with cries of Fifth Column, Quisling and the like. Once let the jury realize that the prisoners were not merely murderers, which might almost be regarded as a personal failing, but spies in the pay of Germany, and there would be no talk of mercy. As indeed there was not. For seven days the trial continued. Counsel for the Defense made a speech lasting nearly four hours. Counsel for the Prosecution was satisfied with an hour and a half. The judge took the better part of a day in instructing the jury, and it was later admitted that he did so with admirable impartiality. The jury took twelve minutes to agree on their verdict, but stayed out for an hour for the sake of appearances. The verdict was unanimous and there was no recommendation to mercy except in the case of Sparkes, who appeared to have jibbed at murder but had been dragged into it by her associates. The judge undertook that this recommendation should be forwarded to the appropriate quarter, but it was ultimately rejected. The temper of the country at that time was against it. And it was significant that even in a country with the strongest possible feeling about the death penalty no one attempted to get up a petition for a reprieve.

"So much for British justice," observed Crook in his unprincipled way on the morning of the triple execution. "Likewise three cheers for British compromise. That trio murdered Sheila Campbell all right, but what they really swung for was espionage. Ah, well, it saved the country valuable ammunition, and from what I can see, it's going to need every bullet it can muster in the days ahead. Whereas the same rope will do for the next murderer who's unlucky."

EPILOGUE

"THERE'S one thing I still don't understand," said Julia when the sharpness of her frightful experience was beginning to blunt a little. "And that is about the girl in Ireland."

Her companion was Colin Bruce and at the mention of the mythical Paddy he had the grace to color richly.

"Well, actually, darling, she's first cousin to Mrs. 'Arris. I mean, there ain't no sich creature."

"But, Colin, you *told* me . . ."

"I know, darling, I know. But—the fact is, I'd bought a pup and I had no intention of starting kennels. I wanted to meet a girl without any likelihood of being regarded as a possible husband. Oh, I daresay that sounds conceited, but, though you don't realize it, I do happen to be a rather eligible party. It's no virtue of mine that my father left me a trifle of two thousand a year, but it was a virtue all right to—certain other people."

"I suppose you never thought of me at all. You didn't think I might believe you and want to scratch the hateful Paddy's eyes out."

"Oh Julia, say that again. Did you really?"

"I couldn't bear thinking about her. I think you were abominable . . ."

"Then you must give me a chance to make it up to you. I swear I'll spend the rest of my life . . ."

"And I'll claim every minute of it. I warn you I'll be the most possessive wife. If you ever dare look at another woman . . ."

He stopped her lips with kisses. Even now he could scarcely believe they were safe. It was part of Julia's good fortune that she had no memory of anything after her sight of Peters' face staring into

194

hers through the glass of the telephone booth until she came round in a nursing home and was told to lie still and not to worry as she was perfectly secure and would never need to be afraid again. It hadn't been necessary at the trial to repeat the history of that terrible night on the railway, since it was Sheila Campbell's death that was in question; and Colin believed that Julia need never know how desperately close she had been to an appalling death. He had obtained special leave for the wedding, and they were going down to Cornwall for ten days to bathe and walk and lie out in the sun of the loveliest summer England had known for years. It was even possible that there they would escape the reporters.

"Not that you're as important as you think, darling," Colin told her. "They're a bloodthirsty lot in Fleet Street, and you did get away. They'd give a hundred times more for Mrs. P.'s life-story than for yours."

"No one can call me a match-maker," said Crook thoughtfully, "and if you ask me there's a lot in what that writin' chap said about a young man married is a young man marred. But there's something about those two that makes me feel quite scriptural. Did you ever learn collects on Sundays when you were a kid, Bill?"

"I wouldn't have known what a collect was," returned Bill, dryly.

But Crook was obsessed with his own thoughts. "There was one I remember—perhaps it wasn't a collect, but it doesn't matter—about a happy issue out of all our afflictions . . ." He brooded, like a great brown bird with half-shut eyes. Suddenly he felt Bill's glance, half-derisive, half-affectionate, burning through his reverie. He jumped up, clapping his brown bowler over his aggressive red brows.

"And what we want right now," he said, "is a double round of old and bitter, and you'd better come along and help me to find it."

THE END

Discover more about
Anthony Gilbert, aka Lucy Malleson

in this fascinating memoir:

THREE-A-PENNY

with an introduction from
bestselling crime writer
Sophie Hannah